Francesca Scana  ther
and Italian father 'een
England and Italy. and
she has pursued an eclectic mixture of career paths, including
working as a technical translator between Italian, English, Spanish
and French, a gym owner in Spain, an estate agent in France, a
property developer in France and Senegal, and a teacher.
Francesca lives in Dorset and currently works as a builder with
her husband. She has two children. *Return to Paradiso* is her
second novel and the second of the *Paradiso Novels*.

Return to Paradiso

Francesca Scanacapra

SILVERTAIL BOOKS • *London*

First published in Great Britain by Silvertail Books in 2021

www.silvertailbooks.com

978-1-913727-09-3

For all those who have knowingly and
unknowingly inspired this story

CHAPTER 1

Pieve Santa Clara, Lombardy, 1950
The dawn of a new decade brought a feeling of optimism. At last the constraints of rationing and the hardships of war were being consigned to memory as Italy entered the throes of the Economic Miracle.

The consumer age rolled in at a galloping pace, blurring the distinction between essentials and luxuries. Slick salesmen brandishing shiny hire-purchase catalogues began to call at every house in the village. They offered every conceivable modern 'necessity', from kitchenware and farming tools to furniture and clothing, and all payable in affordable monthly instalments. The array of domestic appliances and gadgets was quite bewildering.

'Graziella, look at this!' exclaimed my mother. 'A tin-opener which uses electricity. Can you think of anything more ridiculous? As if anyone would want to waste electricity on opening a tin.'

For my mother, the electric tin-opener became a symbol of things having gone too far, but eventually even she succumbed to the allure of hire-purchase. After several weeks of careful consideration she purchased a set of baking trays, although she was reluctant to use any of them until she had paid in full – a process which took six months.

Telegraph poles were installed along the North Road during the summer of 1950 and my aunt paid for the connection of a telephone line. There had been a telephone in the village post office since before the war, but having one in our home made it feel as though Paradiso was connected to the whole world.

'You could even call the President of the Republic if you wanted

1

to, Mina,' said Ada Pozzetti, who had come over with several of the little Pozzettis to witness the wonder of modern telecommunication. One of the Pozzetti twins, who was in a particularly excited state, asked whether it was possible to telephone God.

However, Zia Mina's first call was made not to the President of the Republic, nor to God, but to her foster-mother, Immacolata Ogli, the housekeeper at Don Ambrogio's residence.

It took my aunt several attempts to dial the number correctly as she was unsure whether she was supposed to remove her finger from the dial once she had turned it. When she did finally manage to get through, the conversation lasted under a minute and consisted of Zia Mina and Immacolata asking one another repeatedly whether the other could hear them, followed by confirmation and amazement that they could. They both shouted so loudly into their receivers that they would probably have heard each other just by opening the windows.

The village buzzed with activity and with the noise of new vehicles. Vespas and Lambrettas would pass our house, their engines spluttering and popping and leaving the smell of two-stroke fuel in their wake. Some would have whole families on board, with children clinging on behind or wedged between parents' knees.

Luigi Pozzetti extended his workshop and purchased modern machinery, but the whine of electric saws and rhythmic drone of wood being planed never bothered us. It was a cheerful and positive sound and a reminder that fortune, peace and prosperity had finally arrived. Pozzetti even bought an ex-military truck, which he painted yellow and used to transport both his work and his ever-growing family.

Zia Mina still advertised her produce for sale on the blackboard outside the gate. Salvatore continued to man her market stalls, which had become so popular that Zia Mina was able to employ him officially, and pay him a wage.

The success of my aunt's market garden had allowed her to acquire a second-hand washing machine. It was probably well over twenty years old, but both Mamma and my aunt were thrilled with it. Of course it was not an automatic machine which could be filled and left, like a modern one. It required almost constant supervision. Also, it did have a tendency to walk across the room when spinning, so Pozzetti screwed several pieces of wood into the floor to keep it in place.

The washing machine was not the only improvement. At last my mother and I had our own inside lavatory. A section at the back of the laundry room was partitioned off and a fully flushing indoor WC was plumbed in.

My mother's business was flourishing. She had amassed so much work that often we were forced to eat our meals squeezed up at one end of the kitchen table behind piles of sheets and tablecloths. However, the embroidery she undertook in such enormous amounts was never a chore for her. She would thank her clients for bringing work. It seemed that every new sheet, tablecloth or handkerchief increased her confidence.

My mother knew the price of everything and was meticulous with the money she earned, proud of the fact that she had never had to rely on handouts from the widows' charity. She had even been able to pay for my schoolbooks without having to ask for assistance.

Every week she sat doing her accounts, placing coins and notes in different envelopes.There was an envelope for food, another for firewood, another for household bills. She also had a tin for her business expenses.

At last she began to speak about my father, and whenever she did so, it was of him as he had been before his accident, as though she had decided to close her eyes to the struggle of his disabilities and instead, wished to remember the vigorous and able-bodied man she had first loved. She had been creating her own stone memories. As she recounted stories and jokes he had told, and laughed at them again with me, her affectionate descriptions of my Papá gave me new ways to think about him. I borrowed her memories and made them my own.

The candle she lit every Sunday in church, and for which she paid 100 lire, was for him. She would smile gently as she lit it, kiss her fingers and place it carefully in the holder.

The value of money had changed significantly in the six years since the end of the war. Now, a labourer could expect to be paid between 1,500 and 2,000 lire per day, depending on his skills. It pained me that the 100 lire my mother placed in the collection tin was the same amount that the church had paid my father for each day of his labour.

When I was not at school or helping at home, I spent my time with Gianfrancesco. The acres of fields and orchards which surrounded Cascina Marchesini were our world where we could do and say as we pleased and where our secret kissing could be concealed. As far as our mothers knew, Gianfrancesco and I were just friends. We were both afraid that if our mothers found out about our kissing they would forbid us from spending time together.

I still missed my father, though not in the same way as before. I wished that he could see how things had improved. I wished that I had been able to show him my good grades. And finally, I wished that he had been able to be part of the new post-war world which was emerging. I spoke to him constantly during my prayers.

In truth I spoke to my father more often than I did to God. I found praying to God pointless, since it felt as though my prayers were too small to be noticed. God was obviously too occupied listening to millions of others to hear mine. Speaking to my father was different. He was there for me whenever I wanted, and I could be sure of his undivided attention. Even in church every Sunday I did not pray to God, but communicated with my father. I was not sure whether this was a sin or not, and thought it better not to enquire in case it was and I was told to stop.

I didn't like church very much. I was too old for Sunday school, which I had quite enjoyed because we listened to Bible stories, but Mass I found to be a tedious and mechanical occasion. The repetition of the same rites week after week was so boring that I would spend most of the service sucking in my cheeks to stop myself from yawning.

Although I went to confession regularly, as was expected of me, I kept my sins lightweight. I was not comfortable baring my soul to Don Ambrogio and certainly never told him about Gianfrancesco and our secret kissing.

'Why don't you go to church?' I asked Gianfrancesco.

'Because church is no place for me. I'm an apostate.'

'What's that?'

'Apostasy is the abandonment of religious beliefs. I find the whole concept of organised religion questionable. I'm not even sure there's a God.'

I was aware of the fact that there were people who didn't believe in God, but as far as I knew, I had never met one. Sometimes Don Ambrogio offered prayers for those who had abandoned their faith. Although my own communication with God had been unsatisfactory, I had never questioned His existence. Everybody I knew believed in God. Surely it was impossible for all those people to be wrong?

'God is an unproven unknown,' Gianfrancesco stated. 'So when it comes to God, I'm an agnostic. I would like to be more decisive about it and say I'm an atheist, as my father was, but I'm still an agnostic.'

I considered this for a moment. Then I said: 'Aren't you afraid that if there is a God, you'll anger Him by not believing?'

Gianfrancesco laughed.

'No, not at all,' he said decisively. 'If there is a God, because

I'm not saying there definitely isn't, then I think He, or She, would just want me to try to be a good person. But what I *am* certain about is that I don't need all the rituals and dogma of the Church in order to be a good person. In fact, I think it gets in the way. And the Catholic system of confession where absolution is granted for any sin, even a serious one, simply by telling a priest is a very flawed concept.'

'I sometimes make things up to confess,' I confided. 'Just small stuff. Like being greedy or not having prayed enough.'

'So you lie in the confessional? There's not much point in you going to confession then, is there?'

'I've never confessed about us.'

Gianfrancesco looked at me, slightly perplexed. 'What would you confess about us?'

'Well, we kiss.'

'And you think that's any priest's business?'

'It's supposed to be a sin.'

Gianfrancesco snorted. 'Are we hurting anybody when we kiss?'

I had asked myself this very question many times. 'Well, no.'

'So it can't be a sin, can it? It's not like stealing or murder.'

His words made sense, but I was confused. 'So why would the Church say it's a sin?'

'Because the Church can make up any rules it likes and people will obey for fear of being punished. If the Church banned people from wearing socks on Tuesdays, then people would stop wearing socks on Tuesdays. My father used to say that religion was all about control of the people. He said you should never submit to the authority of the Church in place of your own powers of reason. Catholicism isn't really about God. It's a system of rules and threats to ensure those rules are followed. It's just a form of government and taxation, but with added guilt.'

These were new and radical words to me. I found them compelling, but more than a little unsettling.

'But it's not all bad, is it?' I asked. 'What about heaven – that's not a threat. Don't you think your father is there?' The thought that my Papá looked down at me from heaven had been my greatest comfort since we had lost him.

'The only place I can be certain my father is, is in the cemetery of Pieve Santa Clara,' replied Gianfrancesco.

'But wouldn't you like to think he was in heaven, watching over you?'

'There are lots of things I would like to think, but it doesn't mean any of them are real or true. If you believe something enough you can bend the facts to justify it. But I don't think my father's looking down from a heaven full of harp-playing cherubs and angels any more than I believe he's in hell drowning in a lake of sulphur. He didn't believe in heaven and hell anyway. The Church uses the promise of heaven and the threat of hell to keep control without having the slightest shred of evidence that either exists.'

'The church here helped my father when he couldn't work any more.'

Gianfrancesco looked at me, then looked away again, shaking his head. 'Really?' he said.

'Yes. The church charity gave him work at the cemetery. If it hadn't been for that, he wouldn't have had any work ever again and we could have starved.'

'Graziella, how did your father have his accident, the first one?'

'He was crushed.'

'What was he doing when he was crushed?'

'Repairing the church tower.'

'And he was doing it gratis, wasn't he? He gave his services free of charge because he was a devout man.'

'Yes.'

'So don't you think the church had a duty to help him?'

My mouth was dry. Gianfrancesco's words expressed thoughts which I had never dared to articulate.

'And the second accident. How did your father have his second accident?' Gianfrancesco persisted.

'Removing a wasps' nest from Don Ambrogio's house.'

'And did the church help your mother?'

'She didn't have to pay for the tomb.'

Gianfrancesco looked me in the eye. 'How very magnanimous of the church,' he said.

*

That evening as I sat eating supper with my mother I wondered whether the same thoughts had ever occurred to her. She had cursed Don Ambrogio for instructing my father to climb a ladder to deal with the wasps' nest and refused to let him take my father's funeral service, but she still went to church every Sunday and she still prayed before bed every night.

'Mamma, do you think that the church should have done more when Papá died?' I said.

'More? What do you mean?'

'I mean, should they have taken more responsibility?'

'Well, the parish gave us 5,000 lire.' She shrugged. 'It was better than nothing. And I didn't have to pay for his place in the cemetery.'

'But you were very angry with Don Ambrogio.'

'Yes, of course I was. Asking a crippled man to climb a ladder to deal with a nest of wasps was an irresponsible thing to do. And your father was irresponsible for agreeing. I was angry with them both. But that wasn't the church's fault. It was two foolish men deciding to do something foolish.'

'And have you ever wondered whether God might not exist?'

This made my mother put down her fork. Obviously alarmed by my question, she frowned, then said, 'Why would you ask me that?'

'Just because of a conversation I was having with Gianfrancesco. We were talking about how some people don't believe in God.'

'Is that what he thinks? That there isn't a God?'

'No, of course not. It was just an interesting subject,' I replied reassuringly, not wanting to worry her. I thought it better not to mention apostasy, or agnosticism. My mother seemed relieved.

'Of course God exists,' she said.

'But how do you know?'

'I feel Him in my heart, just as all good Christian people do.'

I didn't question her any further, for I was questioning myself. I didn't feel God in my heart, or my mind, or anywhere else, despite the fact that I considered my behaviour to be that of a good Christian. I tried to be kind and thoughtful and helpful towards others. I had never stolen anything, apart from Zia Mina's sloes. My lies were limited to small untruths, mainly told in the confessional, and to omissions about how Gianfrancesco and I spent our time together.

Doubts which had been chattering in my mind since my days at the convent were becoming louder.

CHAPTER 2

Salvatore had been living at Paradiso for over six years. It was difficult for me to remember a time without him. We all thought of him as family.

One day he took my aunt to one side and said, 'Donna Mina, there's something you should know. I have a project. A plan for the future.'

'It's always good to have a plan. What is it?'

'I am going to open a restaurant again.'

'A restaurant?'

'Yes, but not like the one I had before in Naples. Donna Mina, I am going to open a pizzeria. More and more people know about pizza now and I think it would be very popular.'

'Won't it be rather expensive to set it up?'

'I have been saving my salary, Donna Mina. Almost every lira you have ever paid me,' he said proudly.

'Will that be enough?'

'Almost. Just a few more months, maybe a year, and I will have enough. I have even seen a premises near the cathedral in Cremona. It's in a beautiful old building, with an arched doorway and vaulted ceilings. The current owner wants to retire soon and he said he would give me first refusal. That as long as I could come up with some of the money to start with, I could pay him the rest in instalments once my business gets going.' Salvatore's voice grew excited. 'And right after I had spoken to him, I saw a sign, Donna Mina! A hunch-backed man walked right past the door and stopped and looked at me. He looked me right in the eyes! You know that they say in Naples that it's lucky to see a hunchback?'

My aunt's smile was tinged with sadness as she said, 'So you wouldn't live here any more?'

'I love living here, Donna Mina,' Salvatore replied, 'and I love working for you, but my heart is in the kitchen, not the garden. I will never forget your kindness and your generosity. You are a remarkable woman. But I'm thirty-five years old now and I need to make my own life.' He paused. 'I was thinking that you could be part of it though.'

'How? A restaurant is no place for me.'

'Tomatoes, Donna Mina. You grow the finest tomatoes and if you could grow more, I would buy every single one from you.'

'I would like that,' my aunt said, and she smiled.

'You would?'

'Yes.'

He said shyly, 'Then I have your blessing?'

'You do, Salvatore. And I'm certain you will be very successful.'

Receiving my aunt's approval galvanised Salvatore into action.

'I need your help, *criatura*,' he told me. 'I want you to write a letter, to a man who used to supply mozzarella to my old restaurant in Naples. I'm hoping that he still has his herd of buffalo, and if so, I need to know if he would agree to send fresh mozzarella up to me on the train every week.' Salvatore licked his lips. 'The mozzarella he used to make was exceptional. It came from the creamiest buffalo milk, had the texture of elastic silk and it tasted like … I cannot describe how good it tasted. There was nothing like it.'

Salvatore dictated a letter for the mozzarella man, giving a brief explanation of the circumstances which had led him to remain in Lombardy and proposing a business partnership as part of his new venture. We walked to the village together to post it.

'Maybe I could name a pizza after you,' he said. 'Pizza Graziella with extra mozzarella! What do you think, *criatura*?'

I thought it was a very good idea!

11

Salvatore waited for almost a month for a reply. The anticipation was immense.

'Hey, Graziella!' he called to me one day. 'We've got a letter from Naples!' Handing me the envelope, he said, 'You open it, or I might tear it.' I could see he was as excited as I was.

He began to read it aloud, but barely got past *My Dear Salvatore*, when his mouth dropped open and his words tailed off.

I didn't think it possible for a man as swarthy as Salvatore to go pale, but that is what he did as he read the letter. He stared at it, gaping like a fish, before falling to his knees with a great yowling wail of, '*Madonna! Madonna! O Madonna Mia!*'

Salvatore's cry attracted the attention of both my mother and my aunt, who came running outside, thinking he had hurt himself.

'What on earth's happened?' asked my mother.

Salvatore, still on his knees, could not utter a word. He was glazed and immobile, staring at his letter.

'Graziella! What's happened to Salvatore?' repeated my mother.

'I think he got an answer about the mozzarella,' I said.

My mother and my aunt looked at each other, perplexed.

It took Salvatore several minutes before he could speak, and when at last he managed it, he seemed to have forgotten his Italian. Indecipherable words in Neapolitan stuttered from his mouth.

'*Frátell … Fratemó …*' he sputtered.

'*Frátell?* Your brother? What about him?'

He passed the letter to Zia Mina. His whole body was shaking, his eyes wide and wild.

The letter, it transpired, was not from the mozzarella man. It was from Carluccio Scognamiglio, Salvatore's supposedly deceased brother.

The mozzarella man had received Salvatore's business proposition and had been somewhat surprised as he had thought that Salvatore had been killed in the war. There had even been a memorial service for him, which had been extremely well attended. He had taken the letter straight to Salvatore's brother, who was very much alive and living in Naples.

Carluccio Scognamiglio explained that he had become lost in Eritrea, or rather, he had lost himself to avoid the slaughter. After most of his company had been massacred, he had hidden in the bush, preferring to take his chances with the carnivorous wildlife than face almost certain death in battle. Eventually he was declared missing and presumed dead.

Those few weeks in hiding turned into months and then into years. Had it not been for the kindness of several Eritrean families who had offered him food and shelter, he would certainly not have survived. In the letter, Carluccio explained that it was not until 1947 that he was able to make his way home to Naples, hoping to be reunited with his brother. However, he could find no trace of Salvatore. In the end, he had written to the government who had replied that Salvatore had been killed in Albania.

'Albania?' exclaimed Salvatore once he had calmed down sufficiently to regain the power of speech. 'I've never even set foot in the place!'

Starting afresh by himself had been difficult, Carluccio wrote. There was no sign of any reconstruction work, and their old restaurant was still a pile of rubble.

Almost before we had all had a chance to take in this momentous event, Salvatore had sprung into action. He made me write back immediately. It was a long letter, full of news and information about how he had made his new life in Pieve Santa Clara. He described Paradiso, me, my parents and my aunt. By the time I had finished, it was five pages long and my hand was aching.

I was about to seal the letter in an envelope, when Salvatore stopped me.

'I haven't asked about Carmela,' he said hesitantly. 'I wonder whether I should? I wonder if my brother has seen her, or heard from her? I suppose it wouldn't hurt to ask.'

I added a final line to the letter and cycled down to the village to post it.

One week later, Salvatore received a telegram from Carluccio to say that he would be coming to see him and would be bringing his family with him.

'My brother has a family,' Salvatore said emotionally. 'A family. That means I'm an uncle!'

'How many people are coming?' asked my aunt.

'Carluccio didn't say. The telegram just says *Arriving in 10 days with family*. He doesn't mention how long they're staying either.'

'They can stay in my house, Salvatore,' Zia Mina said briskly. 'Let's just hope I have enough beds.'

I helped prepare the twin beds in her spare room and the Pozzettis lent an extra mattress, just in case two beds were not enough. Zia Mina's son Ernesto's room was out of bounds. It had remained untouched and nobody had slept in his bed since his death.

I took turns with Salvatore keeping a look-out on the date that Carluccio Scognamiglio and his family were due to arrive. Salvatore was beside himself with anticipation. He said he hadn't slept since receiving the telegram.

'I'm an uncle,' he kept repeating. 'I wonder how many nieces and nephews I have? One certainly, but maybe more. My brother's been back in Naples three years.'

Even when it wasn't his turn to be the look-out, he kept coming to the gate.

'You make sure you tell me straight away if you see anybody,' he said. 'Even if it's just one person, or a bicycle, or a cart. Anything. Anyone.'

There were several false alarms. Salvatore went running up the road when he saw two figures appear on the horizon, but they turned out to be a farmer and his wife on their way to the village. Another time he flagged down a car full of nuns.

It was late in the afternoon when a taxi pulled up at the gate, and there was no mistaking that it was Carluccio Scognamiglio sitting in the front passenger seat. He had the same dark, broad face and tightly-curled corkscrew hair as Salvatore.

'They're here! They're here!' I called.

Carluccio was the first to get out of the car, followed by a plump woman with a swarthy young boy who looked about ten years old.

Salvatore came tearing out of the barn at such speed that he nearly fell over, but when he reached the gate he stopped in his tracks. He looked straight past his brother to the woman and gasped, 'Carmela!'

Carmela said nothing. She just nodded and burst into tears. Carluccio took the boy's hand and edged him forwards, towards Salvatore.

'Your son?' Salvatore looked in bewilderment from the child, to his brother, to Carmela.

'No,' replied Carluccio, embracing him. 'Not my son. *Your* son. This is Salvatorino. We call him Rino.'

*

After all the excitement, we came to learn the full story. When Carmela had fallen pregnant in the spring of 1940 her family were furious. They had sent her away to have Salvatore's child in secret, ordering her to surrender her baby to the Church. Carmela had refused, following which they had forbidden her to come back to Naples until they heard news of Salvatore's death.

Despite agreeing to her return, Carmela's family had all but disowned her, which meant that the young woman had brought

15

up her son alone and in straitened circumstances. She had rented a one-roomed garret, scratching a living doing any menial job which came her way. Being the mother of an illegitimate child had rendered her unmarriageable.

When Carluccio finally made his way back from Eritrea, he had met her by chance at the festival of the Madonna Del Carmine. On learning that he was an uncle, he had taken on the responsibility of helping Carmela as best he could.

After hearing the story, the mistreatment Carmela had endured played on my mind. It seemed so wrong that her family had separated her from a man as lovely as Salvatore and in so doing had denied Rino a loving father. Perhaps it was because I missed my own father so much that I was so troubled. When I told Gianfrancesco all about it, a couple of days later, I became very upset.

'How could they?' I burst out, tears welling in my eyes. 'How could they force Salvatore and Carmela apart like that? Our fathers are dead and there's nothing that will bring them back. But Rino had a father all along and Carmela's family kept them apart.' The more I thought about it, the more enraged I felt. 'Anyway, why does it matter so much that people have to be married to have children? Our mothers are raising us alone, but because they're widows people are fine with it. In fact, they think our mothers are brave and admirable. I don't see why being unmarried is such a big deal. As long as people love each other and love their children, why should anything else matter?'

'You're right,' replied Gianfrancesco, 'but illegitimacy is a stigma. It shouldn't matter, but it does. The Catholic Church's grip is strong, and all the rules are made up by old, celibate men. Sadly, it's the women and children who pay for it. No woman has ever got pregnant all by herself, but women are the ones seen as having lapsed morally and they're the ones left looking after the children. A man can deny paternity, but a woman can't deny maternity.'

16

'It's not right,' I said hotly.

'I completely agree, but that's the way it is – and until Italy divorces itself from Catholic morality and drags itself into the twentieth century, that's the way it will always be.'

I sat back with my head resting on Gianfrancesco. He put his arm around my shoulder.

'My family used to take in foundling and orphaned or illegitimate children,' he said. 'We used to entrust them to the workers' families who lived on our farm. That system continued right up until my grandfather's day.'

'Zia Mina was one of them,' I said.

'Yes. She must have been one of the last children to be taken in.'

'Why did you stop taking in children?'

Gianfrancesco sighed. 'After my grandfather's silk business failed, the farm's fortunes plummeted. Most of the workers had to leave, so there was nobody to foster the children.'

*

That evening, Salvatore's newly re-formed family sat together talking in rapid, unintelligible Neapolitan. Excited howls and peals of joyous laughter echoed across the yard.

I liked Carmela very much and it was clear to see why Salvatore was so madly in love with her. There was a spirited bawdiness about her and a sparkle in her eye. She had a way of looking at him which made him blush.

Carluccio turned out to have the same easy warmth and humour as his brother. He told incredible tales of his time in Africa and his numerous brushes with death.

'They came looking for deserters,' he said. 'Those who had run away from the fighting were shot if they were found. Fortunately, my skin had become so black and my hair grew so wild under that African sun that you couldn't tell I wasn't a local unless you came really close!'

My aunt welcomed the family warmly into her home, saying to Carluccio, 'I was expecting you to be with your wife, so I've prepared a bedroom for you to share, but now I don't know how you want to divide your sleeping arrangements.'

Carluccio volunteered to sleep on a mattress in the barn and to leave the bedroom for Carmela and Rino, but Carmela had other ideas. She had no objection to Carluccio sleeping in the barn, but it was not Rino she wished to share with.

My aunt was so overjoyed by the reunion that she put aside her prudery. She didn't even pass judgement when Salvatore and Carmela pushed the twin beds together.

Over the following days Salvatore was uncharacteristically quiet. He just stared at Carluccio and Carmela, but most of all he could not keep his gaze off Rino.

It was taking the boy some time to acclimatise. He was wary of his newly-found father and alarmed by the clawed hand. He would not go near him and hid behind his uncle and his mother. When Salvatore spoke to him, he would not answer. By the evening of the fourth day, Salvatore was beside himself.

'I don't know what to do, Donna Mina,' he said to my aunt. 'My own son is afraid of me. Am I really so frightening?'

'Just give him a bit of time to get used to you,' she said wisely. 'Imagine what a shock it must be when you suddenly discover that a relation you thought was dead is actually alive, especially a father.'

Salvatore sighed and said, 'I suppose so.'

'And perhaps if you didn't stare at him quite so much he would feel more comfortable.'

'Have I been staring?'

'All the time! The poor boy can't blink without you having a look.'

My aunt took Rino into her vegetable garden and they spent the afternoon talking, gathering strawberries and pulling onions. Eventually Zia Mina was able to convince him to go and see Salvatore's lodgings in the barn.

'You see here?' Salvatore told his son, taking down his book of saints. 'I have kept this picture of your Mamma here in this book since before you were born. And every day I have prayed to the Madonna del Carmine to ask her to keep your Mamma well and happy.' He crossed himself and said emotionally, 'She has not only answered my prayers, but She has surpassed them. She has guided me back to my brother, to my love, and She has sent you, Rino. I am the happiest man on this earth.'

Rino smiled, took his father's clawed hand in his and kissed it.

That night, Salvatore and Carluccio prepared a Neapolitan feast. We sat under Zia Mina's vines until long after dark.

'So, will you go back to Naples and open a new restaurant now?' asked Zia Mina. There was no disguising the disappointment in her voice.

Salvatore grinned. 'We are going to open a pizzeria, but not in Naples, Donna Mina. We are going to open it in Cremona, in those premises with the arched door and the vaulted ceiling. And it's going to be quite a place, Donna Mina! Carluccio has managed to save almost as much money as me, so we can afford to furnish and decorate it and make it beautiful. Our mozzarella supply is promised, and I'm sure people will come from miles around.'

Pizzeria Paradiso opened its doors in May 1951.

Salvatore and Carmela were married shortly after, in July, on the Feast Day of the Madonna Del Carmine. Six months later they welcomed a baby girl into the world and named her Carmina.

CHAPTER 3

Although my mother and I now had our own inside lavatory, we did not have our own bathroom. I was accustomed to washing daily at the kitchen sink and going to my aunt's twice a week for a bath. In the past, I had always loved my baths. I would play games, sucking in my stomach to see how much water I could hold in my navel, or counting how long I could hold my breath for under the surface. Now, suddenly, such games seemed childish.

My appearance had never concerned me before, but I began to look forward to my nakedness at bath-time and felt a growing interest in the way I looked.

In the spring of 1951, Zia Mina took delivery of an enormous antique wardrobe. It had been left to Immacolata in some distant relative's will, but she did not have either the need or the space for it, so she gifted it to my aunt. It arrived on the back of a lorry, took three men over an hour to carry it upstairs in various pieces, and four hours to reassemble it.

The wardrobe was a mammoth thing, dating from the early 1800s. Made of walnut, it had four full-length mirrored doors and would not have looked out of place in Gianfrancesco's house.

My aunt did not have enough possessions to fill it and offered a section to my mother to use to store her linen work, or anything else she wanted. Zia Mina said that I too could have a section, but I had nothing at all to put in it. All my clothes fitted into the blanket box I had slept in as a small child and with plenty of room to spare.

Up until then, the only place where I had been able to view

my reflection was in a small shaving mirror which my father had fixed to the wall by the kitchen sink. It was sufficient to see half of my face at a time if I craned my neck, and nothing more. The mirrors in the cloakrooms at school were not much better. They were always crowded with older girls checking their hair and inspecting their complexions. I did sometimes catch a distorted, spectre-like image of myself in the window when it was dark outside, or in the glass frontage of a shop, but I had never had the chance to look at my full-length reflection at leisure. With the arrival of the wardrobe, that changed.

Being an old piece, the glass of each mirror was warped. I looked at myself in the first mirror, bobbing my head up and down, amused at the comical distortion. The second mirror seemed to squash me and the fourth gave me a neck like a giraffe. It was the third mirror which enthralled me. It was the best of the four.

I stood before it, examining myself from head to toe, from the front, from the sides, close up and at a distance. I untied my hair and let it fall loose, like a model on a billboard, then turned my back to the mirror and gave the sultriest pout I could, gazing intensely over my shoulder. I pinched back the fabric of my dress so that it clinched around my waist, raised my skirt to examine my legs and stood on tiptoes, imagining how I would look in high heels.

I was not displeased with my appearance. I had definitely grown. Lots of people had told me that, but my shape was changing. During my second year at middle school my bust burst forth with some pain. Within a year I could not do any of my blouses up. My hips were broadening too and had developed a pleasing curve. They made my waist look smaller. I wondered whether one day I would be fortunate enough to have a waist like Signora Marchesini.

The sudden arrival of pubic hair alarmed me. I had never seen a grown woman naked and was too embarrassed to ask my mother whether it was normal. Genitalia, whether male or female, was referred to as 'the shame'. I couldn't think of any practical reason why hair might grow there, unless it was to hide 'the shame'.

It was the chance discovery in the barn of a nude postcard which alleviated my concerns slightly. The card must have belonged to Salvatore. It consisted of a black and white photograph of a woman wearing only stockings and a top hat. She had full, fleshy breasts and ample thighs, and was pointing to an enormous bush of hair between her legs.

I looked at my own body in the mirror and compared it with the photograph. My breasts were larger than a lot of other girls', but nowhere near as weighty as those belonging to the woman in the picture, for which I was grateful. Thankfully my thighs were not as thickset either. I still wasn't sure how I felt about pubic hair. Mine was rather sparse and grew at funny angles. I didn't know whether less or more was preferable.

Shortly after the arrival of the wardrobe my mother gave me some obscure information about menstrual cycles and I was warned to expect bleeding and not be alarmed. The advice came just in time. I woke one morning to find a bloom of blood on my sheet.

I was shown how to make sanitary pads out of cloth and wadding. Each pad was a small oblong bag into which rags were stuffed. Cotton wool would have been preferable, but it was an expensive option as it could not be washed and re-used. My mother said that during the war when rags were scarce she had resorted to filling her pads with grass. Although this provided a barrier, it provided no absorption, but it was preferable to hay which was spiky and itchy and frequently full of mites.

My mother made me two pairs of enormous knickers with loops sewn into the gusset to keep my pads in place. They were horrid, cumbersome things and I was certain that everybody would know I was menstruating by the way I walked. But I was told not to make a fuss. Menstruation was a nuisance which all women had to endure. Until the arrival of my own periods I had had absolutely no idea of the inconvenience suffered by my mother every month. She had never complained, not even about mites.

The arrival of my period should have been an opportunity for Mamma to explain the facts of life to me, but all she said was that it was part of growing up and that I should not concern myself with any further questions until I was married. The subject of sex remained strictly off-limits.

All I knew about sex at the age of fourteen and a half was that it was a sin and that it resulted in babies, which in itself was confusing. It was called fornication if the people involved were not married, and adultery if they were married to other people. Fornicators and adulterers were destined for eternal damnation. We had been given this information during a religious studies class at school. Several pupils had raised their hands to ask further questions, but the teacher had moved on quickly to the sin of anger, which was explained in far greater detail even though we were all perfectly aware of what anger was.

We all had some rudimentary understanding of the biology of reproduction. Being children of a rural community we knew what livestock did, but translating the mating habits of animals to human sexual behaviour posed more questions than it answered.

One of the boys in the class claimed that he had come across a couple having sex in a field. He had seen the woman's feet poke up above the tops of the wheat. This was not helpful. I could not understand why sex would involve a woman having her feet in the air as in my imagination I pictured the woman doing some sort of hand-stand.

I didn't know whether kissing was sex, or whether kissing could cause a pregnancy. Couples could be fined if they were caught

23

kissing on the mouth in public. Italy had very strict laws concerning public decency.

Gianfrancesco and I spent hours kissing, but I had always been careful that when we kissed, we did not kiss for too long at a time. I would pull away after a while, take a breath and start again. I cannot say now by what reasoning I thought this to be a form of contraception, but as rumours of the connection between kissing and pregnancy were prevalent and I had not fallen pregnant, I guessed there must be some truth in it.

Sex, this forbidden act which happened somewhere and somehow in between kissing and the arrival of a baby, and which had something to do with menstruation and eternal damnation, was mystifying. Trying to extrapolate some truth from speculation and superstition only caused more confusion.

Even Gianfrancesco, who seemed to know everything about everything, was puzzled about the details and frustrated by the government censorship of all things pertaining to sex. The maddening lack of facts and the prevalence of contradictory information only served to fuel our curiosity. By the end of our second splendid summer together our curiosity was growing keener.

It was late August and the heat was so intense that it was visible. The region had teetered on the edge of drought since June. The crops in the fields were parched, and what little wind there was blew through them with a dry, crackling sound, like a flameless fire, whipping plumes of dust into the air. Everybody hoped for rain, but week after week the sky remained stubbornly blue and utterly cloudless. My aunt was worried that her well would dry up. The water from it, which was usually sweet and clear, tasted like rust.

Gianfrancesco suggested we should go to the river to cool off. If he managed to catch a fish I could take it home to my mother for supper.

24

We mounted our bicycles and set off in the scalding heat. By the time we reached the river we were both drenched in sweat and I felt quite faint. Gianfrancesco laid his bicycle on the bank, immediately stripped off his shirt and trousers and jumped into the water.

'Come in!' he called. 'It's lovely, and it's shallow here. You can touch the bottom easily.'

I hesitated for a moment, unsure whether I too should strip down to my underwear.

'Come on – you'll die in that heat,' he said, then disappeared under the surface for a few moments, resurfacing with his wet hair plastered to his face.

'I can't swim,' I said. 'And I don't have anything to wear.'

'Just jump in in your underclothes, like me.'

I looked up and down the river bank. 'What if someone sees me?'

'Nobody will see you. Nobody else is mad enough to be out in this heat.' He disappeared under the surface again, and reappeared further out.

I hid in a thicket and gingerly stepped out of my sweaty dress, which I hung on a branch to air. Then I waited for a moment, looking both ways up and down the bank again. Gianfrancesco was right. There was no sign of life apart from us. We were the only ones foolish enough to be outside in the searing afternoon sun.

I dashed from the cover of the shrubbery to the water. I did not have the courage to jump in as Gianfrancesco had done. Instead I eased my way in slowly, feeling the bottom with my feet. The river bed was soft and a little slimy, but not unpleasant. The cooling of the water was exquisite.

I felt a little less self-conscious once I was in. Gianfrancesco swam up to me.

'Just stay close to the bank if you're afraid,' he said. 'But if you feel like coming out a bit further, come with me.'

He took my hand and we waded out slowly. A fish swimming past me amongst the weed made me squeal and jump, and I almost lost my footing. Gianfrancesco caught me and I clung to his arm.

'Try to catch the next one,' he said, laughing at my jitteriness. 'Then you can have trout for supper. Sometimes I catch really small ones in the streams on the farm, but the ones you can catch here are a good size. You can even catch catfish here. My father caught a huge one once, but my mother said it tasted disgusting.'

The current was strong and I was too nervous for him to let go of my hand, even though the water was only just above waist-deep.

'Do you want me to teach you to swim?' he asked.

When he placed his arms around me in the water with only our thin cotton underclothes separating us it was like being naked together for the first time.

'Let me hold you under your arms. Just lie back against me and let your legs float.'

It was easier than I had imagined. I let myself be carried, allowing the water to lift my legs.

'There!' he said. I felt the breath of his words brush against my cheek and his wet hair dripped down my neck. 'I'm going to move backwards really slowly. Don't worry – I've got you. Just let the water take your weight.'

The sensation of floating was quite lovely, but the sensation of being skin-to-skin with Gianfrancesco was even lovelier.

'If you feel your legs sinking, just give a little gentle kick and they'll come up again,' he said. He kissed my cheek and wrapped his arms around me a little more. I rested my head on his shoulder.

'It's easy, isn't it?' he murmured. 'Once you're used to floating, swimming is easy.'

In that moment I was not really concerned about learning to swim. Our closeness in the water was enough for me and I was loath to separate my body from his, but he insisted that I should try.

'You never know when you might need to swim,' he said. 'It could save your life, or someone else's.'

He pressed his wet cheek against mine for a moment.

'I'm going to release you very slowly. Don't panic. If I feel you start to sink, I'll catch you. And anyway, you can touch the bottom easily here.'

He eased his grip and moved one hand to support the small of my back and the other to support my head.

'Stay relaxed. That's perfect. Now kick gently with your legs.'

Gradually I felt my body master the water. Gianfrancesco's hands guided and buoyed me, and before long I was swimming on my back unaided.

'You're doing really well,' he told me. 'On your back is easiest. It's a bit different swimming on your front, but I can teach you that too, and if you ever feel you're sinking, just flip onto your back.'

We were in the water for a long time. I learned a rudimentary breast-stroke and only swallowed a few mouthfuls of river. In the end it was only the fact that we were cold which made us go back to shore.

As we emerged with our underwear clinging wet and transparent to our bodies, we became very aware of our almost-nakedness. I was still anxious in case someone should walk by and see us – or worse, that some officious witness would report it to my mother. But I left my dress hanging in the tree.

We stretched out together under the shade of a willow to dry off. I watched the rise and fall of Gianfrancesco's chest. He was almost seventeen years old. His body was lean and his shoulders were broadening into those of a man. The muscles of his stomach twitched as he breathed. I was overwhelmed with the urge to touch his bare skin and wondered whether he'd mind if I did.

The more I thought about it the more the fizzing feeling I felt whenever we were close bubbled through my body; then something inside me detonated, making my heart beat fast and liberating such a fervent burning that I thought I should jump back into the river for fear of catching alight.

'Are you all right?' asked Gianfrancesco.

For once I didn't know what to say to him, so I pulled him close and kissed him more keenly than I had ever kissed him before. It was not the cautious, explorative kiss of a young girl kissing a young boy. It was a lover's kiss, filled with passion and meaning and desire.

'Can I touch you?' he asked, breathless, when I finally let him come up for air.

I could not have spoken even if I had known what to say. I lay back on the parched grass without a word, but the invitation was clear. He nuzzled my neck as his hand moved from my waist and softly up over my ribcage, then slipped into my camisole and cupped my breast gently. As he squeezed my flesh his kiss became more intense, as did the burning feeling inside me.

Suddenly I was afraid of the way I felt. Gianfrancesco sensed my tension.

'What's the matter, Graziella?'

'I don't want to get pregnant!' I blurted out.

He smiled, then chuckled. 'You can't get pregnant by letting me caress your breasts. If you did, it would be an immaculate conception, which would be inconvenient, but impressive.' He propped himself up on one elbow and curled a strand of my hair around his finger. 'The only way any woman can get pregnant is if a man releases his sperm inside her, and then it has to be at the right time in her menstrual cycle.'

'Are you sure?'

'Absolutely. I read a medical text on human reproduction last term. An old classmate whose father is a doctor lent it to me. There's no reason for a medical text to lie.'

Still, I was not fully convinced.

'Graziella, I wouldn't ask you to do anything which involved a risk like that. And I would never do anything that you didn't want me to do, or that you didn't like. It's not that I wouldn't want to have sex with you, or that I don't think about it a lot. But it can only happen when we both feel ready. It's a risk we can't possibly take now. The consequences would be far too serious.'

'You think about us having sex?'

'Of course. It's a natural thing. Don't you think about it?'

I couldn't deny that I did, although my fantasies involved little more than guesswork and were overshadowed by the danger of falling pregnant.

'I've been thinking about asking to touch your breasts for ages, but I wasn't sure how to do so. I was hoping you'd offer,' he said. 'But if you're not comfortable with me touching your body and you just want us to kiss, then that's fine. All you have to do is tell me so that it's clear.'

The problem was that clarity was difficult when there were so many chasms in my knowledge. I did want Gianfrancesco to touch me. I had also been thinking about it for ages.

'But what if someone finds out?'

'How is anyone going to find out unless we tell them? I would never tell anyone. Some boys brag about things they say they've done with girls. I would never do that.'

I took his hand and placed it firmly back on my breast.

'I read another book about sex,' he said after a few moments. 'I found it hidden behind some books in my father's library. But it's not a medical text. It's a novel. An erotic novel.'

'What's an erotic novel?'

'Well, something erotic is something sexual, or something that makes you think about sex. Something which arouses desire.'

My desire was aroused simply by the thought of it, which I realised was probably the point.

'What did it say?'

'Lots of different things. It's called *The Garden of Pleasure*. It's about a woman who marries a Count and lives in a palace, but she doesn't love the Count. He's drunk all the time and he can't do sex properly.'

'How does she know he's not doing it properly?'

'She just does. She complains about it a lot. But then she falls in love with the groundsman and he can do sex in a way that she likes, so they have sex. Lots of it. All the time.'

'Does the Count find out?'

'No. And that's intrinsic to the story. She doesn't have sex with the Count so when she has sex with the groundsman she knows she mustn't fall pregnant, because if she does, the Count will know she's been unfaithful. The Countess and the groundsman do things which involve no risk of conception.'

'What do they do?'

'They kiss a lot.'

'Does kissing count as sex?'

'Yes. Part of it at least, if it's passionate. The Countess and the groundsman make an art of it. And they use their tongues.'

'Their tongues? How?'

'They kiss in the same way we do, but they use their tongues at the same time as their lips.'

I thought about this for a moment. I had always been mindful to keep my tongue out of the way when I kissed Gianfrancesco.

'So have we been doing it wrong?'

'No. Not wrong. Just differently, I think.'

I rolled my tongue against the roof of my mouth, considering the technicalities of involving it in a kiss. If we were to try, it would require some practice.

'But they don't just kiss on the mouth,' continued Gianfrancesco. 'They kiss everywhere. All over each other's bodies. When they're naked.'

30

A hot flush rose through me. Gianfrancesco fidgeted and turned to lie on his front.

'And they caress too. They give each other pleasure by rubbing each other's intimate parts.'

This piece of information was so astonishing to me that I gasped, but not as much as I gasped when Gianfrancesco told me that the groundsman kissed the Countess between her legs, as though he was kissing her mouth, and his tongue was very much involved in the process.

Suddenly I had a lot of new complexities to consider. The mystery of sex was a lot more involved than I had thought.

Gianfrancesco rolled back onto his side, pulled me close and placed his hand on my waist.

'Maybe we could read it together some time,' he said, folding me into his arms. 'Because I'm definitely one hundred per cent totally and utterly sure that you can't get pregnant by reading.'

I clasped his face in my hands and kissed him, then tentatively poked my tongue out. It made him cough. As I thought, it would take some practice.

We were roused by a distant rumbling as a gust of wind cut through the grass. The temperature had dropped quite suddenly. A line of brooding black clouds had gathered on the horizon.

'It's going to rain,' said Gianfrancesco, shivering and reaching for his clothes. 'We should get home before we get caught in it.'

*

At last a huge thunderstorm broke the drought. Bruise-coloured clouds released a biblical deluge and lighting cracked the sky in two. Thunder pounded through the walls of Paradiso and made the windowpanes rattle. Gutters overflowed and the yard ran with water.

It rained for several long, dark hours, sometimes so heavily that the garden looked out of focus. When at last the rain stopped, thin wisps of steam rose from the fields and hovered over the heads of the battered crops, but the sky remained thick with clouds, promising more rain.

Although I told my mother that Gianfrancesco and I had been down to the river, I didn't mention that I had learned to swim. I was afraid she might discern something in my expression, or read something in my words which could divulge that my afternoon had not been entirely innocent.

My outward calmness could not have been any more different to the way I felt inside. I could not stop thinking about my afternoon with Gianfrancesco; about our almost-nakedness; about the way we had kissed and caressed under the willow trees; about the fact that he thought about us having sex. But more than anything, I was consumed by a yearning curiosity to read *The Garden of Pleasure*.

My mother was not particularly interested in hearing where I had been or what I had been doing. She was busy working on a very complex piece of lace which involved a lot of counting and multiplying by twelve.

'Go and help Zia Mina,' she said, shooing me away with a wave of her hand as she muttered calculations under her breath.

The long weeks of drought followed by sudden torrential rain had turned the soil in the vegetable garden to ankle-deep mud. My aunt laid planks across the ground to stop her clogs from being sucked off her feet. She was busy pulling up her onions before they rotted in the ground.

'Where have you been?' she asked.

'Just down to the river,' I replied.

'With the Marchesini boy, I suppose.' My aunt frowned and made a tutting noise. 'I wouldn't be letting any daughter of mine out gallivanting with a young man like that.'

'We just went to the river, Zia Mina. We're friends.'

My aunt stared straight at me, her lip curled into a snarl.

'Friends?' she sneered. 'I know that's what you tell your mother and more fool her for believing you. And more fool you for expecting anything from the Marchesini boy.'

'What do you mean?'

'I mean because men of his family's social standing do not marry girls like you!'

With that she turned and left me alone in the garden, muttering something about the Marchesinis. I was very glad that Zia Mina was not my mother.

I didn't lend too much weight to Zia Mina's judgement. It sounded to me as though she had never been in love. Whatever her reasons were for not liking the Marchesinis, she didn't understand how Gianfrancesco and I felt about each other. Past grievances and social standing had nothing to do with it. He and I knew with absolute certainty that we were in love, and that was all that mattered.

Thoughts of reading *The Garden of Pleasure* kept me awake well past midnight. I raced through my chores the following morning and was on the road to Cascina Marchesini within minutes of my mother telling me that I could have the afternoon to myself.

'My mother's out,' said Gianfrancesco, wrapping me in his arms. 'There's nobody here except us. Come in. It's about to rain again.'

He led me inside as the first fat drops spattered on the steps. The house smelled of damp and storm water. There was a puddle in the kitchen, fed by a drip from a jagged crack in the ceiling. The pan which had been positioned to catch the leak was close to overflowing.

'The roof's leaking worse than ever,' sighed Gianfrancesco, casting a resigned look at the crack. 'But there's no money to fix it. I love this place, but sometimes I wish we just lived in an ordinary house.'

We stood contemplating the crack until Gianfrancesco said, 'One day I will bring this house back to life again. I will continue my father's plans to restore it.'

'What about the farm?'

'I intend to get it back up and running again. But not as my father did. He worked with the labourers, which was admirable, but it's pretty much what killed him. I will finish my education and get a well-paid job which will allow me to employ a farm manager to begin with, then I will take over the management myself. I will build it up again bit by bit and not get into debt, as my father did.'

I followed Gianfrancesco out of the kitchen. A mass of furniture and boxes was stacked in the middle of the oval hall.

'I've been sorting through the furniture that my grandfather amassed. We're going to try to sell it to raise some money for repairs. An antique dealer's coming to value it.'

Leaning up against a carved dresser was the enormous portrait of Carlo Marchesini. A bloom of mildew now obscured part of his red jacket. He was still looking down his nose at me.

'I've been sorting through some things upstairs too,' said Gianfrancesco. 'I've managed to clear the master chamber. Come and have a look.'

We made our way up the great curling staircase. I had never been upstairs before. Signora Marchesini was very particular about her privacy and did not like us to be in the house. She allowed us to study in the dining room if the weather was bad, and we had also been allowed into the library, but I didn't like it there. The place smelled of mould and mice and rotting leather, and it was always cold, even in the summer.

Although faded and peeling, the master chamber was spectacular, painted in various shades of blue, with golden cornices and coving. The ceiling was decorated with a fresco of vines. Bunches of sumptuous purple grapes had been painted so skilfully that they appeared to hang down.

34

In the centre of the room stood a vast bed with a draped silk pelmet and a headboard carved with swans and harps. It was much higher off the ground than a normal bed and had a polished wooden box on each side to use as a hop-up.

Gianfrancesco kicked off his shoes, clambered up and reclined against the mass of pillows. I sat back with him, surveying the room. A single streak of light pierced through the shutters where one of the louvres had slipped, making the gilt-work glitter.

'Shall we read?' he asked with a mischievous raising of his eyebrows as he slipped a slim book from between the pillows. It was the size of a postcard, small enough to fit into a pocket, and I could see by the dog-eared corners, the tattered cover and the split spine that it had been in many different pockets. It was *The Garden of Pleasure*.

I settled down onto the bed, my head resting on Gianfrancesco's chest. He held the little book up so that we could both see the print and began to read.

The first half-dozen pages were not dissimilar to any novel. Gianfrancesco read with expression and emotion. The beautiful Countess, her weak and spiteful husband and the handsome, brooding groundsman were introduced. The Count was mean and addlebrained with drink. The Countess was unhappy and friendless, stranded far from her family in her palatial home. On a lonely walk through her gardens, she came across the groundsman. There was instant attraction. There was tension. There was the promise of forbidden passion and lust.

Page eight exploded into an orgy of words, describing feelings and sensations which caused me to catch my breath and Gianfrancesco to falter and lose his place.

The title of the book, *The Garden of Pleasure*, referred not to the garden in which the Countess and the groundsman engaged in their illicit tryst, as I had presumed, but to the Countess' body. What I referred to as my 'shame', she referred to as her 'garden of pleasure'. There was no shame involved.

35

I pictured the Countess with her cochineal-reddened lips. I tried to imagine how it would feel to be kissed as intimately as the groundsman kissed her. The more I imagined it, the harder it was to sit still.

A long paragraph was dedicated to the groundsman unfurling the petals of her rosebud. Gianfrancesco had to explain the euphemism to me. But every description, however veiled or oblique, captivated me. Yet despite the fact that both my mind and my body were ablaze with curiosity and lust, I was far too afraid to act out the pleasures described in the book.

The Garden of Pleasure was a novel and novels were not fact. The author, who remained mysteriously anonymous, could have made things up. Common sense overrode the burning desire which I felt. In the back of my mind the fear of becoming pregnant would not be quiet.

We had some success in kissing using our tongues. I let Gianfrancesco unbutton my dress and kiss my breasts, but when his hands slipped over my hips and his kisses began to meander towards my garden of pleasure, my sharp intake of breath betrayed my trepidation. Gianfrancesco redirected his attention back to my breasts, where it remained until we heard a clock in some distant part of the house strike four.

I kissed him deeply one more time, fighting the urge to stay, and arrived back at Paradiso at precisely the time I was supposed to, conscious of maintaining an appearance of normality.

CHAPTER 4

My final year of middle school was spent without Gianfrancesco. He had secured a place at the Liceo Classico in Cremona. Along with the Liceo Scientifico, which specialised in the sciences, the Liceo Classico was the most demanding of the high schools.

I made him a gift so that he would think of me whilst we were apart. I embroidered a handkerchief with our initials and attempted to reproduce the Marchesini coat of arms on one corner. My mother was always strict about getting a design right on paper before committing it to cloth, but I was in a hurry. I did my best to replicate the image from memory straight onto the fabric. It was by no means my best work, but I gave it to Gianfrancesco anyway.

'Thank you,' he said. 'It's lovely.'

'I could have done better. I know it's not quite right.'

He looked at the coat of arms for a long time and said, 'The herons do look a bit like ducks. And their legs are the wrong way round.'

'What do you mean?'

'Herons' knees work the opposite way to ours. They bend backwards. You've sewn them with their knees bent forwards.'

My heart sank and I took the handkerchief from Gianfrancesco's hands.

'I'll make another one for you,' I said. 'I'll go down to the cemetery and copy the coat of arms properly.'

Gianfrancesco kissed my cheek and took the handkerchief back.

'Absolutely not. I love it just the way it is and I'll keep it with me all the time. And I'll think of you every time I blow my nose.'

I never saw him during the week, and on Saturdays and Sundays our time was limited. The Liceo Classico set an onerous amount of homework. Even during the holidays our time together was dictated by Gianfrancesco's endless assignments. Every subject was taught to a far more rigorous standard than in other schools, and in addition to the foundation subjects there was Greek History, Roman History, History of Art, Philosophy, and a copious quantity of Latin.

I wondered how useful these subjects would be if his intention was to run Cascina Marchesini as a working farm again one day, but when I broached the matter he said, 'A good education is the basis of everything. And the Liceo Classico offers the best education there is.'

'Yes – if you need Latin and Greek and philosophy. But you won't need any of those to look after cows, or manage the fruit harvests. Wouldn't it be better if you went to one of the agriculture schools?'

Gianfrancesco shook his head and said, 'My mother wouldn't have it.'

Nevertheless, he liked his new school and rekindled friendships with several boys with whom he had been at boarding school previously, but for me it was a lonely year. I tagged along with a few girls, but I didn't form any meaningful friendships. Rita, who had regarded my friendship with Gianfrancesco as a betrayal, made it very clear that she was not willing to share her circle of friends with me.

When at last I too finished middle school I passed my exams with good grades and was able to submit my application to the Istituto Magistrale.

My mother would have been within her rights to demand that I went to work as soon as I finished middle school, as the majority of girls in my class had done. Rita, for instance, had taken a job at the hairdresser's in the village. But my mother was wholly supportive of my choice. I would be the first person in my family to continue my education beyond both elementary and middle school.

Within days of receiving my letter of acceptance it seemed that the whole village knew. My mother was not normally one to gossip, but she was so proud that she told everybody she met that I was about to embark on my teacher training. On a trip to the village to run an errand I was congratulated by the butcher, the mayor's secretary and several people to whom I had never spoken before.

The Istituto Magistrale admitted only girls from the ages of fourteen or fifteen. Four years later, providing they had passed their yearly exams, those same girls emerged as capable, upstanding young women, qualified to teach from nursery through to primary school.

Exemplary behaviour was expected both within school and outside. Immoral conduct, consorting with undesirable company, shouting, eating or smoking in the street, the use of coarse language, truancy, stealing or involvement in any physical altercation would lead to withdrawal of privileges, or in the more extreme cases, expulsion.

I quickly adapted to the etiquette. We stood by our desks at the beginning of each lesson and did not take our seats until we were told to do so. If a teacher entered the classroom whilst class was in session, we had to stand and could not sit down again until a greeting had been exchanged and permission to sit had been given. We kept to the right-hand side of corridors and staircases. We held doors open and stood aside to let teachers pass. We always said hello, good-bye, please and thank you. We offered our help to anybody who appeared in need of assistance, and often to those who did not, just to be polite. We never raised our voices.

The feeling of camaraderie between us was strong, even though our backgrounds were diverse. Daughters of doctors and civil servants were seated beside daughters of grocers, carpenters and farmers. Teaching was an egalitarian profession where snobbery was not tolerated. A spirit of solidarity was not only encouraged, but demanded. We were a female army of budding primary-school teachers, united in the cause of education.

The driving force behind the school was its formidable headmistress, Professoressa Soldi, for whom we all felt a combination of fear and admiration. It was no secret that she had been an active member of the resistance during the war and a vocal opponent of Mussolini's views on the subjugation of women within society. She had fought against the Battle for Births campaign, aimed at increasing the population of Italy, and had narrowly avoided imprisonment numerous times. What's more, she had temporarily lost her teaching position when she had refused to take an oath of loyalty to the Fascist regime.

When metal had been requisitioned for the war effort, Professoressa Soldi had ordered the Fascio ironwork to be removed from the front doors of the school. The Fascio, a symbol depicting a bound sheaf of wooden rods and an axe, was the image from which Fascism had been named. It symbolised strength through unity.

The removal of iconography which Professoressa Soldi considered to be dangerous and backward had been a bold move and one which had made its point to the authorities, who were nevertheless in no position to refuse any donation of metal during a time of national emergency. After the war the doors were re-furnished with plain ironwork.

On our first day we were called to congregate in the main hall. Professoressa Soldi took her place on the podium and cast her steely eyes over her new recruits.

'Welcome,' she began. 'Firstly, I would like to congratulate you all on your choice of school and ultimately, your choice of profession. As you embark upon this new stage of your young lives, I would also like to remind you all that you are here by virtue of the fact that women who have gone before you have striven to make it possible. Many have made great personal sacrifices. Some have even laid down their lives for it. This must never be forgotten.'

We sat in silence, mesmerised by her words.

'Nevertheless,' continued Professoressa Soldi, 'we have not stepped out from beneath the shadow of the black banner of Fascism into a shining Utopia. There are many things for which we must continue to strive. We have the vote, but there are no women in the government in our country above local level. We have the right to enter university, but female doctors, lawyers and engineers make up an infinitesimally small percentage of those professions. That is because there are men who believe that owing to our lesser physical strength, our mental abilities must also be inferior; that we are unfit both in constitution and temperament to hold any position of influence. Those archaic, patriarchal attitudes are falsehoods which must be fought against and beaten, not with our fists, by means of force and violence, but through *education.*'

She spoke the word 'education' with emphatic purpose.

'Education is not simply the teaching of numbers and letters, or facts from history. It is the moulding of young minds. Your students will be like empty vessels, and the power to fill them with principles which are just and rational will be yours. Learn to use that power wisely.'

She ended her speech by reciting the school motto, *Virtus Scientiae Decus* – virtue is the sign of wisdom.

In 1950s Italy 'feminism' was an unknown term. Women's liberation had not yet entered the vernacular, and gender equality was a fledgling concept. Nevertheless, we were imbued with a sense that we lived in a time of change. The economy was booming. There was no war to fight. Nobody was starving.

Literacy was improving. Technology was advancing at an astonishing rate. Unlike the majority of our mothers, we had the choice of education and of living independently. We were not constrained by laws which confined us to the kitchen.

My decision to enrol at the Istituto Magistrale had been based on little more than a small girl's wish to be just like her primary school-teacher, but I was both glad that I had made the choice and grateful that I had been able to make it.

By the end of my first year I felt transformed in ways which occasionally bewildered my mother. She had been more than a little alarmed by my decision to attend a Women's Day march. I had left the house dressed in yellow, my hair woven with mimosa flowers and a banner made from an old sheet rolled under my arm.

The slogan on my banner was a demand for equal employment rights and pay. The Fascist regime had put in place quotas limiting to 10 per cent the proportion of women allowed to work in both the public and private sectors. Although the law had been repealed, many employers still refused to employ married women of childbearing age.

The idea that by being in the workplace, women were taking jobs which were rightfully intended for men was a stain which was stubborn to shift; as was the principle that men should be paid more than women, even if they were doing the same job. Professoressa Soldi herself was paid well over a third less than she would have been, had she been a man. I was beyond thrilled when mine was the banner she chose to hold.

I threw myself into my studies. Along with the core subjects we studied psychology, child development and law. I took pleasure in them all and relished the classroom debates. We were encouraged to read, not just the books included in our syllabus, but anything and everything which made us think.

But not all the reading material at school was of the academic variety. Cheap romance novels, which were available to buy from newspaper kiosks for as little as 50 lire, were circulated and exchanged between students. We were mesmerised by titles such as *Condemned to Love*, *Cruel Passions* and *Souls in Torment*.

We also devoured weekly magazines which, amongst the advertisements for kitchenware and bust-firming creams, printed thrilling tales of love, jealousy and intrigue. My favourite was *Grand Hotel*, where stories were told through cartoons and photographs, with the characters' words expressed in speech bubbles and their feelings in thought bubbles. Every possible human emotion was explored.

The problem pages were not only a source of advice on matters of the heart, but also the source of great entertainment. We would read them aloud to one another, offering up our own advice and opinions, laughing and gasping at the predicaments in which unfortunate readers found themselves and gleaning a vicarious pleasure from their problems.

Troublesome boyfriends, fiancés and husbands were the most common subject-matter. Infidelity, or the suspicion of it, always made for a torrid read.

Professoressa Soldi did not approve of such tawdry material, which would be confiscated if we were caught reading it during school-time.

'You will find better things to fill your heads with than *this*!' she said, dropping a copy of *Grand Hotel* into the waste-paper bin as though it was a soiled handkerchief.

But we couldn't get enough. Although we all strived to be strong, independent, modern women, we also wanted to be just like the heroines in the stories who won the hearts of the heroes. We longed to be adored. We craved romance and adventure.

However, there was still one subject which remained strictly off-limits in every book and magazine we read, and that was sex.

The dictate was that girls should be pure until married. Even once married, bedroom activities were not to be spoken about. Young women lived under the constraints of chastity and abstinence, and most did so unquestioningly. Amongst the students, in particular those from more middle-class families, the notion of sex was utterly distasteful. The preserving of an impeccable reputation was vital. Like virginity, once gone it could not be reclaimed.

Some girls had boyfriends; others claimed that they did, or that certain boys were in love with them. It was acceptable to admit to kissing and to holding hands, but anything more was not. Any girl violating this code of behaviour could be turned upon by her peers. One girl who alluded to having let a boy put his hand up her skirt was branded a slut. It was a label which stuck to her throughout her time at school, despite the fact that she was a very pleasant girl who had a beautiful singing voice and a great talent for playing the flute.

Of course I had spoken to my friends about Gianfrancesco, but I was very careful never to mention anything that might suggest that I had let him touch my breasts, or behaved in any way immodestly. I certainly didn't tell them about *The Garden of Pleasure*. We had read it together numerous times and although I had been very close to trying the pleasures it proposed, I had not been brave enough. Gianfrancesco had been very accepting of my reticence, assuring me each time that he would never demand that I do anything I wasn't ready for, but as my sixteenth birthday approached, I felt my readiness increase.

The government's censorship of all matters pertaining to sex extended to the teaching of sex education in schools, but Professoressa Soldi considered it important that we should be warned about the perils of sexual exploration. During my first two years at the Istituto Magistrale, four girls in the years above me had left suddenly to get married. The number had been higher in the years directly following the end of the war. There was only one common denominator. And Professoressa Soldi was determined that ignorance should not be the cause of pregnancy.

In order to circumvent the legal restrictions concerning sex education a lesson was to be given as part of a Child Development class.

A letter was sent to parents informing them that the lesson would be taking place and assuring them that no explicit nudity would be shown. Nevertheless, some parents refused to let their fifteen- and sixteen-year-old daughters participate and kept them at home on the day in question. One girl forged her father's signature in order to be allowed to attend the class. My mother did not object. I think she was relieved that she would not have to field any questions herself.

Our Child Development teacher was Professoressa Pagliacci. She was a small, stout, stand-offish woman and nobody's favourite teacher. Her teeth, most of which were the colour of milky coffee, appeared to have sprouted not only in a state of chaos, but sideways on. Unlike the majority of our teachers, she was a spinster.

Professoressa Pagliacci greeted us with a business-like smile, briefly exposing her zig-zag teeth. It was clear that she was keen to get the lesson over and done with.

Pinned to the blackboard behind her was a copy of a classical painting of Adam and Eve. The Professoressa began by pointing to the image of Eve and explained that our bodies were like Eve's because we had vaginas and ovaries. Ovaries made eggs. Eggs were the first necessary ingredient in the making of babies. This was not new information. We had already covered the subject briefly during a lesson on menstrual hygiene which had been given at the very start of term; too late for all but one girl in the class.

The Professoressa then turned her attention to Adam. A muffled titter spread through the back rows. At this, she flared her nostrils and cast a disapproving look over all of us, not just the errant gigglers, cleared her throat loudly, then pointed vaguely at Adam.

'Men's bodies are different by virtue of a small tube called a penis and two glands called testicles. Testicles make sperm and the penis is used to deliver it. Sperm is the second ingredient necessary in the making of babies.'

In the name of public decency all the offending parts mentioned were obscured by fig leaves.

'In order for the man's sperm to reach the woman's eggs, an act of physical intimacy must take place. The man's penis becomes rigid. In response, the woman's vagina becomes slimy. This is a sign that the vagina is ready to receive the penis. The act of receiving the penis is called copulation.'

Professoressa Pagliacci demonstrated this not by means of a diagram, or by drawing a picture on the blackboard, but by straightening the middle finger of her left hand to illustrate the penis and by forming a circle with the thumb and forefinger of her right hand to illustrate the vagina. She then proceeded to simulate the penis entering and exiting the vagina, repeatedly, and at some speed.

'As we have already learned, the man's testicles make sperm,' she said, continuing her mime as she spoke. 'After a short time he will feel that the sperm wants to come out.' She gave her middle finger an impatient wiggle. 'When the sperm comes out, copulation is complete and the man will remove his penis. His sperm will swim to meet the woman's eggs and that's how babies are conceived. Any questions, girls?'

There was a considerable amount of shuffling and sideways glancing. Some girls looked perplexed, others horrified. A few were still suppressing the urge to laugh. But no questions were forthcoming. Professoressa Pagliacci seemed relieved.

'Of course it will be several years before any of you are married, so you have nothing to be concerned about now. When the time does come, it's perfectly normal to be worried. Girls ask whether it will hurt and yes, at first it will. There might be blood. It might be awkward at first. But it's like anything. Remember how it was, the first time you rode a bicycle? It was difficult to get your balance. I expect most of you fell off a few times. It's the same with copulation.'

We were dismissed shortly afterwards and filed out of the classroom quietly.

'I will never, ever, *ever* do *that*!' exclaimed the girl who had forged her father's signature.

She had a point. Professoressa Pagliacci's description of sex, reduced to a perfunctory act of penetration was enough to make any girl want to keep her slimy vagina to herself. But I knew otherwise.

CHAPTER 5

Modest dress was compulsory at school. All buttons had to be done up. Tight skirts were not allowed and certainly no hemlines above mid-calf. Our clothing had to be clean and pressed. Visible patches and mends had to be neat. Only laced or buckled shoes were allowed. Heels higher than three centimetres were absolutely prohibited, as were sandals, even in the summer.

I owned two dresses, two skirts, four blouses and two cardigans. None had been purchased new. They were by no means shabby and there were other girls whose clothes were decidedly more rustic and threadbare than mine, but I wished that my clothes could be better. I was aware of the fact that girls from wealthier backgrounds wore nicer clothes than girls like me. They also had more of them.

Along with romance books, fashion magazines were read and exchanged at school. I loved the full skirts, the nipped-in waists, the sweetheart necklines and the seductively scooped cuts across the shoulders. I would stand before the third mirror of Zia Mina's wardrobe holding a picture of a style which I found particularly appealing, imagining myself wearing the real thing.

I had a best dress for church, donated by a client of my mother's. I had been grateful when I had been given it, but the more I wore it, the less I liked it. It was a rust brown, simply-cut thing, not much better than a housecoat, and similar to any number of cheap dresses worn by women of all ages in the congregation. It certainly did not flatter my complexion or my newly-emerging womanly figure.

My mother had basic dressmaking skills and had always made

our clothes, or altered what we were given, but she saw no need for our clothing to have anything other than a practical use. As long as what we wore was warm in the winter and cool in the summer and was not tatty, it was fine.

She had moved the buttons and sewn darts into the bust of my church dress, which had improved the fit a little, but my dress had been made with fabric economy in mind. It was impossible to turn it into anything remotely elegant. The new styles required many more metres of material. The fancy fashions of the 1950s were a statement that the frugality of wartime no longer needed to be respected.

I longed for a lovely dress, but I knew that asking my mother for such a luxury was wholly inappropriate. I never asked her for anything that was not an absolute necessity. She worked hard so that I could remain in school and although we never wanted for anything, her budgeting was always tight.

I supposed that it was not beyond me to make my own, but making a dress was impossible without fabric.

Amongst my mother's rolls of material were ones of stiff linen for tablecloths and softer cotton for sheets, all in plain white. It was not unfeasible to make a dress out of sheet or tablecloth material, but I didn't want that. I wanted a vibrant colour and a bold pattern, just like the dresses in the magazines.

'What are you doing?' my mother wanted to know as she found me rifling through her stock of fabrics.

'I was wondering whether I could make a dress with a full skirt,' I replied, holding up a picture of a blue polka dot frock. I then added, 'For church.'

I thought she might scold me and tell me to be grateful for what I already had, but luckily I had caught her in a good mood.

'A dress like that requires an awful lot of fabric and a proper pattern,' she said. 'I'm no dressmaker, but if you'd like to learn, you could ask Signora Grassi. She's a very experienced seamstress and used to work for a fashion house in Milan. Dressmaking would be a very useful skill for you to have.'

Signora Grassi was a newcomer in Pieve Santa Clara. It was impossible not to notice her. Her hair was bleached peroxide blonde and she would be seen in church wearing high heels and bright jewel colours. In her finest Sunday plumage she stood out like a parrot in a flock of sparrows.

'I've spoken to her several times,' said my mother. 'She's very friendly. If I see her, I'll ask.'

A few days later a length of yellow daisy-patterned fabric appeared on the kitchen table. My mother said it was for me.

'Where did you get it?' I asked.

'From Signora Grassi,' she replied, looking rather pleased with herself. 'I saw her this morning at the baker's and I told her that you were interested in learning to make clothes. She let me have this off-cut at a very reasonable price and said it would be enough to make a skirt in your size. She lent me a pattern too. She said it would be simple to follow for a first attempt.'

A skirt was not quite the fashionable dress I had in mind, but the daisy print fabric was very pretty. It was definitely better than my drab church dress. I hugged my mother so tightly that I made her cough.

Having never used a pattern before it was difficult to know where to start, but with my mother's help I did eventually manage. Had I been more experienced, I would have aligned the print more squarely and done a better job of fitting the zip, but for a first try it was not bad at all. I even had enough fabric left over to make myself a little bag and a hairband.

I wore my new creation to church the following Sunday. Signora Grassi remarked that, considering the fact that it had been my first attempt, I had done rather well.

'If you're looking for a bit of pocket money, come and see me. I'd be glad to have some help over the summer,' she said.

It was a tempting offer and one which was encouraged by my mother, but all I wanted was to spend my summer holiday with Gianfrancesco.

The end of term could not come fast enough. I had reached the midway point of high school and would be starting my third year of Istituto Magistrale the following September, but my mind was not on my studies. I was ripe and ready for a summer of love.

I spent a long time preening myself in front of the mirror. Gianfrancesco hadn't seen me in my new skirt, nor had he seen me wearing the lipstick I had found at the bus stop outside school. It must have fallen out of somebody's handbag. It was not new – in fact, there was very little left of it – but it was enough. I didn't dare to put it on before I left the house because my mother might not have approved. It was only when I reached the turning to Cascina Marchesini that I stopped and applied it, checking my reflection in the bell of my bicycle.

I felt red-lipped and pretty, with my hair tied up in my new hairband and fluttering behind me in the breeze. I found Gianfrancesco sitting on a bench under the portico reading, but he didn't mention my new skirt or the fact that I was wearing lipstick.

'Your gastrocnemius looks very beautiful when you pedal,' he said as I rested my bicycle against the wall.

'My what?'

'Your gastrocnemius. Your calf muscle.' He laughed and held up his book. 'I'm learning about muscles of the human body.'

I sat down beside him and peered across at the pages. He ran his finger slowly up the leg diagram and said, 'I've been giving a lot of thought to caressing your adductor magnus.'

I took his hand, placed it on my knee, then guided it slowly under my skirt and up the inside of my bare thigh.

'Are you wearing lipstick?' he asked as he put his other arm around my waist and drew me towards him. I breathed in the scent of him and felt the hot, fizzing wave rise through me as I squeezed his hand between my thighs.

'Is your mother here?'

Gianfrancesco understood the implication behind my question.

'She's in her room, but she's taken a sleeping pill so she'll be asleep for hours. We could go to my room. She won't know. But only if you think ...'

I didn't let him finish his sentence. Instead I locked my lips with his and ate kisses from his mouth. He cast aside his book, took my hand and led me into the house. We crept quickly and quietly up the immense marble staircase and slipped into his room, shutting the door silently behind us and turning the key in the lock.

Being alone and locked in his room unleashed such a feeling of lust that for a moment I could barely feel the floor beneath my feet. All my fears had vanished. We both knew this was the moment I was ready.

'I'll only do what you want me to do,' he said.

'I want everything,' I replied as I stepped out of my skirt and unbuttoned my blouse. 'You be the groundsman and I'll be the Countess.'

I untied my hairband and let my hair fall loose – and just as the Countess had done in her first moments alone with the groundsman, I turned around for Gianfrancesco, letting him drink in my body, then peeled off my underwear teasingly slowly and stood before him naked.

It was not the first time I had stripped seductively. I had rehearsed the moment numerous times in front of Zia Mina's wardrobe mirror, practising the most alluring way to undo my buttons and lower my straps, studying every movement of my body and inspecting myself from every angle in preparation for that moment when Gianfrancesco would see me naked for the first time.

'Only if you're sure you're ready, Graziella,' he said.

I could not have been more sure. I could not have been more ready.

I unbuttoned his shirt and began to kiss his chest, leaving red lipstick prints where my lips touched his skin. I felt his breathing quicken and the beat of his heart against my face as his hands gathered up my hair. I covered every inch of him in kisses. Every inch of me was covered in kisses too, even my garden of pleasure ...

*

Although my mother had no idea quite how intimate our relationship had become, she had no doubt that we were now more than friends, but she didn't forbid me from seeing Gianfrancesco as I had feared she might. She trusted that I was a good girl who would not behave inappropriately. That trust was acutely misplaced.

We were in a whirlwind of desire and discovery; a time of utter wonder. Every moment that we could steal was steeped in sex. We explored one another everywhere and anywhere that was unobserved: in bedrooms, barns and fields. I was so utterly filled with love and lust for Gianfrancesco that it seemed to overflow from my every pore and crackle through my veins like electricity. It was a shining, glorious feeling.

When I was not with him there were moments when I was so overcome with desire that I thought I would lose my mind.

One day, finding ourselves entirely alone in the house when Signora Marchesini had gone to Cremona, we barely took the time to speak to one another. We flew into a frenzy of kissing and unbuttoning. Gianfrancesco told me he'd dreamed about me and the dream had been so real that when he had woken he had looked for me in the bed beside him, certain that I was there. He described his dream in the minutest of detail. I drank in his words, whispered fervently into my ear as his hands explored me.

He picked me up and laid me back on his bed. I curled my legs around him and drew him as close as I could. My whole body yearned for him.

'We have to be careful, Graziella,' he whispered, 'because right now I could be really reckless and we can't take a risk like that.'

Yet despite knowing all I knew about the perilous consequences of sex; despite knowing that we were playing with fire; despite everything, I felt an irrepressible lust for him, like lightning bolts through my body. The touch of his mouth and his hands on my skin made me quake. I knew the risk, but I was overcome with such frenetic yearning that I begged him and he did not refuse.

*

It was just over a week later when I was woken by a knocking at my window. Sleepily, I roused myself and peered through the panes. Gianfrancesco was outside in the yard. There was a troubled look on his face.

'What time is it?' I yawned, opening the window and rubbing the sleep from my eyes.

'It's a quarter to six,' he replied. 'I can't stay long. I have to get home before my mother wakes up.'

He took a deep, joyless breath. 'I came because I've got something to tell you,' he said, and I felt suddenly afraid. 'I'm being sent away to summer school.'

'Summer school? Why? You passed all your exams.' I was fully awake now, and my heart was pounding.

'Because my mother knows about us. The maid found your lipstick on my sheets and showed it to my mother. She was furious. She gave me an almighty lecture on responsibility and threatened to tell your mother.'

I felt myself go pale. 'Do you think she will?'

'I hope not. She's going to stay with some friends whilst I'm at summer school, and I'm hoping that by the time we come back it will all have blown over and she will have calmed down.'

'When are you coming back?'

'September – just before term starts. I'm sorry, Graziella.' He kissed me hurriedly, promised to write and pedalled off at speed.

Our summer of love had come to an abrupt halt. The only relief was that the day after Gianfrancesco's departure, my period arrived. Luck had smiled upon us.

Nevertheless, I was miserable to the point of irrationality; feelings which were compounded by a fear of what Signora Marchesini might report to my mother. I checked for post every morning, not just in the hope of receiving a letter from Gianfrancesco, but also fearful that Signora Marchesini might write to Mamma.

My mother tolerated my despondent state for a few days before telling me to pull myself together and stop moping. In order to distract me she gave me endless lists of chores. It was not the best way to re-focus my mind.

A letter arrived for me a week after Gianfrancesco's departure. The summer school was situated near Lake Como. He said it was nice and that the other students were friendly, but nothing was mentioned about the reason for his absence. The letter could have been for anybody. Clearly he had been mindful of it falling into the wrong hands.

My mother had gone down to the village for groceries. I cleaned the windows, swept and mopped the floors, then sat on the doorstep in the sun, waiting for the floors to dry whilst I re-read Gianfrancesco's letter. The more I read it, the more banal it seemed.

When my mother returned from the village I thought she would give me a new list of jobs, but instead she wedged herself between me and the flower pot which covered the missing brick, then reached into her basket and took out a bag of figs.

'Here,' she said, splitting open one of the figs. 'These need to be eaten. They'll be past their best by tomorrow. I only wanted four, but the grocer gave me eight for the same price. You can take some to Zia Mina later.'

We sat shoulder to shoulder with our legs stretched out, soaking up the warmth of the sun and the sweetness of the over-ripe figs.

'Papá used to sit right here reading his newspaper and you'd climb up his legs,' smiled my mother, pressing the skin of her fig to squeeze out the last of the flesh. 'He used to pretend he hadn't noticed you. Then you'd peep over the top of the newspaper and he'd pretend to be surprised.'

'He did? I don't remember.'

'I don't suppose you do. It was before he had his accident. You can't have been any older than two and a half or three at most.'

'I think I'm forgetting things about him,' I said.

'It's normal. You were little when he died.'

I loved the moments when my mother spoke about my father, especially when she told me a story which was new to me. It seemed she had saved so many moments in her head, like a bank. Every so often she would withdraw something new – a little domestic vignette, a ridiculous coincidence, a slapstick moment.

'Do you miss him?' I said.

My mother sat forwards, resting her elbows on her knees and her chin on her hands. I could see she was giving some thought to what she was about to say.

'For a long time I missed the man I had married. You see, your father died twice, Graziella, and I grieved for him twice. The first accident and the medication killed the man I married. The second accident killed what was left. The first time was the hardest.'

'Would you ever re-marry, Mamma?'

'I don't know. I'm used to not having a husband and I don't mind it. I suppose it would be different if I wasn't able to support us.'

'How did you meet Papá?'

'I met him when I was in service, near Cremona.'

'Why were you in service when you were so good at embroidery?'

'My parents sent me away,' she said, suddenly looking a little coy, as though she had carelessly divulged something she had rather not have mentioned.

'Why did they send you away?'

My mother sucked in her cheeks. I felt her prickle, then she laughed. 'I was very young and I did something very silly.'

'What did you do?' I asked, smelling a whiff of scandal.

'It was all to do with a boy. As so many things are at that age.'

My mother looked out across the yard and seemed reluctant to say more, but I persisted until finally she conceded, a smile twitching on the corners of her mouth.

'I met a boy when I was fifteen. He wasn't from my village – he was from a place called Pomazzo about ten kilometres away, just outside Bologna. But my parents weren't at all happy about us courting.'

'Why?'

'They didn't like him. They said he wasn't from a good family. His father cared more for wine than for work and he'd been in trouble with the law a few times. So when I announced that we wanted to get married, my parents were not at all pleased.'

'You were going to marry him?'

'Oh yes. I was absolutely determined that I would. And my parents were absolutely determined that I wouldn't. And the more they forbade it, the more obstinate it made me.' She sighed. 'I didn't always get on very well with my parents. I argued with my mother about it, and my father locked me in my room. He even slapped me a few times – but that just made me worse. So the boy and I decided to run away together and get married. We had a plan to slip away in the middle of the night and go to Bologna

57

together. It was pure madness, of course. We didn't have a single lira between us, or anywhere to stay. But we set a date and I gathered together a bag of possessions and crept out of the house in the middle of the night.'

I listened open-mouthed. I had no idea that my mother had once had such a disobedient and adventurous temperament.

'We didn't get very far though,' she said. 'It was January, which we realised very quickly was not the best time of year to run away. It was pitch black and freezing cold. Then it started to rain. We hadn't brought enough clothes and hadn't thought to bring any food. Suddenly running away didn't seem like quite such a good idea.'

'What happened?'

'I wanted to go back home. I think he did too, but he just got very angry with me for changing my mind. I didn't like being shouted at or being called names, so I told him that I didn't want to marry him any more. He was even angrier after that and walked off, leaving me all by myself in the middle of nowhere in the middle of the night.'

'So you just went back home?'

'I tried to. I hoped that I could sneak back into the house and my parents would never know, but I completely lost my bearings in the dark. I'd been walking for hours with no idea where I was until at last I happened upon a farm and thought I'd shelter in the barn until daylight. It was so cold! I couldn't feel my hands or my feet and my clothes were soaked through. But my arrival set the farm dogs barking and woke the farmer. He found me hiding in a cowshed. At first he thought it was thieves. It was lucky he didn't fire his shotgun at me! But then he saw I was just a young girl. A very cold, very wet, very frightened young girl. He took me into the farmhouse, gave me hot milk and biscuits and let me dry off in front of the fire. He was so kind to me, and the next morning he took me back home at first light. I'd never been so happy to be home.'

'What did your parents say?'

'They were furious, quite rightly so. And I ended up in bed with a feverish cold for a week. It was a disaster, but nothing compared with the trouble I would have found myself in if I'd really run away.'

'So that was the end of it with the boy?'

'More or less. The way that he'd abandoned me in a rage made me come to my senses very abruptly. I didn't hear from him again. However, about a month after our failed escape, I learned that he'd been arrested!'

'Arrested? What for?' I knew my eyes were open wide.

'He'd been caught stealing chickens.' My mother sighed, then laughed, before telling me: 'Good things can come out of bad, for it was thanks to my unsuccessful escape that I met your Papá.'

'How?' I was intrigued to hear more.

'Well,' began my mother, 'my parents were so concerned that I would do something foolish again that they organised for me to take a position as a domestic servant in a big house near Cremona. I didn't want to go, as I knew I would hate domestic service and wanted to do embroidery, like my grandmother and great-aunt. What's more, I had hardly been out of my village before then, so sending me to Cremona was like sending me to the moon! But my parents were determined to keep me away from that boy. They insisted that my employers should lock me in my room at night and also that they should send all my wages back to them for safekeeping so that I couldn't plot an escape. When I arrived at the house I wonder now what kind of girl my employers assumed they were taking on. Surely a very unruly and wayward girl.'

Unruly and wayward were two words I would never have associated with my mother, but by this point I could see she was thoroughly enjoying telling me her story.

'So I began work at the big house. The family were pleasant enough and they soon realised I wasn't going to be any trouble.

They certainly didn't lock me in my room at night. However, they were demanding. I had to work very long hours and never felt I had anything to show for it because, as requested, they were sending the entire sum of my wages back to my parents for safekeeping. But to be fair, Graziella, I can't say I was unhappy there. The other staff were nice, especially the cook. She was a wonderful lady. Dear Signora Brocchi had a heart of gold. I don't know what I would have done without her. I was so young and so completely inexperienced, and away from my home and my family. Signora Brocchi took me under her wing and was like a mother to me. In fact, to be absolutely honest she was a good deal kinder than my own mother.'

Mamma closed her eyes for a moment, lost in her musings.

'Signora Brocchi was an important person in my life. Sometimes you can know someone for many years but they never really affect you, not significantly. But other times you can meet somebody and perhaps only know them for a short while, but the effect they have on you transforms you. That's how I felt about Signora Brocchi. I wished that my mother had been like her. My Mamma was a waspish woman. She could be selfish and unreasonable, and sometimes I think I brought out the worst in her. She made me feel like a nuisance. But Signora Brocchi was warm and compassionate and I felt loved in a way that I just hadn't experienced before.' She turned to me. 'And when you were born, Graziella, I made a promise to myself that I would never make you feel the way my mother made me feel. Instead, I would try to be like Signora Brocchi. I have tried, Graziella. I want you to know that.'

She ran her hand along my arm and laced her fingers with mine. We were sticky with fig juice.

'Sometimes I can be impatient,' she said, 'I know that. Sometimes I need quiet and nothing more than my own company – and perhaps that comes across as cold. But I always try to be kind and I always try to be reasonable.'

I rested my head on her shoulder. It felt good listening to her and it was rare for her to talk about herself so openly.

'Anyway,' she continued, 'I didn't like the domestic work, but I did it without too much complaint. However, as soon as I was able to show the Signora that I could embroider and that I was really rather good at it, she took me off my cleaning duties and set me to work on her linens and mending anything which required a needle and thread. I liked that far better.'

My mother's eyes were still closed. The sun caught her cheek. Time had engraved her face with concentration lines from hours of embroidery, but in that afternoon light she looked very beautiful and exceptionally serene, almost dream-like, with a little smear of dried fig juice on the side of her chin.

'I had been working at the house a couple of years and I was not far off my nineteenth birthday when some work needed doing on the garden walls. A builder from Cremona had been charged with the repairs and your Papá was his apprentice.'

She opened her eyes and smiled again, seemingly transported back to the moment.

'We'd caught each other's eye but neither of us was brave enough to do anything about it. Then one day I was sitting outside hemming dishrags when he came to ask for some water. To be honest, I was a bit embarrassed. I wished he'd found me embroidering something beautiful so that he'd be impressed. He had such a cheerful smile. And he was very polite, and I liked that.'

My mother rested her chin on her hands.

'We spoke a little that first day, and again the next day. Signora Brocchi saw what was happening and she started sending me out with water and food for the builders, and each time I would talk to your father a little more. Just before they were due to finish the work on the garden walls, your father asked if he could accompany me to church on Sunday. Signora Brocchi gave me

Sunday afternoon off until five o'clock. So Papá called for me in the morning, we walked to church together, attended the service and spent the afternoon walking and talking – and that was it. That's how everything began.'

'But did he have to leave when the work was done?'

'Yes. He came to see me whenever he could, but it was a complicated journey for him. He would take the train from Mazzolo to the other side of Cremona, but the house where I worked was almost ten kilometres from the nearest station. Sometimes he could catch a lift on a cart, but most of the time he walked. By the time he got to me he'd spent all day travelling and he must have been exhausted, but he never complained. He couldn't stay in the house, of course. He would spend the night in one of the stables.'

My heart fluttered. I wondered whether from time to time my mother might also have spent her night with him in the stable.

'And when the weather was really bad and the days were short I didn't want him to make the journey. I was afraid he would catch his death and I couldn't bear the thought of him sleeping out in a stable in the winter. So during those times we wrote to each other. We wrote a lot, sometimes every day. I used to walk to the local village to post my letters in all weathers. I didn't have access to any money but Signora Brocchi was kind enough to give me a few lire every week for stamps.'

My mother told me, 'I liked the fact that he could write, and he wrote well. It was rare in those days for ordinary country people like us to be able to write so well. He even used to draw little pictures around the edges of his letters. Your Papá always had a talent for art too. He even had a portrait photograph taken, and he sent it to me with a little drawing of the two of us on the back. I used to keep it on my bedside table.'

'You had a photograph of Papá!' I exclaimed. 'What happened to it?'

'I don't know,' she replied sadly. 'It was lost at some point after we moved in here – I can't think how. But we were married by then, so I didn't need a photograph because I had him right there with me.'

'And your parents didn't object to you marrying Papá?'

My mother pursed her lips. The tone of her voice changed.

'They objected all right – to the fact that I would no longer be sending my wages back to them. I'd been very naïve in thinking that they'd been putting them aside so that I'd have a bit of money to start off married life when in actual fact, they'd spent the lot. I had absolutely nothing to show for nearly three years' work and I'd just given up my job to get married. And although your Papá had finished his apprenticeship by then and was working for a wage, he had no savings. As an apprentice he'd been given his food and board and a few lire each week for personal necessities, so it had been impossible for him to put anything aside. But we still decided to get married and we managed. We rented a little room. People were helpful and they gave us bits and pieces. Zia Mina and Zio Augusto gave us blankets and firewood as a wedding present. Pozzetti's parents gave us a cooking pot and a milk pan. But for the first few months we would eat our food off a shared plate because it was the only one we had. Bit by bit, week by week, we managed to furnish our home with the things we needed. Your father's wages covered the basics and I'd managed to find a bit of embroidery and sewing work by then. Starting with nothing made us appreciate everything. And when Zia Mina offered us a permanent home here in return for Luigi restoring the house, it felt as though we'd won the Christmas Lottery ten times over.' Her eyes sparkled.

'It's funny,' I said. 'If it wasn't for a chicken thief I wouldn't be here.'

My mother turned to me and squeezed my hand.

'I suppose that's one way of looking at it,' she said, amused.

'But let it be a lesson, Graziella. I know you have feelings for Gianfrancesco, but don't pin all your hopes on him. I remember how it felt to be fifteen and in love, but things can change so quickly when you're young. Don't think that the first boy who takes your heart is the one who will have it for ever.'

Her words made a lump rise in my throat, but I knew that my love for Gianfrancesco could not possibly be compared to my mother's infatuation for the chicken thief. Nevertheless, that half-hour spent sitting on the step with my mother, sharing figs and listening to her talk so openly, was a precious moment. I resolved that I would make it a stone memory, for it was the first time that I felt she was speaking to me not as a child, but as a young woman. It made me realise how relationships re-mould over time. Children grow up, but their parents grow up with them.

My mother smoothed out her skirt and got to her feet.

'Those floors must be dry now,' she said. 'Go and take Zia Mina the rest of the figs and ask her for some zucchini, then come in and help me prepare them. I've bought some fresh pecorino, and I shall need you to grate some breadcrumbs.'

That evening as we feasted on stuffed baby marrow, I decided that I would not waste my summer doing chores, feeling despondent and missing Gianfrancesco. I would take up Signora Grassi's offer of a job.

CHAPTER 6

Mechanisation and cheap food imports had decimated jobs in agriculture. Rural Italy was undergoing massive and irreversible changes. Small farms were swallowed up by cooperatives. Smallholdings became redundant. Young people, specifically young men, could no longer count on employment on the land and there was a mass migration to find work in the industrial towns and cities further north.

Many communities became nothing more than ghost villages, but fortunately, this was not the case with Pieve Santa Clara. Although we did suffer from an exodus of youth, our village was saved by its proximity to the railway line, which made it an attractive and affordable place for people employed in Cremona to relocate. With the advent of diesel trains, the journey from the station in Mazzolo to Cremona took less than half an hour.

The newcomers cared little for the old, traditional properties with their basic facilities, draughty windows and damp problems. Many old houses were demolished to make place for contemporary constructions. Several new streets branched out from the North Road.

Signora Grassi's was one of a number of villas recently built on a brand new residential road halfway between Paradiso and the village. It was very modern, with central heating and two bathrooms, one of which had a shower cubicle, something I had never come across before. The garage was situated on the ground floor, with the accommodation above. Instead of traditional shutters, there were mechanised blinds. The villa also had a fashionable style of garden, planted with grass, roses and cacti.

Hearing this, my aunt sniffed and said that planting gardens with things that could not be eaten was a waste.

I was nervous. It was not just the prospect of my first job which made me anxious, it was Signora Grassi herself. She had an effusive, gregarious manner and a loud, cigarette-laced cackle. She called everybody 'darling'.

She greeted me on my first morning wearing an orange georgette blouse. I could see her brassiere through it. The top three buttons were undone and revealed more of her quivering bosom than would normally have been considered appropriate.

'Come along in, darling,' she said. 'Don't be shy! I don't bite.'

The atelier was in a large, bright room adjoining the garage. It had two enormous floor-to-ceiling windows which looked out across the garden and flooded the space with so much light that being inside was almost like being outside.

My eye was drawn immediately to the posters and photographs displayed on the walls. They were all pictures from fashion shows. Signora Grassi said she had worked on all of them. Apparently, she had learned her skills from a famous couturière in Milan. In her time, she told me, she had made and altered garments for many esteemed clients, and assured me that if I worked hard, I too could be dressed in the height of fashion very soon – a promise which caused me great excitement.

In the centre of the atelier was a long table for setting out patterns. One wall was shelved and stacked with rolls of fabulous dress fabrics, boxes of buttons and bundles of zips. Three mannequins stood in the corner, each clad in a different piece of work at varying stages of production. Signora Grassi had made padding for each one which corresponded to her individual clients' proportions.

She tested my hand-sewing first. Although I had spent countless hours of my life sewing by hand, my nerves made my hands clammy. I was so mindful not to make any mistakes that it took me far longer than normal to form my rows of stitches. When I finally showed my work to Signora Grassi she was pleased enough.

'Rather slow, darling,' she said, 'but your work is very tidy and your stitches are nice and regular.'

She was also pleased with my cleanliness. Just like my mother, she was obsessive about it.

'Always wash your hands before you set to work. Fabric is like a sponge for smells. Especially bad ones.'

Signora Grassi had a special soap scented with Parma Violets with which she would wash her hands, twice, after each time she had been outside to smoke a cigarette.

'And keep your nails filed short, darling, but not too short. You need enough to be able to pick a stitch.'

The atelier contained two sewing machines – a traditional treadle machine and a large modern electric one. Signora Grassi showed me how to thread the treadle machine first; it was a complex process. Two colours of thread could be used at the same time, something which delighted me.

'Make sure you keep both feet on the treadle, darling, and push down with your heels. If you push with your toes you'll end up with calves like the footballer Carapellese.'

I spent several days on the treadle machine, sewing seams and practising different stitches on scraps and off-cuts of fabric. I was amazed by the speed at which it was possible to work. Miles of edging and hemming, which was so tedious and time-consuming when done by hand, could be completed in minutes with absolute accuracy.

Once I had mastered the basics of the treadle machine, I was introduced to the electric one. This was an altogether different experience. The complexity of the machine bewildered me. It had dials for tension, switches for different bobbins, thread-winders and spindles. It was connected to a series of spools which hung from the ceiling. A light touch on the foot pedal would make it clatter into action at incredible speed. The needle would pump up and down so fast that it became no more than a blur. If used incorrectly, it could gobble up fabric, snagging and puckering it into a knotted mess. I was always afraid that it would catch my fingers, despite there being a guard to cover the needle and pressure foot. Loading the spindles involved clipping a spool between two stiff springs, which had a tendency to snap back. I had my thumbs bitten repeatedly. Signora Grassi laughed at me each time. It was also hot work. The heat from the electric motor blew into my face and I had to keep stopping to mop my brow for fear of staining my work with sweat.

Signora Grassi was a demanding employer, but as I was a disciplined student and also used to my mother's strict tuition, I acclimatised quickly to her teaching.

Initially I was tasked with making cotton dust-covers, which were used to protect garments. Signora Grassi said it was easier to learn on thicker fabric. She was pleased, but still pressed me to improve the speed at which I worked.

Once she was sure that I could be trusted working the machine and could produce a perfect cotton dust-cover in under ten minutes, I was allowed to work on garments. I was only given simple straight seams and hems to sew, but with each item came a deadline. Signora Grassi's time limits were always very tight, although she insisted they were far more generous than when she had been learning.

A steady stream of clients came through the atelier. Signora Grassi's reputation was excellent and women came from quite a distance to engage her services. She would go out of her way to compliment them in terms which verged on the sycophantic, gushing about their lovely legs, their graceful shoulders or their elegant posture, and all the time suggesting the best way to enhance and flatter their figures.

'You have to make clients feel special, darling,' she said. 'I've never met a woman who couldn't be won over with a few compliments.'

One extremely fat lady, who was obviously very conscious of her size, was complimented on her flawless skin and beautiful eyes. Signora Grassi had suggested a style of dress with an empire line, which clinched under the bust, the narrowest part of her ample figure. Although the dress was flattering, it was not miraculous. The lady looked herself up and down in front of the mirror and thanked Signora Grassi with an air of resignation – but Signora Grassi had a special trick for the larger ladies. She would place a spool of thread on their heads and tell them to stand up straight so that it did not fall off, then she would say, 'It's all about posture, darling. Anyone can lose five kilos just by standing correctly.'

Without a doubt, the lady had left the atelier with an increased feeling of confidence.

It was only when she had gone that Signora Grassi turned to me, shook her head and said, 'It's going to take more than standing up straight to sort that one out. I would suggest she also spends less time *sitting* at the dining table!'

At first I was not sure whether I was supposed to laugh at such comments, but they came thick and fast. A client would come in, be measured, fitted and flattered – and when they left, Signora Grassi would speak the truth. She would refer to their physical imperfections as their 'problems'.

Of course, not every client was physically flawed. Numerous ladies with beautiful figures came to have outfits made and altered. Signora Grassi fussed over them, obliging them with extra care and adulation as she said they were the best possible advertisement for her business.

The radio was always on in the atelier. As we did not have a radio at home I had little knowledge of the wonderful variety of music being broadcast. I loved the cheerful voice of Renato Carosone, who sang humorous songs in Neapolitan. Signora Grassi said she couldn't understand a word he said, but I had been subconsciously schooled in Neapolitan by Salvatore and was able to translate.

I would even find myself singing the tunes I had heard through the day on my way home. I suggested to my mother that she should buy a radio as I was certain she would also enjoy the music. But she said she appreciated silence when she worked and had no need for such a distraction. My aunt was not keen either. She would go to Don Ambrogio's to listen to radio broadcasts by the Pope with Immacolata from time to time, but she considered modern music noisy and the lyrics immoral.

Signora Grassi had been very interested to know about Gianfrancesco. I was missing him, but I was so busy and enjoying my work so much that I had little time to brood over his absence. We had written to each other. He was also busy and enjoying himself, and clearly not brooding over his absence either. He had been horse-riding and canoeing. Summer school to me sounded more like a summer camp.

'I recently altered some garments for your young man's mother,' Signora Grassi told me. 'She got so pitifully thin after she lost her husband. How tragic that he should have died so young. I don't suppose she'll find another suitable man around here, not even with her looks. Now there's a truly beautiful lady. You could say she looks a lot like Sophia Loren, couldn't you? Those big eyes, those full lips … And haven't you done well, bagging that handsome son of hers! You'll be the lady of Villa Marchesini if you play your cards right, darling.'

Signora Grassi did not have any children. She had been the second of eight and said she had seen enough babies to know she never wanted any of her own. Instead, she had concentrated on her career and had not married her husband until the age of thirty-four, which in marriage terms at the time was ancient.

'How old do you think I am, darling?' she asked one day, combing her fingers through the ends of her bleached hair.

'I don't know, Signora. Forty?'

Signora Grassi squealed with delight. 'Oh! Say it again – tell me I look forty!' She threw back her shoulders and rearranged her bosom inside her blouse. 'Actually,' she said in a lower voice, 'I'm going to be forty-nine this year.'

My incorrect guess pleased her so enormously that she gifted me several of her own garments, which she had made years before but which no longer fitted her. I was so grateful that for a moment I felt giddy, as though I was about to faint with excitement. Laid out before me on the cutting table was an array of beautiful dresses in a spectrum of gorgeous colours.

Signora Grassi told me to feel free to alter her old clothes in whatever way I wanted as she had absolutely no hope of ever getting into them again. The only good thing about wartime and post-war rationing, she said, was the fact that they had kept her slim. Not so now in this time of plenty.

'What I wouldn't give to have your figure, Graziella,' she sighed. 'Enjoy it whilst you have it, darling. You are a perfect advertisement for me. I know – we'll use each garment as a lesson, and that way I won't be frightened of you spoiling my clients' clothes when you come to work on them. If you make mistakes, you'll have to live with them. I will help you as you go along.'

It was an excellent way of teaching, and my dressmaking skills advanced very quickly. In a few short weeks I learned countless techniques and created a smart selection of garments for myself. My shapeless, dowdy old clothes were a thing of the past.

My favourite new dress was a turquoise blue gingham frock with capped sleeves and a neckline shaped like a keyhole. It had a stiff petticoat to give the skirt volume. My mother was concerned that it would catch in the spokes of my bicycle wheels, so whenever I wore it I would walk to and from work. It was a very small sacrifice to make.

I offered to create some garments for my mother, but she said the clothing she had was just fine. She didn't always approve of the new clothes I wore. To her mind they were too bright and showy and she told me in no uncertain terms that I was not to raise my hemlines any higher than two centimetres below my knee. As for my necklines, anything which showed any hint of décolletage or too much shoulder was prohibited.

Signora Grassi taught me the importance of wearing the right underwear so that clothes would fit more alluringly.

'Underwear is like scaffolding, darling,' she said. 'It holds everything in place. And by the time you get to my age, unless you've got good support you'll find your titties chafing against your knicker elastic.'

With help from Signora Grassi I made myself a padded balconette brassiere, which I copied from a photograph in a magazine. I used two condiment bowls to shape the cups. It gave me a cleavage like Jayne Mansfield. My mother absolutely forbade me from wearing it.

Still, I felt like the best-dressed girl in the village. Other girls eyed me enviously. Boys wolf-whistled as I passed. I couldn't wait for Gianfrancesco to see me in my lovely new clothes. Meanwhile, my mother warned me not to become vain.

I would have been more than happy to work in exchange for clothes, but Signora Grassi also paid me for helping her. I could hardly believe my good fortune.

My wages of 1,000 lire per week seemed like an enormous amount of money, but I was not free to spend my earnings on frivolous indulgences. The money I brought home each week was strictly managed by my mother. She allowed me to keep 500 lire for myself and the rest she put away for me in a biscuit tin, which she kept along with her own money box tucked under one of the sinks in the laundry room. Every time she did so, she would lecture me on the importance of saving.

But I was so busy that I had no time to spend the little bit of money which I was allowed to keep, and there was nothing to spend it on in Pieve Santa Clara anyway, apart from stationery and stamps for my correspondence with Gianfrancesco and the occasional ice cream. The little bar in Pieve Santa Clara had recently acquired a refrigerator. Sometimes I would take a detour down to the village after work and treat myself to a cone.

I did put aside 2,000 lire of my own money with the intention of buying a pair of high-heeled shoes, but Mamma overruled me, saying that high heels were impractical. And anyway, I already had smart shoes for church. Having a second pair was wholly unnecessary.

Of course I couldn't tell her that church was not the place I intended to wear my high heels. I had seen a picture in one of Signora Grassi's magazines of a model wearing high heels and stockings and a balconette brassiere very similar to mine. It was a look which I thought Gianfrancesco would appreciate very much.

Signora Grassi was not prudish and would often crack bawdy jokes or make risqué remarks which my mother would have found inappropriate and my aunt would have found outrageous. Professoressa Soldi would certainly not have approved. Some of my more straight-laced classmates would also have been shocked.

After a particularly miserable lady came in for a skirt alteration, the moment she'd gone, Signora Grassi tutted and said, 'What a dismal woman! You know what she needs, Graziella? She needs a good seeing-to. I can always tell when a woman isn't getting any.'

And then she threw her head back and laughed. Whenever she made an off-colour comment, she would cackle like a magpie. She derived great pleasure from shocking me.

'If my husband didn't come up with the goods at least twice a week I would have to find myself a young lover,' she said mischievously. 'One with big, strong hands and plenty of stamina. And I'd want him well-catered for in the gentleman department, if you know what I mean. Let's be honest, most women would prefer a good-sized salami to a little sausage!'

Many newspapers published articles on *The Kinsey Report*, which was a ground-breaking study on the sexual behaviour of Americans authored by Dr Alfred Kinsey, who in Italy gained the nickname of 'Doctor Sex'. Some people campaigned for the prohibition of its translation into Italian; but the more progressive supported its research.

I read whatever I could, keen to glean information, but in truth there were more column space dedicated to the war of words between the opposing factions than there were details of the report itself.

Sex was still full of contradictions and paradoxes. What was clear was that Italy lived under two sets of morals: those of outward appearance – and those of reality. Outwardly, people exhibited a veneer of propriety in which sex was not spoken about and only happened within marriage. The reality was different. People had sex before they were married. People did not necessarily marry the people they had sex with. Married people had affairs. Babies turned up notwithstanding their parents' marital status.

Pictures in magazines and on billboards used sex to sell their products. Pretty, scantily-clad ladies lounged on the bonnets of new cars or gazed out alluringly with their come-to-bed eyes, enticing consumers to purchase furniture polish, washing machines and tinned meat.

Even the Church had had to acknowledge that times were changing. The Pope had conceded that the rhythm method was acceptable within marriage, although he had specified that what he was countenancing was not contraception, but the control of fertility. It made absolutely no sense to me.

I read several articles on the rhythm method with great interest, but not one of them gave a clear explanation of how it worked, let alone any details of how to calculate it.

Gianfrancesco and I wrote to each other every few days to begin with, but as the summer advanced, his letters became less frequent. During the last three weeks of August I received no letters at all, despite the fact that I had written seven. I would hurry home from work filled with hope that a letter might have arrived for me, but I would be left disappointed.

I finished my time with Signora Grassi as the summer holiday came to an end. I had learned a lot. I had fabulous new clothes, money in my purse and savings in a tin. I should have been very happy, but I hadn't heard from Gianfrancesco and I was worried that something had happened to him.

One day, I ventured down to Cascina Marchesini hoping to find Fiorella. She was bound to know when he would be back. I could not have been more surprised when she informed me that he had been home since the beginning of the month.

'I think he's in the library,' she said, wiping her hands on her apron. 'I'll go and have a look for you.'

I waited on the doorstep for a long time in a state of bafflement. When at last Gianfrancesco came to the door, he looked uncomfortable. He stepped back when I moved forward to kiss him.

'Why didn't you tell me you were home?' I asked. 'I've been writing to you at summer school.'

He ran his hands through his hair, looked down at his feet and said, 'I'm sorry. I had to study.'

It was a flimsy, feeble excuse and we both knew it.

'When were you planning to tell me?'

He shuffled uneasily. He was still looking down at his feet.

'The thing is, Graziella,' he began, sucking in his bottom lip, 'that I'm about to start my final year of Liceo. I'm going to have

75

to prepare for some very difficult exams and there won't be any time for us to see each other. And once I've passed my exams I'll be sitting more exams to get into university. I'm planning to go to university in Rome because it's the best university in Italy for Classics. And if I take on extra courses in Medieval and Gothic Literature, then I won't even be back for the summer holidays. I can't expect you to wait for me when I go to university. I'll be gone for four or five years and then I'll be getting a job and I don't know when I'll come back here permanently. And then ...'

Words and excuses tumbled out of him until I interrupted him. 'What are you saying?'

He swallowed hard and said, 'I'm saying that we have to calm things down between us. We can't be together any more as we have been.'

His words hit me like slaps. I stood open-mouthed on the doorstep.

'We can still be friends. I'm sorry. I'll write to you.'

With that, he closed the door.

I ran to my bicycle and flew off down the driveway, my legs pedalling for all they were worth. I cycled faster and faster, kicking up sharp shards of grit, hurtling down the avenue of cypress trees and towards the old gateposts. I didn't stop when I reached the North Road. Didn't even slow down or look out for traffic. I flung myself around the corner, skidded, came off my bicycle and bounced along the asphalt before landing legs up in the ditch opposite.

My lovely turquoise gingham dress was torn. I knew that I was hurt, but I didn't stop. I got back onto my bicycle and raced down the road towards home, the taste of blood in my mouth and my vision fogged by tears.

When at last I tumbled into the yard I threw my bicycle to the ground and crumpled onto the doorstep sobbing, drops of blood from my chin pooling in my lap.

'Dear God, Graziella! What happened?' gasped my mother. 'Did you come off your bicycle?'

I nodded, screwing up my eyes to seal in the tears.

'It's only a graze,' I whimpered, picking pieces of grit out of my arm.

'It's more than a graze! Let me have a look at you.'

My chin was split open. My hip and shoulder were grazed and bruised. I had skinned both my elbows. My dress was ruined. Every part of me throbbed. But my physical injuries and my torn dress paled into insignificance beside the news I had just received.

My mother went to fetch iodine and tweezers. She crouched in front of me, dabbing at my wounds and plucking road chippings from my flesh.

'You'll mend,' she said, 'but your dress won't. How fast were you going? Did your skirt catch in your spokes? I told you not to ride your bicycle wearing that dress!'

*

I began my third year at the Istituto Magistrale in a subdued state. Everybody wanted to know what had happened to my chin. I told them I had fallen off my bicycle, but I didn't tell them why. My mother had taken me to the doctor to have the split stitched, a process which had been more painful than the injury itself. I still have the scar.

I held on to the hope that Gianfrancesco would change his mind, or at least write to me as he had promised, or come to see me as a friend, but his silence was absolute.

During October I wrote him a long letter. I wanted to know how our years of love and friendship could have ended so abruptly. He didn't reply. I wondered whether he had met somebody else at summer school.

I rode my bicycle down to Cascina Marchesini several times,

but each time found the house closed up. I rang the bell at the side and I rapped on the enormous front door, but if anyone was there, they didn't respond. I couldn't ask Fiorella for any information. She had got married at the end of the summer and moved away.

Nobody in the village had any news of Gianfrancesco, except to say that he wasn't there any more, and as with all gossip and second-hand information, there were discrepancies. Someone said he had already left for university in Rome and that his mother had gone with him. Someone else said that he had secured a government job. One man conjectured that he had gone to South America as a missionary. I was certain that there was absolutely no truth in that. The only thing I knew for sure was that both Gianfrancesco and his mother were gone. It was as though the Marchesinis had evaporated.

November brought wretched weather and impenetrable fogs. I could barely see my hand in front of my face as I walked to and from the piazza to catch the school bus. I was afraid of the cars which passed, their headlights barely able to pierce through the soup. A man had been knocked down early one morning and had lain by the side of the road with a broken leg for three hours before anyone had found him. Another time, a truck had ended up in the canal on its roof.

Still there was no communication from Gianfrancesco.

In December I took the bus into Cremona on a day when I should have been at school and made my way to the Liceo Classico, where I waited outside hoping to catch a glimpse of Gianfrancesco. All I wanted was to talk to him, to get some sort of explanation and some kind of closure.

Hordes of students spilled out as the lunchtime bell rang. I scoured the crowd, but there was no sign of him. I approached a group of boys who seemed to be of the right age to be his classmates.

'Excuse me,' I said. 'I'm looking for Gianfrancesco Marchesini.'

A short, spotty boy with glasses so thick that they distorted his eyes said, 'He's moved school. He's not here any more.'

'Do you know where he is?'

The boy shook his head. 'Sorry, no. But Gaudini might.'

Gaudini was called over from another group of boys. Gianfrancesco had mentioned him before. He was the doctor's son who had lent him the medical text on human reproduction.

'I'm trying to find Gianfrancesco Marchesini,' I said.

'You won't find him here,' Gaudini told me. 'He's moved to Milan to live with some relations.'

This was yet another piece of inconsistent information, but before I could ask anything else Gaudini said, 'Are you Graziella?'

'Yes,' I replied.

'We've heard all about you,' he grinned, then called over to his group of friends. 'Hey, you lot! Come and see. This is Marchesini's girl, Graziella.'

The group made their way over, circling around me and examining me as though I was some sort of exhibit.

'Do you have an address for him?' I asked, trying not to seem intimidated by the crowd which had gathered.

'No,' replied Gaudini with a leering grin. 'But if you're lonely, sweetheart, I'll happily give you mine.'

I was embarrassed. I didn't know what Gianfrancesco might have told them about me. I pushed my way out of the scrum as quickly as I could, ignoring the chorus of comments. Somebody pinched my bottom. I had not expected Gianfrancesco's friends to be such a loutish bunch.

As Christmas approached, my shattered heart was showing no signs of mending. It was almost four months to the day since I had been dispensed with.

On Christmas Eve I walked down to Cascina Marchesini again. Clearly nobody had been anywhere near the house for weeks. The only footprints in the light carpeting of snow were mine. I left a card in the letterbox anyway, wishing Gianfrancesco a Merry Christmas.

*

The one and only sighting of Gianfrancesco came the following April, just before Easter, when Signora Grassi glimpsed him passing in his mother's car. Knowing that he had been back home and had not come to see me was the final insult to my injured heart. Signora Grassi did her best to comfort me.

'I know you're heartbroken, darling,' she said, 'but unrequited love is pointless. It's like trying to clap with one hand.'

Signora Grassi was right, but it didn't make things any easier.

Soon afterwards, I made one final trip to Cascina Marchesini and found the enormous ornate gates padlocked. I couldn't even go as far as the house.

It was then I knew that I had been truly discarded for once and for all. Gianfrancesco had extricated himself from my life totally and absolutely.

Very slowly my wounded heart scarred over, but a lingering pain remained. It hurt that Gianfrancesco didn't even want to be my friend.

My mother urged me to be pragmatic and told me not to expect the first boy who took my heart to have it for ever. She related the chicken-thief story again.

My aunt was altogether less sympathetic.

'I told you not to expect anything from the Marchesini boy,' she said.

CHAPTER 7

The summer of 1955 was oppressively hot. Humidity weighed down the air and made even the thinnest cotton clothing stick to sweaty skin. We were plagued with swarms of mosquitoes. Zia Mina's repellents made with vinegar, lemon juice and basil proved useless.

'I haven't known mosquitoes like this since I was working in the rice fields,' she said, scratching at her ankles. 'You'd think that with all the chemicals they use on the land these days they'd have killed them off, but I swear it's made them worse.'

The heat imbued me with a deep apathy. I was bored and I was lonely. I tried to distract myself by reading magazines, but all they did was to make me long for the unattainable. Even the problem pages, which I had spent months scouring for advice on dealing with a broken heart seemed ridiculous and glib.

That summer's editions were filled with holiday romances. Beautiful people with sun-browned bodies fell in love on sun-kissed beaches. They took long moon-lit walks, hand-in-hand. They made promises of eternal devotion as they gazed into each other's eyes. Everything was perfect. Girls were beautiful. Boys were handsome. It was never too hot, or so humid that their clothes clung to their backs. Nobody had sweat patches under their arms. There certainly weren't any mosquitoes.

My horoscope predicted that I would have an unexpected romantic encounter. On reading this, I heard myself sigh out loud. I longed for a romantic encounter, unexpected or otherwise. I had attracted the attention of various boys in the village, but they were rough, or dull, or both. They didn't interest me at all.

I had hoped to spend my summer working for Signora Grassi again, but my mother had been suffering from recurring migraines and had fallen behind with her work. She was fretting about money, so I felt obliged to help her instead.

We sat together, working at opposite ends of the same bed-sheet, reproducing the same cutwork patterns over and over again. Hemming which would have taken minutes on a sewing machine had taken us all day. I had suggested to my mother that a sewing machine would be a sound investment for her. There were various different models available on hire-purchase. I had even asked Signora Grassi's advice on the best one to buy, but my mother had refused.

'I won't be replaced by a machine,' she said.

Signora Grassi's chatter and the coming and going of different clients through the atelier made the day pass quickly, but sitting in silence in the kitchen sewing with my mother and without the distraction of the radio made each day feel interminable. It gave me too much time to brood about the fact that I missed Gianfrancesco. There was still no news of him.

The quiet in the kitchen was absolute, except for the occasional rustle of linen and the soft clicking noise my mother made with her tongue each time she threaded her needle.

Then, one afternoon and out of nowhere, the shuddering boom of a motorcycle engine resounded through the house, making the crockery dance across the table. It stopped suddenly and was followed shortly after by footsteps on the gravel outside. A young man appeared at the door.

'Is this Teresa's house?' he asked. His accent was not local.

'Yes,' replied my mother.

'And are you Teresa?'

My mother squinted at him through her spectacles. 'Yes. Who are you?'

The young man grinned. 'I'm Giovanni,' he announced. 'Ugo's son.'

'Ugo? Who is Ugo?'

'Your Cousin Ugo!'

It took my mother a few moments to process the information, and when she did, her face lit up.

'Oh my goodness,' she gasped. 'Giovanni! You were a baby the last time I saw you.'

I had never met any of my mother's family. Plans for a trip to visit them had been scuppered by my father's accident and then by the war. As a result, my mother had lost touch with most of her relatives. The sporadic exchange of letters with uncles, aunts and cousins had dwindled over time. People had moved on, died or simply lost interest in swapping news.

I had never heard of Cousin Ugo, nor of his son Giovanni, who now stood in our kitchen with his arm around my smiling mother.

'What brings you all the way out here?' she asked.

'I'm on a road trip with my friend, but we've got problems with his motorcycle and we're not sure we'll make it back home. We were wondering whether you could put us up for the night so we can get it fixed tomorrow.'

'Of course. You can stay in Mina's spare room. But where's your friend?'

'He's outside, at your neighbour's.'

'Graziella, go and get Giovanni's friend,' said my mother.

A miasma of petrol fumes, the tang of hot metal and the smell of road-worn rubber filled the yard. An enormous red and silver motorcycle was parked by the door to Pozzetti's workshop, its spoked wheels dazzling like rays of the sun and the heat from its huge chrome exhaust pipes making the air shimmer. I had never seen such a gleaming steed of a machine before.

A young man was standing beside it talking to Rita and smoking a cigarette. By the look on Rita's face I could tell she was very pleased that he had stopped to ask for directions at her house. She stood with her hand on one hip, throwing her head back and laughing. There was much pouting of lips and fluttering of eyelashes.

The moment he saw me the young man cut their conversation dead, turned away from Rita, dropped his cigarette and ground it into the grit.

'Are you Ugo's Cousin Teresa?' he asked.

'No. I'm Teresa's daughter, Graziella,' I replied.

He grinned, grabbed my hand and pulled me towards him with such energy that I almost lost my footing, then he kissed me enthusiastically on each cheek, leaving a little spot of spit on each side.

'Gino Bianchi,' he announced, looking straight into my eyes and not letting go of my hand.

Gino Bianchi was a very fine-looking young man. His dark hair was slicked back and he was wearing jeans. I had never seen anyone wearing blue jeans, except in magazines, which reported that they were all the rage in America. They fitted his stocky, strapping build perfectly.

I was in my new favourite dress – a gorgeous, rose-pink full-skirted frock which I had made from scratch. It had required more than eight metres of fabric. Signora Grassi had shown me how to bring out the shoulders and pleat the hips. It gave me a wasp waist like Signora Marchesini.

Rita was wearing a faded old button-front housecoat. She was no longer laughing or fluttering her lashes. Her arms were crossed and her lips were tight. The looks she was giving me made it clear that she could happily take a pair of scissors to my dress.

It was then that Pozzetti emerged from his house, tousle-haired and yawning. He had obviously been roused from his afternoon nap.

'It would awaken the dead, that thing,' he said, tucking his vest, which was generously smeared with the remnants of his lunch, into his trousers. 'But my word, what a machine! What is it?'

'She's a Moto Guzzi Falcone,' replied Gino, although he was not looking at Pozzetti, or the motorcycle; his gaze was still firmly fixed on me.

'It's a work of art. I expect it goes like lightning.'

'She does, normally. Top speed of 135. But she's playing up.'

'What's the problem?'

'I don't know. She started running really rough and losing power. And when I was trying to see what was wrong I knocked the spark plug cap and cracked it, so now the plug cap doesn't fit properly, which means that the clip detaches and then the engine cuts out. I've had to stop every few kilometres since Asti to screw it back in. I'm going to have to get her looked at. Where's the nearest garage?'

'You'll have to go to Cremona.'

'Cremona? Nothing closer than that? Don't people have cars or motorcycles round here?'

'You could try Galletto. He's got a workshop up in Mazzolo and can probably fix it for you. He's a grumpy old sod, but he can repair just about anything.'

'I can fix it myself as long as I can get the part I need.'

'Well, if Galletto manages to sort it out, you can take me on a little blast up the road.' Pozzetti took one last long, admiring look at the motorcycle and went back into the house.

Gino grinned at me and said, 'I'd rather take you for a blast up the road.' Rita rolled her eyes and followed her father back into the house.

*

Giovanni and Gino were loud. I wondered whether the long ride on the noisy motorcycle had numbed their hearing. I was surprised that my mother didn't ask them to quieten down, but she was so eager to quiz Giovanni for news of her family and of her old home that it didn't seem to concern her.

'So where are your parents living now? Still in the same place?' she asked Giovanni.

'Oh no. We moved down to Pomazzo just after the war.'

'Oh? Why there?'

'Because they built an industrial area there and new housing. Pomazzo's practically a suburb of Bologna now. Since they put in the new road you can get to the centre of Bologna in twenty minutes and there are buses every quarter of an hour.'

'Goodness! It must have changed so much. Pomazzo was no more than a church and a handful of houses when I was a girl.'

'It's still expanding. You wouldn't recognise it now. My father's been working at the ceramics factory since 1947. And my parents have got a nice flat. Brand new. It's on the fifth floor, but there's a lift. My mother still won't stop going on about the wonders of central heating and hot baths. Says she doesn't miss the old place at all.'

Giovanni carried on talking to my mother, while Gino carried on gazing at me. He sat with his chin resting on his hands, looking at me as though I was the only girl he had ever seen.

My mother cast a wary glance in Gino's direction at the very moment his foot touched mine under the table. She hadn't noticed him blowing kisses at me each time her back was turned, although later that evening, after Gino and Giovanni had retired to bed, she commented drily that Gino had been ogling me like a hungry dog drooling after a bone.

I went to sleep that night imagining myself riding on the back of the motorcycle.

Early the following morning Gino set off to find Galletto's workshop. I settled into my day's sewing, but I had barely started when the thumping roar of the motorcycle sounded outside.

'That was quick,' my mother said as Gino came back into the kitchen.

'I couldn't find it,' he shrugged.

'It's at the end of the lane which runs behind the station in Mazzolo. It's hard to miss. Didn't you think to ask someone?'

'I was wondering if you could spare Graziella for a bit so she can show me.'

I assumed my mother would forbid it, but she didn't. Although she had enjoyed catching up with Giovanni she hadn't warmed at all to Gino and I think she was keen for him to be on his way.

'As long as you go slowly and it's only to Galletto's,' she said.

'You don't have to worry about me going fast, Signora. I can't do more than thirty at the moment and I'd bring your daughter straight back.'

Although I had pictured myself riding on the back of the motorcycle, with the wind in my hair and my arms around Gino, the reality of riding on such a monstrously powerful machine, even slowly, frightened me. I had been given a ride into the village on a Vespa once before, and even that had made me nervous. I had been able to ride on the Vespa wearing a skirt, in a side-saddle position, something which was not possible on a motorcycle.

My first difficulty was getting on in a ladylike manner. I wrapped my skirt around my legs and perched tensely behind Gino, wishing that I owned some trousers.

'Hold onto me,' he said. 'And sit a bit closer.' He then opened the throttle and pulled onto the road. The motorcycle jerked and bounced. We were still within sight of Paradiso when it cut out.

'Shit!' Gino got off, adjusted something whilst muttering some very colourful curses in Bolognese dialect and we limped our way up the North Road towards Mazzolo.

Despite the noise and the bone-shaking vibrations, I rather enjoyed the ride. It was nice to feel a cool breeze blowing on my face and legs. It was the coolest I'd been all summer.

There was nothing else on the road apart from a group of grubby little boys playing a stick-throwing game on the bridge over the canal. The boys stopped their game and ran along beside us cheering as we spluttered past. The motorcycle cut out twice more before we reached Mazzolo.

'Turn left up here,' I called out as we passed the station.

'I know,' replied Gino as we approached Galletto's. 'I found it earlier. But I wanted an excuse to take you out.'

Galletto's workshop was little more than a ramshackle hut, almost indistinguishable from the piles of scrap and decaying vehicle carcasses which surrounded it. The premises were guarded by a mangy, dirt-caked dog, who barked and strained on his chain as we rode in.

'Is this guy any good?' asked Gino as he steered the motorcycle carefully around puddles of oil, then parked it in the cleanest patch he could find. 'This place is a total dump.'

The sound of metal grating on metal emanated from the hut. We picked our way through the detritus and went in. It was dark inside and filled with the smell of solvents, rubber and rust. The walls were hung with time-worn tools, used tyres, buckets and cans. The only light came from a single bulb suspended from the rafters. It was so dim and dirty that there seemed little point in having it there at all.

Galletto stood at his workbench behind a colossal vice, sharpening an ancient-looking axe with an equally ancient-looking rasp. A blizzard of little sparks flew from the file with each stroke.

Although he saw us and heard our greeting, he ignored us and continued rasping. We tried again, but still he ignored us. Finally Gino shouted, 'Oi!' at the top of his voice.

Galletto put down his rasp slowly and looked up at us with an expression of deep displeasure. He was not a pretty sight. His jaw was missing from chin to ear on the left side of his face, making his cheek sag into the void and his mouth droop open on the afflicted side. He could only blink his right eye.

Galletto had been decorated for bravery during the First World

War, but had been too old to fight in the Second. He had volunteered his services anyway as an emergency mechanic. The story, which had become something of a local legend, went that a starter-handle had jammed, then recoiled, smacking into his face and demolishing his jaw. Once he had regained consciousness he refused any medical intervention, but simply spat out his loose teeth and shattered bone, and carried on fixing the problem.

The loss of a quarter of his face had done nothing to improve his disposition. People did not visit Galletto to enjoy his cheerful company or his amiable conversation. They only called on him because he had a reputation of being able to repair anything and everything. Galletto could fix the unfixable and mend the unmendable.

'What d'you want?' he asked, engulfing us in a billow of halitosis. His remaining teeth were as black as his overalls. He eyed Gino, me and the motorcycle suspiciously as Gino began to explain the problem, but Galletto didn't seem to be listening.

'This yours then?' he interrupted before Gino could finish.

'Yes.'

Galletto circled the motorcycle twice, rubbing the remaining part of his chin. 'Bit young to afford something like this, aren't you?' he grunted.

'I'm twenty-one and I've got a good job,' replied Gino indignantly.

'Got anything to prove it?'

Gino took out his wallet, exposing a sheaf of banknotes as he fished for his documents. The old mechanic's good eye lit up as he eyed the money. He took his time looking through Gino's papers and circled the motorcycle again.

'Fire her up,' he said.

Gino kick-started the motorcycle with some difficulty. Galletto listened to the struggling engine for a while, then placed his hand on the tank and closed his right eye, seemingly attempting to diagnose the problem through some sixth sense. His blind eye remained wide open.

After a minute or so he nodded and removed his hand. The smear of black fingerprints he left on the shiny red paintwork did not please Gino at all.

Galletto then disappeared into his hut and returned with a length of rubber hose, which he dipped into the petrol tank and sucked on. He sloshed the petrol around his mouth as though he was tasting wine, pinching together his lips on the jawless side with his oily fingers to avoid any of the liquid leaking out. Eventually he spat it onto the ground and said, 'You've got water in your fuel.'

The problem was easily solved by draining the tank and replenishing it with fresh fuel. When Gino re-started the engine it coughed for a while, then ran smoothly.

Galletto then sorted the plug cap problem with a provisional repair using a piece of wire. When he'd finished, he announced, 'That'll be 3,000 lire.'

'*How* much?' exclaimed Gino. 'All you've done is twist a bit of wire round the plug and put a few drops of petrol in the tank!'

'It's my expertise you're paying for,' replied Galletto. 'But if you're not happy with the price I'll take the petrol out and you can push your motorcycle to the next petrol station. Closest one's seven kilometres.'

Gino growled and handed over the money, then asked, 'What about the new plug cap?'

'What about it?'

'Can you get one today?'

'Today? Does it look as though I can drop everything for you just because you've swanned in here on a flash motorcycle? I've got a lot of other customers waiting. You'll have to wait your turn. I can probably fit you in the day after tomorrow.'

'The day after tomorrow?' Gino glared at him. 'It would be quicker if I rode back to Bologna and got it myself!'

'Suit yourself.' The old mechanic shrugged. 'But that plug cap you've got on there now won't take much more tampering with. If it shears off completely you'll be going nowhere. So do you want me to get you one or not?'

'Is there anywhere else I can get one round here?'

Galletto ran his tongue over his remaining teeth. 'No,' he said smugly.

'All right then.' Gino raised his hands in exasperation. 'Yes.'

Galletto's face twitched, which I assumed was the closest thing he could manage to a smirk.

'Right. I'm going to need you to pay for it now though.'

Gino took out his wallet again. Galletto licked his teeth as he eyed the money. 'What about the fitting? I'll need that upfront too.'

'I can fit it myself.'

The old man shook his head. 'That's not the way I work. I have to be sure it's done properly. How do I know you won't mess it up or break it then come running back complaining I've sold you a faulty part?'

Gino rolled his eyes. 'It's what I do for a living,' he said. 'I'm a mechanic.'

'Not a very good one,' Galletto snorted. 'You couldn't even work out that you had water in your fuel.'

As we rode out of the yard Gino called him a dick-head. He was angry and embarrassed, which made the journey back an altogether different experience. Any notion of enjoying the ride or appreciating the views vanished. The fields flew past on either side of the North Road as we powered towards Pieve Santa Clara. The old gateposts at the entrance to Cascina Marchesini passed in a blur.

The only traffic we encountered was a farmer weaving down the centre of the road on a bicycle with a crate of chickens strapped to the back. Seeing him, Gino revved his engine and signalled to him to get out of the way. The startled man jumped and wobbled, momentarily losing control of his bicycle and almost veering into the ditch and losing his chickens. He shook his fist at us, cursing as we sped past him. Gino called him a dick-head too.

CHAPTER 8

Giovanni could not stay as he had to return to work, so he caught the train back to Pomazzo. I was thrilled that Gino would remain with us until his motorcycle was properly fixed. My change in mood and the reason for it did not go unnoticed by my mother. She had her reservations about Gino, but seemed relieved that I was no longer miserable.

My mother was not gregarious by nature. Although she had enjoyed catching up on family news with Giovanni, I could see she was tired. She was pale with shadows under her eyes. I noticed her turn from the light and rub her temples.

'Are you getting another headache, Mamma?' I asked.

'Yes,' she said wearily. 'It's this heat. I've been trying to ignore it and wish it away, but not very successfully. I'm not sure I can work today.'

It was far easier than I thought to convince her to let me go out with Gino on the motorcycle. Zia Mina made her disapproval very clear, saying that allowing me to ride pillion was unbecoming and could lead to immoral behaviour. It was hardly a deterrent.

As we pulled out of the gate and powered up the road, the pounding of the motorcycle throbbed through my body, unleashing such a feeling of exhilaration that I squealed. I loved the roar of the engine, the kick-back of the acceleration and the tension in Gino's arms as he opened the throttle. The way our bodies leaned into the bends felt as though we were defying gravity.

We rode out together along roads that were new to me, even though they were only a few kilometres from Pieve Santa Clara.

Since my stay at the convent I had never been much further than a bicycle ride from home, apart from the occasional trip to Cremona on the train and the school bus ride to and from high school.

Gino thought it was funny that I didn't know where we were, even when we were less than a twenty-minute ride away from Paradiso. We had no itinerary or scheduled route. We just went wherever the roads took us.

We rode south, following the river. The bright sunlight streaked across the new industrial rice fields on the banks of the Pó. Processing plants rose out of the flat landscape, their tall chimneys puffing out feathery plumes of smoke and steam.

Whenever we stopped, people would gather round the motorcycle to admire it. Somebody even fetched a camera to take photographs. Gino enjoyed the attention and I did too. I felt as though I had landed on the pages of a romance novel, out with a fine-looking young man on his gleaming Moto Guzzi Falcone.

Cremona at night was a wholly new experience for me. The centre was full of activity, but not the daytime routines of working and shopping. The brightly lit shops and restaurants sparkled with life and with the sound of people socialising, chattering and celebrating.

Gino was amazed that I had never been to the cinema before, although my regular consumption of magazines had made me very knowledgeable about new releases. He had already seen all the films being shown at the main cinema in the centre of town, so we found a smaller cinema down a side street which was showing a film neither of us had heard of. I was so keen to experience the big screen for the first time that I didn't really mind what we watched.

A beautiful girl toyed with the affections of two admirers, dithering between her dependable first love and a morally unscrupulous Lothario. There was not much to the plot or to the characters, but the lack of creative depth was made up for by the exposure of a lot of flesh. The girl wore a bikini throughout, even though she was nowhere near a beach. It made Gino fidget.

The cinema was filled with couples making the most of the darkness. Few were paying any attention to the film. Gino pulled me towards him and kissed me.

For a moment I felt transported on a wave of romance and transfixed by the touch of his lips, but it was only for a moment. It was not the kind of melting, desire-inducing kiss I had experienced with Gianfrancesco. Gino seemed to be trying to suck out my teeth and chew my tongue. I ended up with a lot of saliva on my chin. But the clumsy kissing didn't bother me. I was enjoying an adventure – a welcome distraction from my heartache.

As we made our way through town we passed a restaurant which was so busy that a sizable crowd was waiting outside. It was not until Salvatore came flying out of the arched doorway that I realised we were standing in front of Pizzeria Paradiso.

'*Criatura!*' he exclaimed, hugging me tightly. 'What a surprise! I'm so happy to see you! Have you eaten?'

He didn't wait for an answer. We could have been on our way back from a banquet and Salvatore would still have insisted on feeding us.

'Come in, come in,' he said, leading me by the hand through the crush of waiting customers. 'If you'd called ahead and said you were coming I'd have saved you a table outside. But I've got a lovely table in one of the alcoves. Carmé!' he called through the throng. 'Come and see who's here!'

Carmela, who had now grown so fat that she had to squeeze in between the tables sideways, flung her arms around me, gushing her greeting in thick Neapolitan and covering my face with kisses.

'Ah, there's nothing like young love,' she sighed, looking from Gino to me and back again with misty eyes. 'Isn't that right, Salvá?'

95

'There's something to be said for old love too,' replied Salvatore, giving her enormous bottom an affectionate tap. Carmela squealed and said something in Neapolitan which I could not quite understand, but it made Salvatore swallow hard.

A lot of work had been done to the inside of the restaurant. Panels of fresh new plaster set off the high vaulted ceilings. Long strings of chillies in every shade of orange, red, yellow and green were strung from the beams. Paintings of the Amalfi Coast and characters from Neapolitan folklore adorned the walls. In pride of place was an enormous reproduction of the Madonna Del Carmine, glittering with gold leaf and looking down benevolently over the spread of full tables.

The air was laden with mouth-watering aromas: the hot, yeasty scent of home-baked bread, roasting meat, sweet vanilla, basil, pepper, the zing of fresh lemons. Above all there was the scent of pizza: sizzling ham and sausage toppings, oozing puddles of mozzarella, and rich, fresh tomato.

Carluccio and Rino stood behind a great marble-topped counter spread with bowls of ingredients. They were engaged in a frenzy of activity as pizza orders were called, prepared and dispatched. Their black hair was dusted white with flour and their faces were red from the heat of the huge brick oven behind them.

'See our new oven?' smiled Salvatore. 'Carluccio and I built it ourselves. I wouldn't have known where to start unless your dear Papá had shown me.'

He hurried off then brought us more food than we could eat. '*Magna, magna!* Fill your plates,' he entreated us. 'Have anything you want. It's all on the house.'

I told Gino the story of how Salvatore had come to live at Paradiso, about Carluccio's miraculous return from the dead, and about Carmela and Rino. I showed him the Pizza Graziella with extra mozzarella on the menu, but he didn't seem very interested. It wasn't too long before I realised that I was doing all the talking.

When I spoke to him about school, he just said, 'I hated school. Waste of time.'

I looked at him as he stuffed food into his mouth and decided that apart from the good looks, fashionable clothes and flash motorcycle, there really wasn't much substance to Gino.

*

On our final ride on Gino's last day, as we were approaching Mazzolo the unmistakable shape of Signora Marchesini's Alfa Romeo appeared on the road ahead. Gino caught up so that he could admire the car.

'Wow!' he said. 'Never seen that model before. And in blue …'

He pulled alongside to take a better look, but it was the last thing I wanted. My heart was in my mouth at the prospect of seeing Gianfrancesco, and of him seeing me riding on the back of Gino's motorcycle. I couldn't decide whether it would be a good thing or not. But he was not in the car. Instead I stared straight into the dark, disapproving eyes of Signora Marchesini.

She accelerated away, but Gino was not deterred.

'Hah!' he shouted. 'You wanna race me, lady?'

He opened the throttle until he caught up again. This time, Signora Marchesini kept her gaze fixed straight ahead, but clearly she was not wanting to race. She seemed frightened.

'Don't!' I shouted. 'You're scaring her.'

'I'm only trying to have a look at the car!'

Signora Marchesini put her foot down again. The Alfa Romeo's engine roared. Undeterred, Gino caught up and rode within touching distance alongside. This time, Signora Marchesini's nervousness was clear. She was hunched forward, her nose just millimetres from the steering wheel.

'Stuck-up bitch!' yelled Gino, swerving in front of her so suddenly that I thought I would be whipped off the motorcycle.

Signora Marchesini was forced to brake hard. I hoped she had not hit her face. I had to cling to Gino for fear of falling off.

As we passed her, Gino swore and made an obscene gesture at her. I buried my face in his shoulder praying that she had not recognised me, but I knew that she had.

*

My brief holiday romance came to an end after three days when Gino had to return home. He promised that he would call me and that he would come back to see me. I doubted whether he would and I was not troubled by it. My adventure had helped to patch up my heartbreak, to some extent at least. But I was about to embark on the most important year of my schooling, by the end of which I would be a qualified primary school-teacher. I was determined that nothing should distract me.

Less than a week after the beginning of term as I was walking home from the bus stop, Signora Marchesini swept past me in her car, peppering road chippings in my direction. As I approached Paradiso, I saw the car parked outside the gate. The ultramarine-blue paintwork was blanketed in dust. One of the back mudguards was dented and there was a scuff on the door.

I hesitated and lingered by the gate for a while, feeling more than a little unnerved. Perhaps she had come to report the incident on the road with Gino to my mother; or worse, she had finally decided to tell her about the lipstick-stained sheets. Perhaps both.

I dithered, going over every possible reason why Signora Marchesini was calling at the house. Eventually I took a deep breath and went in. Whatever business she had, I was about to find out.

My mother and Signora Marchesini were in the kitchen. Signora Marchesini was still very beautiful, if a little less glossy.

Her hair was no longer expensively coiffed, but instead was tied back in a neat bun, fixed with a tortoiseshell comb. She acknowledged my arrival with a regal nod.

'Good afternoon, Signora Marchesini,' I said nervously.

My mother glanced up at me over her spectacles, then looked away. She was copying something into her sketch book from a book on the table.

'I hope I'm not putting you to too much trouble, Signora Ponti,' said Signora Marchesini. 'Your suggestion of hyacinths, peonies and orange blossoms is excellent.'

'It's no trouble,' replied my mother, although obviously it was. She turned her sketch book so that Signora Marchesini could see what she had drawn. It was a beautiful but impossibly intricate design of a garland of hyacinths, peonies and orange blossoms.

'How lovely!' Signora Marchesini congratulated her, clasping her hands together. 'Now, Signora Ponti, do you have some fabric samples for me to choose from?'

My mother went to fetch a roll from the corner by her workspace. 'This is the best fabric I have for what you require,' she said, laying a roll out on the table.

Signora Marchesini ran her elegant fingers over the fabric. I saw that her nails were varnished in pale pink.

'This is cotton, Signora Ponti,' she said, frowning.

'Very good quality cotton,' added my mother.

Signora Marchesini shook her head. 'Oh, no. I insist that it must be silk.'

'That will be rather expensive.'

'I am not expecting it to be cheap, Signora Ponti. This will be a once-in-a-lifetime gift for a once-in-a-lifetime event.'

She then turned her attention to me. 'Have you heard from my son recently?' she asked coolly.

'No,' I replied.

'I see. Then you haven't heard the exciting news?'

'No.'

'Gianfrancesco is engaged to be married,' she announced.

For a few moments I was certain that I had misheard, but Signora Marchesini carried on talking.

'Gianfrancesco is very happy. Anna is a lovely girl. She is from a very good Milanese family; her father is a very well-respected judge. Oh! Before I forget, Signora Ponti, we haven't discussed the monograms.'

My mother turned over the page in her book. She had sketched a G, an A and an M with tendrils that formed a heart.

'That is very pretty, Signora Ponti. I adore the way you are planning to intertwine the initials. I'm certain that Gianfrancesco and Anna will love it too.'

Signora Marchesini took her leave shortly afterwards, leaving a wad of money on the table to cover the purchase of the silk, and a promise to pay for the work when it was done.

My mother said nothing as she cleared away her fabrics. I too was silent. I was in a state of shock. It couldn't be possible that almost exactly a year to the day since discarding me, Gianfrancesco was engaged to be married. I feared that if I opened my mouth to speak I would cry, so I said nothing.

Later that evening I sat at the table, broke bread into chunks and watched them sink into my soup. It was my mother who finally broke the silence.

'Graziella!' she said sharply.

I looked up. She gazed back at me gravely.

'You have to be less foolish about Gianfrancesco.'

I sat with my elbows on the table and my head in my hands, staring at my untouched food.

'He's got engaged so quickly,' I said.

'Yes,' replied my mother, raising her eyebrows. 'There's usually a reason for that.'

This made things worse.

'You think his fiancée's pregnant?'

'That's usually the reason for getting engaged very quickly.'

My tears landed in my soup. Despite the feelings of rejection and anger that I had felt, despite the fact that I had done my best to persuade myself not to love Gianfrancesco any more, and despite the distraction of Gino, I had never let go of the hope that one day our paths would cross again and that something of the love and friendship Gianfrancesco and I had shared would resurge. It was agony knowing that during the year I had spent attempting to gather together the pieces of my broken heart, he had fallen in love with somebody else and that he loved her enough to marry her.

Signora Marchesini had not only ordered an extravagant design for Gianfrancesco and Anna's wedding sheets, but she had also requested cut-outs of broderie anglaise along the entire top hem. She had even ordered six matching pillowcases.

'Six pillowcases,' tutted my mother. 'Who needs six pillows?'

The next day she went to Cremona and purchased a very expensive roll of bedding silk, then prepared her work area with extra care. I watched as she sat down, took off her spectacles, wiped them on her handkerchief, put them on again and took them off.

'See this?' She indicated Signora Marchesini's design on her sketch pad. 'I can't do it.'

'Why not?'

My mother's eyes welled slightly and she blinked away the tears.

'I can't see well enough any more, Graziella. Not even wearing glasses helps. And if I keep my head down for more than a few minutes, I get a migraine.' She rubbed her temples and groaned. 'These damned headaches – they're the last thing I can do with. And I can't turn this work down. We need the money.'

'You should go back to the doctor,' I said. It was not the first time I had suggested it.

'I know,' she sighed. 'Your aunt keeps nagging me about it too. But all he'll tell me to do is rest my eyes.'

I looked at the design on the paper.

'Where do I start with this one?' I asked. It was more complex than anything I had ever attempted before.

'Mark out the sheet every twenty centimetres, ten centimetres from the hem. Start there and work outwards in the usual way. When you've repeated the pattern once you'll see what works best.'

My mother left it entirely to me. The top sheet alone took over a month of late evening and Sunday work to embroider. The six pillowcases took even longer and ate into the time I should have spent studying. By the end I was so sick of it that I took the set down to Signora Grassi's and did all the seams and hems on her electric machine. I was even able replicate broderie anglaise by using the button-hole setting.

My mother had to admit that what I had been able to do on the machine was impressive. For a moment I wondered whether she had changed her mind about purchasing one, but she was anxious that Signora Marchesini would complain about it not being done entirely by hand. I did not share her concern. I wanted to finish the set and to have it gone.

At last, when everything was complete, my mother laid the work out on the table.

'You've done such a beautiful job,' she said. 'I couldn't have done it any better myself. Even when my eyesight was sharp.'

There was no doubt that I had produced excellent work. My mother was quite emotional about it. 'It's fit for a king,' she said.

The praise was little comfort. All I could think of was Gianfrancesco making love to Anna, surrounded by my silk flowers. It was the only thing I had thought of with every stitch.

Anna, the judge's daughter, was probably nothing like me. I imagined her as beautiful as Signora Marchesini, with a sharp wit and the benefit of an expensive education. I would never be as clever as her, or as lovely as her. I was no competition. As Zia Mina had said, men of Gianfrancesco's social standing did not marry girls like me.

I listened desperately for news of a wedding, or of a baby, or both, but nobody knew anything. Being aware that Gianfrancesco had moved on should have brought me closure, but all it did was to re-open the wound.

I wrapped the completed work in brown paper and left the package on the table, ready for Signora Marchesini to collect, then went to school. By the time I returned home, it was gone.

CHAPTER 9

My mother's headaches became so ferocious that the doctor prescribed her very strong medication and complete eye rest. The medication helped with the pain, but it made her drowsy and blurred her eyesight further. Sometimes she suffered from dizzy spells. I began to worry about leaving her during the day but she said very firmly that she refused to be treated like an invalid for the sake of the odd migraine.

Despite being told not to, she would attempt to sew using an enormous magnifying glass, but even then she could only deal with small amounts of simple work. Very quickly that also became impossible for her.

She would set out her materials at her seat by the window, wash and dry her hands carefully and sit down to work just as she had always done, as though her eyesight was perfect and nothing had changed. She would then endeavour to sew, squinting and straining as she fumbled with her needle and thread. Eventually she would put down her tools, rest her head against the wall and sit in silence, either with her eyes closed, or staring into whatever distance she could see, deeply withdrawn into her thoughts. Sometimes she hardly seemed aware of me.

I returned home one day to find her sitting in her seat, her work on her lap. Clearly she was not herself. She was unresponsive and remote. She hadn't even said hello.

'Are you all right, Mamma? Does your head hurt?' I asked.

There was no reply.

'Mamma, does your head hurt?'

Still no reply.

'Mamma?'

'Of course my head hurts! My head always hurts! Don't ask me stupid questions!' she cried.

I was taken aback by her outburst. She had never spoken to me like that before.

'I'm sorry,' she said with a long sigh. 'There was no need to snap at you. Yes, my head does hurt, but no more than usual. The medicine helps with the pain, but it makes my eyes worse.'

She tried to smile, but the attempt was feeble.

'I have been able to work a little today,' she said. 'I've done this collar. What do you think? Is it all right?'

I looked at the piece and felt desperately sorry for my mother. It was not all right. The stitching was shambolic and dotted with spots of blood from where she had pricked her fingers.

'I'll do a bit of finishing off for you,' I said, trying to sound positive. 'Just some of the fiddly bits.'

But my mother knew I was not being truthful. 'Be honest with me, Graziella. It's a mess, isn't it?'

'It's not great, Mamma.'

She screamed in frustration and hurled her basket of threads and needles across the room. I ducked as spools and pins bounced off the wall and flew like shrapnel around the kitchen.

'Mamma! Just leave it! I'll do it!'

She buried her face in her hands and began to sob.

'Of all the things to lose,' she wept. 'I'm nothing without my eyes. I'm useless – redundant! Just a burden. I'd rather have my feet cut off than lose my eyes.'

'Mamma, we'll go back to the doctor and see what he says. And if he can't help you we'll find another doctor who can. Maybe there are other medicines which will stop the pain but won't affect your sight.'

Ignoring me, she rocked back and forth, crying, 'It's gone. My sight has gone and I know it won't come back.'

Her words dissolved into a fit of frenzied weeping. I wrapped my arms around her, felt her sobbing pulsate through me. I had only seen my mother cry properly twice, once when Ernesto had been killed and the second time when my father had died, but this was different. This was not grief for someone else. She was grieving for herself. It was a piteous mixture of hopelessness, frustration and fear. When she finally quietened and wiped her cheeks on her apron, she was still trembling.

'Graziella, today I turned down work for the first time in my life. The haberdasher from Cremona came with linens for me and I had to tell him I couldn't take the work. I have never, ever said no to *any* work. And it was a terrible feeling. What am I going to do? How am I going to keep us if I can't work?'

'I'll do as much of your work as I can, Mamma. You rest. And there must be a medicine which will help.'

My mother pressed her face against mine and gripped me tightly.

'You're a good girl,' she said. 'You're such a good girl. But I can't ask you to take on my work. You must concentrate on your studies.'

I did try to help all I could. In the evenings after school I would do my mother's work until my eyes watered with fatigue and I wondered how long I could continue before my own eyesight failed me also. But I was not as experienced as my mother at embroidery and although my work was of a good standard, each piece took me considerably longer than it would have done if left in my mother's skilled hands. I also began working at Signora Grassi's on Saturdays to earn a bit of money.

There was little time for my schoolwork and for the first time since starting at the Istituto Magistrale, I fell behind. Within a very short time we became entirely reliant on the small amount of embroidery I could do each evening and my pittance of a wage from Signora Grassi. I began to miss days of school, sometimes several at a time, so that I could earn some money.

'We can use some savings from my box,' said my mother.

When I looked in her box, hidden under the sink in the laundry room, I found that it contained almost 15,000 lire, but with the approach of winter and the imminent need to purchase firewood and pay the household bills, I reasoned that it would not last very long. My own savings in the biscuit tin had already been used.

My mother became increasingly confused and forgetful and I became more and more concerned. I found myself having to remind her what day it was. Even small domestic tasks began to challenge her. She boiled the soup dry two nights running and burned her fingers by shutting them in the stove door. When I insisted that she should go back to the doctor, she made excuses.

'He'll just tell me to rest my eyes again,' she said. 'Or offer to give me the same medicine that he gave your father. I won't touch it. That stuff changed your father and I'm not going the same way.'

My brave, resilient mother was scared – and seeing her so fearful and fragile was a frightening thing.

It was a Thursday in late December when I returned home from school to find her collapsed on the kitchen floor. She was conscious, but dazed. Her spectacles were beside her, broken. She had crushed them during her fall.

Pozzetti took us straight to the hospital. My mother wailed and wept, clutching her head as the truck shuddered down the road. We had to stop twice for her to be sick.

As soon as we reached the hospital, she was laid out on a trolley and wheeled away. Pozzetti sat with me in the waiting room. We waited over two hours before a doctor came to find me.

'We want to keep Signora Ponti here,' he said. 'She is in a lot of pain and we can help her with that.'

'Do you have any idea what's wrong with her?' I asked. 'The doctor in Mazzolo said migraines and eye strain.'

107

The doctor considered this for a moment, then said, 'I would not concur with that diagnosis, but I cannot give you an alternative answer until we do some tests and receive the results. Go home, Signorina. We will look after your mother.'

'Can I see her before I go?'

'She's asleep now. We have sedated her. But if you wish …'

My mother had been positioned in such a way that for a hideous moment I was reminded of my father in his coffin, but she seemed to be sleeping very peacefully. There was a plum-coloured bruise on her cheekbone from where she had hit the floor.

Seeing her made me shudder. The anxiety I had felt after my father's death, the awful feeling that something terrible would happen to my mother, had returned; except that this time, it had come true. The heaviness in my head, which I had not felt for so long, resurged.

My aunt was waiting for news with Ada Pozzetti when we returned home. I gave them both what little news I had. Zia Mina let out a wretched wail.

'She's going to die and it's my fault,' she cried. 'I'm cursed!'

Ada Pozzetti put her hand on my aunt's arm.

'We can't rush to any conclusions, Mina,' she said comfortingly. 'Until the doctors know more we can just pray that Teresa remains comfortable. Medicine has advanced so far now. They can cure almost anything now.'

I went back to the annexe, locked the doors and barred the shutters. I had never spent a night alone before in Paradiso.

The next day I returned to the hospital with my aunt, who stood at the foot of the bed and prayed quietly. I sat at my mother's side and held her hand. She was heavily sedated and she had no idea that we were there. Zia Mina raved all the way home that my mother's illness was due to a curse.

Over the week which followed, the hospital carried out

numerous tests. As I arrived exactly a week after Mamma had been admitted, a doctor greeted me with a grave welcome and took me aside to a small office. The results had come in. He explained that they revealed that my mother had a brain tumour.

I thought immediately of Ada Pozzetti's assertion that advances in medicine could cure almost anything.

'What can you do about it? What treatments are there?' I asked.

'I'm afraid there is very little in the way of treatment for conditions such as this.'

'There must be something.' I knew I sounded desperate.

'Some medical practitioners have attempted to tackle tumours with radiotherapy, but the outcomes have rarely been positive. Radiotherapy is extremely potent and it can indeed kill off tumorous tissue, but in so doing it also kills off healthy tissue. The brain is very delicate and easily damaged, and at this stage in your mother's illness ...'

'How about an operation?'

The doctor clasped his hands together and replied solemnly, 'It is possible to operate, and in some cases this can have a moderate level of success in terms of prolonging life. But equally, it can cause further problems, or even worsen the situation. The brain is a complex organ which we are only just beginning to understand. I am sorry, Signorina, but we are not equipped to carry out such procedures here. There are hospitals in Milan and Rome which can, in some cases, perform operations of this type. But you must understand that these operations are very experimental.'

'It is possible then. There are things you can try.'

There was a resigned kindness in the doctor's expression. He leaned across his desk and spoke softly.

'I have discussed this option with your mother,' he said, 'and she has expressed a very clear wish not to submit to any surgery, nor to any treatment other than analgesic medication.'

'But surely she's in no fit state to make a decision like that?'

'I know that this is very difficult for you, and I wish that I could offer you a miracle, but I can't. Nor can I make promises which will give you false hope.'

'If I'd brought her to you sooner, would you have been able to cure her?' I asked.

The doctor shook his head. 'No. Your mother has an aggressive tumour. Her condition is terminal. There is nothing you could have done at any point which would make things different now.'

'So what *can* you do?'

'We can manage your mother's pain. The level of pain she has been enduring up until now is quite staggering. But as long as we keep her here we can medicate her in such a way that we can make the pain tolerable. That in itself will be an immense relief for her.'

I returned home that night so numb that by the time I reached Paradiso I had no recollection of the train and bus rides which had brought me there. When I broke the news to my aunt, she said, 'Your Mamma knew she was dying. She felt death coming for her months ago.'

'What?'

'I've seen enough death to know when it's coming and your Mamma saw it clearly.'

'Did she say that?'

'She didn't need to. I knew she knew. I could see her preparing herself for the end.'

*

My mother suffered frequent fits and her decline was rapid. She had always been slim and it took only a couple of weeks for her to become emaciated. I watched her shrink away a little more each time I saw her. Her skin turned the colour of old paper.

Most of the time she was so heavily sedated that she had no

idea I was there, but occasionally she would be awake enough to speak to me briefly. She knew she was going to die and was remarkably accepting of her fate. In a rare moment of lucidity she said, 'I'm sorry that I'm leaving you so much responsibility. Look after your aunt, Graziella. She's not always easy, but I know you'll be all right. In a way I'm glad it's like this. I'm glad this is going to kill me quickly. I would rather have lived a shorter life being useful than live a long life blind and a burden.'

I sat as close to her as I could but I knew she could barely see me.

'I've left things in order,' she said. 'As much as was possible. There's money in my savings box and I collected everything that was due to me before I came here.'

But when I looked in my mother's box under the sink in the laundry room expecting to find the 15,000 lire, it was empty. I searched for the money in other places, in the dresser drawers, in her purse, under her mattress, but there was no sign of it.

'Zia Mina, can you think of anywhere Mamma might have put some money? There was 15,000 lire in her box just before she went into hospital, but it's not there now.'

All my aunt could do was to suggest that I look in the places where I had already looked. It was impossible that my mother had spent it, and improbable that it had been stolen. I turned the house upside down trying to find it. I even looked in the stove and in the pizza oven, but it was not there. When I asked my mother during a brief moment of consciousness, she said, 'I put it in my box.'

Zia Mina ordered several masses to be dedicated to my mother and became angry with me when I refused to go. Prayer seemed futile. No amount of praying could heal Mamma.

My aunt only accompanied me to hospital once a week, saying that seeing my mother deteriorate so horribly was more than she could bear. She would stand at the foot of my mother's bed each time, reciting prayers and babbling incessantly about the people she had lost. She spoke about Mamma as though she was already dead.

'It should be me lying in that bed, not her,' she said. 'Your mother has done nothing to deserve this. If I could, I would swap places with her in an instant.'

*

After Christmas I stopped going to school entirely. It was not just because my worrying made learning impossible. I had to earn money. The haberdasher from Cremona had ceased to bring work as soon as he learned that my mother had been taken seriously ill. I offered to do it instead, but he declined politely, saying that his clients required work to be undertaken by an experienced embroiderer. I wished I had been able to prove my abilities by showing him Gianfrancesco's wedding sheets.

Signora Grassi was kind and understanding and offered me a full-time position, albeit a very poorly paid one. But a little money was better than no money and I accepted gratefully. Suddenly I was faced not just with the responsibility of fending for myself, but also with the expense of travelling to and from the hospital. It was a long journey.

I took the bus to the station in Mazzolo, caught the train there and once arrived in Cremona I took another bus to the hospital. After I had spent an hour or so with my mother I would replicate my journey in reverse, except that by the time my train arrived back in Mazzolo there were no more buses to Pieve Santa Clara and I would be obliged to walk four kilometres home.

My long journeys gave me time to think. My father's death had been unexpected and I could not decide which was worse: the shock of a sudden loss, or the dreadful wait for an imminent one.

I felt a bitter, anticipatory grief. I was consumed with worries about how my life would be without my mother. Completing my final year of school was obviously going to be impossible. My studies had been wasted.

Sometimes as I sat by my mother's bed watching her dwindling body rise and fall and listening to her laboured breaths, I would have to remind myself of who she was. The tiny, bone-thin, grey woman before me did not look or feel like Mamma. All that was left was a fading shadow. It was made worse by the fact that she, who had always been so anti-mechanisation, was hooked up to pumps and monitors, and what was left of her life was being stretched out by machines.

Home felt dismally empty without her and the thought of losing her was so unbearable that often it was easier to pretend that she was not dying in her hospital bed, but simply away. She was visiting family, I told myself. She would be coming back.

Other times I would try to convince myself that it was all just a dreadful misunderstanding. If one doctor could be wrong about migraines, another could be wrong about a brain tumour. But my mother would not be coming home. Her condition was real. And my solitary evenings at home were just as distressing as the hospital visits and the train journeys.

As the winter closed in and the days became shorter, the long walks home from the station seemed to become even longer. Although it was not as foggy as it had been in previous years, it was dark and the night air was very cold. I would arrive home late, frozen and exhausted. My aunt had offered to let me stay in her spare room, but being around Zia Mina with all her talk of death and loss only made me feel worse.

By April it was clear that Mamma could not last much longer. A new fear consumed me – the fear that I would not be there in her final moments. I didn't want her to die alone, or holding the hand of a nurse or a doctor. I wanted to be with her.

But I could not be at her bedside around the clock every day.

Each evening when I left her, the heart-crushing feeling that it could be the last time I would see her alive overwhelmed me.

On one particular evening, I alighted from the train carrying a feeling of deep dejection. I hadn't eaten all day. Faced with the choice of spending my last few lire on food or a train fare I had chosen the latter.

The visit to my mother had been particularly distressing. She had lost two of her front teeth during a fit. I had sat beside her and watched her sleeping, open-mouthed. Her cheeks were so sunken that I could see the contours of her molars through them.

The station platform was dimly lit. I was vaguely aware of a man sitting on a bench in the half-light by the glow of a cigarette floating through the darkness. I walked past with my head bowed, lost in my thoughts. It was only when I heard his voice call my name that I stopped, turned and looked at him properly.

'Gino? What are you doing here?'

He dropped his cigarette and stepped out of the shadows.

'I thought you must have lost my telephone number because you hadn't called me. I've tried phoning you lots of times, but nobody ever answers. Then I finally spoke to your aunt yesterday and told her I was coming. Didn't she tell you?'

'No.'

'Your aunt told me about your Mamma. How is she?'

'She's very ill indeed and they can't make her better.'

'Your aunt said you walk all the way back from the station every night.'

'Every other night.'

'It's a long way, and in the dark. It's not safe.'

'I have no choice.'

'You do tonight,' he said.

Gino's motorcycle was parked outside the station. Some boys were gathered around it. He shooed them away. I seated myself behind him, wrapped my arms around his waist and he took me home.

The house was very cold. I had not lit the stove all week to save on firewood and had been sleeping with my father's socks on under many layers of blankets.

'I'm surprised you haven't frozen to death,' Gino said, shivering.

'I just keep my coat on,' I replied tiredly.

'I'm starving. I haven't eaten since breakfast. Is there anything to eat?'

'I could cook some rice,' I suggested. It was the only thing I had in the house. 'But I'll have to ask my aunt for some butter and some vegetables.'

'Really? Is that what you live on?'

'Or I could make some soup.'

Gino thought about this for a moment and screwed up his face. 'I hate soup. Let's go to the trattoria in the village.'

'I don't have any spare money,' I said. I had 20 lire left in my purse.

'My treat. I've had a long trip, and I need a good, hot dinner.'

The warmth and scent of food in the trattoria was an instant comfort. I was grateful for the meal, for the company and most of all for the concern which flooded from Gino. By the time I had finished eating I felt better than I had for a long time.

As we stepped out into the cold night, Gino turned to me and said, 'I've been thinking about you a lot. Every day, actually. I haven't been able to get you out of my mind since last summer.'

He gripped both my hands in his.

'The fact is, I'm crazy about you and I want you to be my girlfriend. I mean like a proper girlfriend. And I want to be your boyfriend. Officially.'

With that, he pulled me towards him and tried to kiss me, but I held back. Although I was grateful for his concern, I was in no mood for any romance. He seemed to understand. When we arrived back home he took himself off to sleep in Zia Mina's spare room.

Gino came with me to the hospital the next day. He was obviously shocked by my mother's condition. She was frighteningly thin, as though her bones were trying to force their way out through her skin, but we found her unusually animated.

'Your mother had a bad night,' said her nurse, 'so the doctor changed her medication. She isn't in any pain at the moment, but she's really not herself. She's been talking about her husband coming to visit her.'

'My father's been dead for years,' I said.

'I know,' replied the nurse.

My mother was euphoric. Her hair hung in a dishevelled tangle around her shoulders. The nurses were very good about brushing it and tying it back for her, but she had pulled out the combs and pins, which were scattered on the sheet.

'Your Papá is coming to see me!' she exclaimed. 'Isn't that wonderful? He's coming on the train!'

I didn't correct her. There didn't seem to be any point. My mother purred with pleasure and clapped her hands. Her fingers were so thin that her wedding ring spun around as she moved her arms. After a while her head rolled back and she fell asleep with a smile on her face.

Gino looked shaken as we left. 'How long do they say your mother has to live?' he asked, lighting a cigarette.

'They can't be sure. But she hardly eats and that doesn't help.'

'I would be devastated if I lost my mother,' he said and began to sob. I put my arms around him, feeling his tears land on my neck.

Gino left early the next morning. Before leaving he asked me to be his girlfriend again and I gave a vague answer about not being in the right frame of mind. It had been nice of him to come and see me and I didn't want to hurt his feelings, but nor did I want to be his girlfriend.

I did miss having company though, so I made the effort to light the stove and eat a meal when I returned from work. I could not bear to be both lonely and cold.

When I visited my mother again she was quiet and even more shrunken. She had deteriorated significantly over just twenty-four hours. The pillows which supported her seemed to be swallowing her.

At first she did not realise that I was there. She raised her head in a bleary, drug-numbed stupor and hesitated, squinting in my direction. It took her a while to formulate her words, and when she did, they were slurred.

'Graziella?'

'Yes, Mamma. It's me,' I replied, taking her hand.

She moved her head almost imperceptibly. Her lips twitched gently.

'Are you thirsty, Mamma?' I reached across to the jug on her bedside table. There was a sponge on a saucer beside it. I dipped the sponge into the jug and placed it against my mother's lips. She opened her mouth with some effort and sucked feebly.

I sat by her bed, stroking her arm until she made a noise of irritation and said, quite clearly, 'Promise me you'll finish school. There's a bit of money to see you through. Not much, but enough if you're careful.'

I just held her hand and told her not to worry.

My mother grunted in frustration and waved in the direction of her jug of water. I placed the sponge against her lips once again. She sucked harder this time, her sunken cheeks trembling. I wiped the excess from her chin with my handkerchief.

'You're a good girl,' she murmured so quietly that her voice was little more than a breath. 'I know you'll make the best of everything. Everything will be all right.'

With that, her head nodded forwards, then rocked back against her pillows and she drifted off, snoring gently.

I cannot be certain whether these were my mother's last words.

They were certainly her last words to me. That night she fell asleep and never woke again. She was just forty-two.

CHAPTER 10

The whole village descended upon Paradiso once the news of my mother's death was announced. People came to offer their condolences, bringing gifts of food and flowers.

When I broke the news to Gino he said he would take time off work and come down to be with me for the funeral. I was touched, but I told him not to trouble himself. He turned up a few hours later anyway. He must have left home minutes after speaking to me.

'What are you going to do now?' he said.

'I have to organise the funeral, then I'll go back to work.'

Gino reached forward and took my hands. 'Come to Pomazzo,' he said. 'We can get married and live with my parents until we have enough money to get our own place.'

'What?'

'I love you, Graziella. Let's get married.'

It seemed like such a ludicrously rash, foolish suggestion that I did not reply, but nor did I express a clear refusal – and for Gino, that was sufficient.

The church was filled with so many mourners that there was not enough room for everybody to sit. People packed the pews, leaned against the columns and crowded at the back. I was overwhelmed by the number of people there. My mother was not native to Pieve Santa Clara and had never been particularly sociable, or a collector of friends, but it seemed that the whole village had taken time to come to pay their respects. Some of the shops even closed for the afternoon.

One after another they expressed their admiration for her – for the strength she had shown when faced with my father's disabilities, for the way she had risen from the misfortune of widowhood, and for the way she had raised me without assistance. They praised her modesty, her dignity and her dedication to her work.

It was not Pozzetti, but the municipal mortuary who prepared my mother for burial. I went to see her only once and decided that I would not offer her body for viewing. She would have been unrecognisable to anyone who had known her before her illness and I did not want her to be remembered like that.

My last image was of her shrouded in pale pink satin. It was a colour she had never cared for much. The undertakers had arranged her hair in an odd bouffant style, rouged her cheeks and applied lipstick to her lips. She looked like an old, grotesque china doll.

So many flowers were brought to the church, from formal bouquets and wreaths, to bunches picked from gardens and little posies gathered from fields and hedgerows. As I looked at the mountain of blooms which covered the casket and spilled down the altar steps, I thought that there was probably not a single one which Mamma had not reproduced at some time in her embroidery.

It was Don Ambrogio who took the service, something which stuck in my gullet as I knew Mamma would have preferred it to have been a different priest. Nevertheless, he spoke kind words and I believed them to be heartfelt. His eyes had welled and he had placed his arm around my shoulder when he had paid a house-call to go over the arrangements. He still smelled of sweat, wine and mothballs.

My mother's tiny coffin was placed into a tomb near my father's. I watched as it slid into its pigeon-hole and disappeared from view. It didn't seem possible that she could fit into such a small box.

Gino shook everybody's hand and introduced himself as my fiancé. People offered their condolences for the loss of my mother and congratulations on my betrothal in the same breath. I couldn't find the strength to tell them that it was a ridiculous idea and that I had no intention of marrying him. I couldn't find the strength to tell Gino either. I didn't want to cause a scene.

*

Zia Mina did not cope well with my mother's death. She became increasingly obsessed with her superstitions, professing that death had installed itself at Paradiso and that the place was cursed. She placed crucifixes on every windowsill and hung rosary beads from her door handles, then arranged a shrine in her kitchen, just as Salvatore had done for his brother. She also called upon Don Ambrogio to visit the house and requested an exorcism, which he refused. He provided a blessing and a small plastic bottle of holy water shaped like the Virgin Mary instead. My aunt was only slightly placated.

During the funeral Zia Mina wailed so feverishly that she made herself hoarse. I thought of Signora Marchesini having to be given an injection to calm her down after her husband had died and wondered whether I should ask the doctor to do the same for my aunt. She stood leaning against the cemetery wall, her face as white as the marble slabs behind her and slowly crumpled to the ground, rocking with grief.

Immacolata took me aside and said, 'I think it would be best if Mina stayed with me tonight. She's in a bad way and it wouldn't be fair on you to have to deal with her right now. We'll stay at Don Ambrogio's residence for the night and I'll get her back home to you tomorrow if she's feeling better.'

Little by little the mourners dispersed and I was left standing alone with Gino in the cemetery.

'Come on. Let's go,' he said, taking my hand. 'I hate these places.'

We walked back to Paradiso slowly. We didn't talk. I felt emptied of energy and emptied of words and beyond tired; overcome by such a deep exhaustion that I felt that if I did not lie down I would fall down. It was as though my bones and my muscles had turned to water. I curled up on my bed and let Gino hold me. I just needed to be still, sad and quiet.

He said nothing. Perhaps he understood my need to be still, sad and quiet. Perhaps he simply didn't know what to say.

It was dark when I woke up with no idea of what time it might be. I was very cold. I tried to get under the covers, but Gino had wrapped himself in the bedspread and was fast asleep. In my attempt to move him, I woke him. When I slipped between the sheets, still fully dressed in my funeral clothes, he wriggled in beside me.

'Come here,' he said quietly. 'You're frozen. Let me warm you up.'

We lay curled together like quotation marks for a while, until he became restless. His hand slid over my hip and down along my thigh until it reached the hem of my skirt.

'What are you doing?' I asked, although I knew perfectly well.

'It's all right,' he said, his hand working its way back up my thigh as he lifted my skirt. 'I love you.'

He pecked little hard, wet kisses on my skin. His kisses made me shiver. It was a chilly, prickly frisson, like biting down on a fork.

'I'll make you feel better,' he whispered, the rough skin on his palms snagging against my stockings. 'I'll be gentle. It'll be nice. And I'll pull out before I come. I promise.'

I didn't want him, but somehow it was easier to submit than to resist. He tried to push himself inside me, but I was unready, unwilling and tense.

'Try to relax,' he said.

'You're hurting me.'

'Don't worry. It's normal that it hurts a bit the first time. Just try to relax and it will feel good.'

I didn't tell him that it wasn't the first time, nor that the first time it had not hurt. I had been ready and willing and filled with desire and it could not have been more different to the way I felt in that moment. It was a brief and unsuccessful coupling. Within a few minutes he was snoring.

At some point during the night Gino stirred me again. His hands were on my hips and I could feel him prodding his way inside me. I pretended to be asleep. I let him grunt, grope and fumble. After a few minutes he groaned loudly and rolled away. I wiped my thigh on the corner of the sheet and fell back to sleep.

He left the next morning, saying that I must go to Pomazzo as soon as possible to meet his parents, something which I had no intention of doing. Instead, I waited until he telephoned me the next day.

There was a long silence when I told him that I wouldn't marry him, followed by a tirade of angry words about how I had made him look like an idiot in front of all the people at the funeral. He called me a slut for having let him have sex with me and said that he never wanted to see me again.

I didn't argue. I didn't even react when he called me names. It was a relief. I was certainly not upset, for I had far greater things to be upset about.

Although I had been living at home alone for over five months, the finality of my mother's departure consumed me. I would awake each day to silence in the house – a silence which felt deeper and more absolute than it had when she had been in hospital. No sound of her moving in the kitchen, or of the door to the laundry room opening and closing; no clatter of the milk pan, or crackle of the stove being lit.

My emotions seemed to bleed into one another. Pain bled into anger; anger into sadness; sadness into denial; denial into a shock; the shock back into pain. It was a constant cycle and I couldn't decide which part of it felt the worst.

It was Signora Grassi I turned to for succour. She offered words of comfort and told me not to worry about work. However, I had no choice but to go straight back to work because I needed the money.

'Just take one day at a time, darling,' she said. 'There will be good days and bad days, but the grief will work its way out eventually.'

Most days at work were bearable. Signora Grassi didn't mind if I didn't finish all my work within her strict time limits. She even insisted that I eat my lunch with her as she said that I was looking worryingly thin. She also obliged me to take a fortifying tonic which had the consistency of phlegm and tasted like fish. It was so foul that it made me sick.

Being at home alone was the hardest. I had already experienced loss, but the loss of my mother felt deeper than the loss of my father. My mother had taken part of my father with her. I knew that there were memories and stories about him that she hadn't yet shared and that they were lost for ever.

For over a month I kept everything at home exactly as Mamma had left it. Moving any of her things seemed wrong. Her basket of sewing equipment sat on the windowsill beside her workspace. Her bed was made and her nightdress was folded under her pillow. Her shoes were by the door.

Sometimes I would wrap myself in her cardigan, bury my face in the sleeves and breathe in what remained of her scent, just as I had done with my father's jacket after his death. I don't know what had become of my father's clothing. It must have been given away at some point. I wasn't sure what I would do with my mother's clothes, but the thought of parting with them seemed terribly wrong.

Nevertheless, as the weeks passed I reasoned that being surrounded by her things was not healthy. I had no choice but to adjust to life without her. Ridding myself of her possessions was unthinkable, but I could put them away in Zia Mina's wardrobe until I decided what to do with them.

My mother had a few changes of clothing, a coat, a spare pair of shoes, some heavy winter boots and a couple of hats. There was very little I could use for myself. And apart from the hats, there was nothing that would fit Zia Mina.

When I went to offer the hats to my aunt I found her kneeling in front of her shrine, deeply immersed in prayer.

'Zia Mina, I've been sorting through Mamma's things. Is there anything you would like?'

My aunt did not look up. 'Have you gone through the items in the wardrobe yet?' she said.

'No.'

'There are things in there too, but it's locked. Your mother kept the key in the left-hand drawer of her kitchen dresser, right at the back, hidden inside a glove.' She then turned away, crossed herself and continued her prayer.

I went to stand in front of the huge wardrobe and took a long look at myself in the third mirror. There was a spent tiredness about me, as though the life inside me had been switched off. I combed my hair with my fingers and rubbed at the shadows under my eyes. Signora Grassi had been worried that I was not looking after myself and she was right. I was pale and thin. I could fit three fingers into the waistband of my skirt.

I stood up as straight as I could, but it made me look even thinner. Signora Grassi's trick of appearing to lose five kilos by standing up straight worked every time.

'Make a fresh start,' I said to the pallid, skinny girl in the mirror. She looked back at me with sad eyes and nodded, but she didn't seem convinced.

When I found the key, exactly where Zia Mina had told me, I unlocked my mother's section of the wardrobe and was surprised at how full it was. Each shelf was neatly stacked with linens and boxes. I began to empty out the contents and laid them on the bed. There was set after set of beautifully embroidered household linens: bedding, tablecloths of various sizes, napkins, cushion covers, doilies and mantelpiece cloths. I recognised them all as items supposedly destined for the haberdasher in Cremona.

I thought that I should probably contact him, for despite Mamma having said that she had left everything in order, perhaps in her confusion she had forgotten to return the completed work. Perhaps she was even owed money for it.

By the time I had emptied the top two shelves, the entire bed was covered in linens. Although money would be helpful, I hoped that the haberdasher would not want all the work returned. Now every piece, which had seemed so commonplace before, was precious.

The lower shelves were packed with boxes and things wrapped in newspaper. I found six stemmed wine glasses, some white china coffee cups, a pretty painted fruit bowl and various ornaments and mismatched items of household crockery. I had never seen any of them before.

Wedged in right at the back was a large package wrapped in brown paper. I eased it out; it was very heavy. I undid the string and opened it to reveal a set of sumptuous silk sheets. At first I thought my eyes must be deceiving me, for laid out before me were Gianfrancesco's wedding sheets, obviously untouched since I had finished and packaged them.

I thought of the countless hours I had spent torturing myself about Gianfrancesco and Anna making love on these very sheets, but there they were, completely unused. Perhaps Gianfrancesco was not married after all! I felt a moment of hope, then told myself not to be ridiculous. He had made it clear that he did not want me, and now was not the time to be trawling back over heartbreak and dredging up feelings of rejection.

As I tried to make sense of what I had found I was interrupted by my aunt's footsteps on the stairs. Moments later she appeared in the doorway. She looked terrible, with sunken, grey-circled eyes, as though she was more dead than alive.

'You've found everything then,' she said.

'This was all Mamma's?'

'It's yours. It's your dowry for when you get married.'

'All these linens? And this crockery?'

My aunt nodded. 'Yes. Your mother had been putting things aside for years. When she got married, she had nothing. She got married in her church dress and borrowed shoes, and she and your father didn't have a dishcloth between them. She didn't want it to be the same for you. Everything in that section of the wardrobe is for you.'

'Signora Marchesini's sheets are here. The wedding sheets I spent so long working on.'

'Ah, yes,' said my aunt. 'She never came back for them.'

'Why?'

'I don't know. Your mother wasn't going to go looking for her, so she kept them.'

'Should I give them back?'

'Not unless she comes and pays for them. But you have a use for them now. They can be your wedding sheets.'

'Zia Mina, I'm not getting married,' I said.

My aunt's expression hardened. 'What?'

'I'm not marrying Gino.'

'Why?'

'Because I don't want to, Zia Mina! And I barely know him.'

'Gino's a good man. He's a mechanic and that's a very useful profession. And just look how quickly he came when he knew your Mamma was ill, and how he came here as soon as you told him she had died.'

'I hardly think that's enough of a reason to marry him.'

My aunt cast her eyes over Gianfrancesco's wedding sheets spread out on the bed.

'I see. You are still obsessing over the Marchesini boy, is that it?' she said, curling her lip. 'I suppose you think he loved you, do you? He didn't love you, you silly girl! I told you before, men of his social standing do not love women of your social standing. They might pretend to, to get what they want, but it's not love. He will use his good looks and fine words to charm girls, just as his father did and his grandfather before him and all the other Marchesini men before them. The Marchesinis are a womanising, philandering, no-good lot. They can't resist a fresh-faced, pretty country girl. You're not the first and you won't be the last. I warned your mother – I warned her many times, but she didn't listen. She was a fool!'

'Mamma was not a fool!' I said hotly. 'How can you say that?'

'And you're a bigger fool than her for believing anything could ever have come of a relationship with a Marchesini,' my aunt sneered. 'You didn't see your precious Gianfrancesco at the funeral, did you? Did he even send you a note to offer his sympathies? No, he didn't. And you can't argue that he wouldn't have heard that your Mamma had died. Everybody in the village and for miles around knew! Why, there wasn't enough room for all the mourners in the church. Graziella, think, girl! If you have any sense, you will marry Gino. There's nothing for you here in this accursed place. Bologna is a rich area with lots of industry. People have good jobs and earn good money there. Gino will be a good provider and give you security. Have you seen any young man around here with a motorcycle like his? A young man here is lucky to be able to afford a bicycle. Mark my words, that young man will make a fine husband.'

'*You* marry him then, Zia Mina!' I cried.

At this, my aunt turned around and padded back down the stairs, muttering to herself.

I didn't take out any more linens, or look in any more boxes. I crammed everything back into the wardrobe without bothering to wrap or fold anything. I just stuffed it all in, went back to the annexe and locked the doors, including the door which led to the laundry room and through to Zia Mina's part of the house.

My aunt's outburst unleashed such feelings of anger that I spent an hour pacing the kitchen, circling the table again and again, my fists clenched. It was not just rage at what my aunt had said about my mother and about Gianfrancesco. It was rage that Zia Mina's grief was so selfish. We should have been supporting one another, but she was so wrapped up in herself that she didn't even seem to be mourning my mother. It was all about her. *Her* losses. *Her* grief. Ceaseless nonsensical babbling about Paradiso being cursed.

I tried not to let it, but the discovery of the wedding sheets re-opened the cracks in my patched-up heart. Questions kept invading my thoughts. I wished that someone would confirm that Gianfrancesco was married so I could put an end to the speculation and persuade myself not to be in love with him any more. But even more than that, I would have given anything in that moment to feel the warmth and comfort of his friendship again.

Over the following days I kept out of my aunt's way. Ada Pozzetti and Immacolata called in as often as they could, but Zia Mina was certain that she was cursed and nobody could convince her otherwise. Even Salvatore, whose good humour could always be relied upon to cheer my aunt, was unable to lift her spirits.

*

Before long, it was 26 June again: the seventh anniversary of my father's death and almost seven weeks since I had lost my mother. The rose shrub in the pot which covered the missing brick on the doorstep was in full bloom, lacing the evening air with the scent of roses. I sat quietly, remembering the time I had sat there with Mamma eating figs and listening to the story of the chicken thief, and her words of caution about losing my heart to Gianfrancesco. The feeling of being utterly alone gnawed through me.

My life seemed broken and it was impossible to see how I could fit the pieces together again when there were such important pieces of it missing. Despite my mother's wishes, I had no hope of ever going back to school. I simply couldn't afford it. The fact that I had been within touching distance of obtaining my teaching diploma made the whole thing worse.

I was plagued by a constant queasy feeling in the pit of my stomach which put me off my food. Even the scent of the roses was making me feel nauseous.

Zia Mina was out. She had taken to visiting the cemetery every day, sometimes twice. I knew it wasn't healthy, but when I had tried to say something to that effect, she had flown into a rage and screamed something about a curse again.

As I was turning to go back inside, a car pulled up by the gate. Don Ambrogio was sitting in the front seat next to the mayor. Zia Mina and Immacolata were sitting in the back. It turned out that my aunt had been found lying collapsed on the ground in the Garden of Little Angels by the graves of her babies.

We took her inside and sat her down. She was expressionless, almost catatonic. Immacolata sent Don Ambrogio and the mayor packing in her usual forthright way. She had brought with her an enormous bag of oranges, which she set about peeling.

'Come now, Mina,' she said encouragingly. 'Come and get some of these in you. Let's lift your spirits.'

My aunt just sat and stared at the oranges.

'We need to get her to a doctor,' I said, but Immacolata immediately pulled me to the side.

'Don't you go saying that in front of her!' she hissed. 'What do you think a doctor would do for her? He'd either fill her so full of pills she wouldn't know up from down, or send her straight to an institution and right into the hands of quacks who amuse themselves tearing people's heads apart. Mina don't need no institution and she's not going anywhere near one. She just needs time and a bit of looking after. I promised her years ago that for as long as the Good Lord sees fit to keep me on this earth, I'll see to it that she don't get put in no institution.'

Immacolata crossed herself fervently several times and cast her eyes up sternly, as though she was not just warning me, but God too, not to interfere. Then she sat down beside my aunt and slowly began feeding her segments of orange, clucking gentle words of encouragement.

'Come now, Mina,' she said. 'Let's get you straight again.'

It took over an hour to feed my aunt a whole orange, but gradually she emerged from her stupor. She was groggy and disorientated, and had no memory of having gone to the cemetery or having been brought home in the mayor's car.

'I'm so tired, Mamma Imma,' she said at last.

'Of course you are, dear. Best we get you up to bed now and you'll be right as rain in the morning.'

Zia Mina settled immediately, sank into her pillow and fell fast asleep.

As she was waiting for the mayor to come and fetch her, Immacolata came to find me in the annexe.

'Poor Mina,' she said. 'She's such a sensitive soul. She takes death very hard. Says she can feel it coming.'

'She thinks she's cursed.'

'If my luck had been as rotten as Mina's I might think the same myself. But she's been like it since she was a youngster. She blamed herself for her mother's death, see, and she's never shook off the guilt.'

'What happened to Zia Mina's mother?'

Immacolata puffed out her cheeks, shook her head sadly and

said, 'The poor girl died in childbirth. Weren't no one's fault – but if anyone should of felt guilt, it was me. I didn't even know she was with child. Maybe if I'd known, or if I'd got to her in time I could've saved her. I've never forgave myself for it. She took herself off to have her baby all alone in secret. We searched high and low for her. By the time I found her it was too late. It was a miracle that Mina survived.'

'Where did you find her?'

'Don't you know? She gave birth to Mina in a field.'

'In a field?'

'Yes. In one of the mulberry fields where we used to work. The master, old Carlo Marchesini, was very good about it. Said it broke his heart that one of his farm girls had died like that. He gave Mina to me to care for. It was him what had her christened Gelsomina – but that was such a mouthful we always called her Mina. He always had a fondness for her. He used to call her "the little mulberry". There was a lot of people who wasn't keen on the master, and many for good reasons, but he did all he could for Mina.' Immacolata dabbed her eyes on her cuff and sighed.

'What about Zia Mina's father?' I said.

Just then, a car horn sounded from outside and the headlights of the mayor's car flashed through the gaps in the shutters. Immacolata gathered herself and stood up to leave without answering my question.

'I expect Mina will sleep soundly tonight, but please look in on her before you turn in, will you? And if you're worried, call Don Ambrogio on the telephone and I'll come up, even if it's the middle of the night. Don't you worry about disturbing him. I'll be back first thing.'

She made her way out, leaving the remainder of the enormous bag of oranges on the table for me.

'You have them,' she said, adjusting her cauliflower hat. 'You look as though you could do with some feeding. I've left more in

Mina's kitchen. It's Don Ambrogio's colleague from Sicily what's sent them. Seven crates of the things! He must have thought we're all suffering from scurvy or something up here.'

I checked in on Zia Mina later that evening. She was sound asleep with her mouth wide open. But when I went to bed, sleep was nowhere to be found.

I gave up when I heard the church clock strike three. I wrapped myself in my mother's cardigan and wandered through to the kitchen, where I stood trying to think of something which might help me sleep. I felt sick and regretted having eaten four oranges for my supper. Heartburn was rising up in my throat.

For a long time I just stood and looked around the kitchen. Little had changed during my lifetime, apart from the picture of the Pope. The same table, most of the same chairs, the same dresser, a few knick-knacks, the bed in the corner, my mother's workspace by the window, it all felt as though it belonged to another time; it felt as though the world had moved on, but my home, filled with my parents' furniture, was stuck somewhere in a pre-war past.

I had seen photographs of modern interiors in magazines. Perhaps it would do me good to cheer the place up. I could cut out pictures from magazines and stick them to the walls and maybe even paint over the whitewash in a vibrant colour. Maybe one day I could afford to buy a rug and an armchair and create a cosy sitting area in place of my mother's bed. Having a bed in the corner of the kitchen was no longer necessary.

By the time the church clock struck four I was no closer to sleep. I looked for some chamomile, but the tin was empty. I knew that Zia Mina would have some.

A silvery sliver of moonlight pierced the darkness of my aunt's kitchen and lit up the shrine with an eerie, other-worldly light. As I searched the dresser shelves for chamomile I was startled by a groaning noise. My aunt was not in bed. She was on the floor, hunched before her shrine, half asleep in a position of prayer. I turned quietly to leave, but she saw me and screamed, 'Teresa!'

She clapped her hands together and began to chant unintelligible gibberish, crossing herself feverishly, then stared at me shiny-eyed through the semi-darkness and continued to scream my mother's name.

'Teresa! Teresa! What do you want? What do you want?'

'I'm not Teresa. It's Graziella. And I'm looking for some chamomile, Zia Mina.'

My aunt shrieked, then prostrated herself on the floor and began to beat at the tiles with her fists. I crouched down beside her.

'Zia Mina. It's *me* – it's Graziella. You should go to bed.'

My aunt would not look at me. She buried her face in her hands.

'Have you come to take me?' she wailed. 'It should have been me, not you! Take me! Take me! I'm ready!'

'No, Zia Mina. Nobody's taking you anywhere. You really need to go to bed. Let me help you.'

I couldn't move her, but after a few moments she quietened down and fell asleep, whimpering. I covered her with a shawl, stepped around her and went back to the annexe.

I did fall asleep eventually, but was awoken with a start at first light. My aunt was standing at the foot of my bed in her crumpled nightdress. Her hair hung around her gaunt face in a dishevelled tangle. She looked like some ghastly, faded spectre.

'Your mother came to me!' she exclaimed with a look of crazed, goggle-eyed consternation.

'No, Zia Mina. That was me.'

But my aunt was not listening. 'She came to me and spoke to me,' she jabbered.

'No. She didn't speak to you.'

'I know what I saw, girl! Her spirit came to me. She was young again. She was dressed in a long, white gown.'

134

I had run out of patience. 'I think you should try to get some sleep,' I said.

My aunt turned and left, placing a string of rosary beads around my bedpost.

As it turned out, believing that my mother had appeared to her and had not chosen to take her seemed to comfort Zia Mina. Within a few days she was tending her garden again and her cemetery visits became occasional as opposed to daily. She still prayed at her shrine, but only in the evening before bed.

*

When September came around, which was the beginning of term and the time I should have returned to school to complete my final year, I had resigned myself to the fact that it would never be possible. There was no point in getting too upset about it. I had to make the most of what skills I had.

There were worse jobs than dressmaking and Signora Grassi had increased my wages a little. I was certainly not rich, but as I didn't have to pay rent, I could manage. I would divide up my money every week, just as my mother had done, and every week I would save something, even if it was just 20 lire. She would have been pleased.

Gradually things began to improve and I settled into my new routines. There were still moments when my nerves overcame me and I felt sick, but my nausea was no longer constant. I felt a sense of relief that the worst of my grieving was over and that everything would be all right.

It was partly true. The worst of my grieving was over but everything, it soon transpired, would be far from all right.

CHAPTER 11

I married Gino for two reasons. The first was that I was pregnant and the second was that neither of us was given any choice in the matter. The reasons for us *not* to marry numbered significantly more than two – but faced with the facts of the situation, they did not count.

For months I had ignored the signs. Gianfrancesco and I had taken so many risks and suffered no consequences, so I refused to believe that the brief fumble with Gino on the night of my mother's funeral could have resulted in conception. I told myself that my nausea was due to nerves. I was grieving. I was worried all the time. It was enough to make anybody feel sick. Even my missed periods could be explained. Menstruation was not an exact science. It could be affected by shock, or by trauma, or by weight loss. I had suffered all three.

Whenever I looked down at my thin, depleted little body it seemed impossible that it could contain another human being. And so I managed to convince myself that I could not possibly be pregnant. I remained suspended in this rigorous state of denial, telling myself that my period would arrive eventually and carrying on with my daily routines as normal, but despite checking regularly for blood, my gusset remained stubbornly unstained.

By the end of October the signs could no longer be ignored. My waistbands were growing tighter by the day and every time I lay down I would feel a subtle bubbling in my stomach.

Signora Grassi remarked that I was still alarmingly pale. I assured her that I was fine, probably just going down with a cold, and set about my day's work, but when I stood up from my sewing machine vomit rose in my throat and the room dissolved. I came round with Signora Grassi kneeling by my side, fanning me with a sewing pattern. Despite my protests, she insisted on taking me straight to the doctor.

'When was your last menstrual period?' he said.

'I don't know.'

'Have you had sexual intercourse, Signorina?' He emphasised the word 'Signorina' with undisguised disapproval.

'A little,' I said.

'A little is sufficient, Signorina.'

He examined me and he was not gentle. It was a deeply unpleasant experience.

'As I thought,' he said as he washed, then wiped his hands, looking at me as though I was something dirty. 'You're pregnant – I would estimate well over twenty weeks. I'm surprised you haven't been to see me before now. I suggest you start making your wedding preparations very quickly.'

When I sat unmoving, rigid with shock and dismay, the doctor tapped the notepad on his desk and cleared his throat loudly.

'Signorina Ponti, I do have other patients to see,' he said. Then added grudgingly, 'It's common to feel light-headed. If you feel faint again, just sit down or lie down and let it pass. Your nausea is quite normal too. The body becomes hyper-sensitive during pregnancy, but it will subside. However, you are rather thin. I would recommend you eat some good food and get plenty of rest. That's all. Pregnancy is not an illness. Come and see me again next month.'

There were many unknowns for me to consider, but amongst them was one certainty: I did not want to marry Gino. We hadn't spoken since he had said he never wanted to speak to me again, and I reasoned that it would be best if things remained like that. He lived a long way away and need never know about the baby.

Perhaps it was naïve of me to think that I could raise my child alone and that Zia Mina would be accepting of it, but when at last I found the courage to break the news to her, something which took several days, she was anything but accepting. She let out a piercing shriek and slapped my face so hard that my ears rang.

'You would deprive a child of a loving father?' she spat. 'You selfish, *selfish* girl! You of all people, who had a father who loved you more than anything else on this earth, and who knows how it feels to have a father's love. It's something that *I* never had.'

'But I don't love Gino.'

'You loved him enough to spread your legs without a second thought for the consequences.' She poked an angry finger into my face. 'And you did it under my roof with your mother barely cold in her grave! Fornicating in my house is one thing, but I will not have you living in my house raising an illegitimate child. Have you no shame? And do you think it's up to me to support you? Do you think it's up to me to feed and lodge you and your child? This is *my* house, not yours, and *I* decide who lives here!'

Despite my begging her not to, Zia Mina telephoned Gino's parents. Between them they decided that we should marry as soon as possible. The fact that neither of us wanted to was irrelevant.

'My father said I have to fulfil my responsibilities,' said Gino glumly. 'If I don't marry you, I'm on my own. He'll kick me out and he'll disown me.'

Both our situations were precarious, although mine was significantly more precarious than Gino's.

Zia Mina could not get rid of me fast enough. Within a week of the news being broken Paradiso was no longer my home.

*

The Bianchis lived on the third floor of a modern six-storey building on the edge of Pomazzo. It was part of a new estate, built

138

post-war. The future of housing was vertical – vertical towns and vertical villages; people stacked on people. A great space-saver, just like the pigeon-holes in the cemetery.

A pressure cooker was simmering on the stove when I arrived, filling the apartment with the smell of boiled meat. My nausea returned immediately.

Considerable efforts had been made for my welcome meal. The table had been set with the best linen and cutlery. Gino's father sat at the head of the table, absorbed in his own thoughts, stabbing at his food and consuming it quickly. He was a large, barrel-chested man. The circumference of his neck was greater than that of his head. Gino's mother sat at the opposite end, and Gino was seated across from me. We had barely spoken since my arrival.

Halfway through the second course, Signora Bianchi turned to me and took a deep, resigned breath before she said: 'Please understand that you and Gino living under the same roof before you're married is not something that we would consider appropriate under normal circumstances. But in view of the situation you find yourself in, having lost your mother so recently and all the rest, we feel we can make an exception. We do want the wedding to take place as soon as possible, but we would rather you didn't mention your *condition*. We haven't told anybody outside the family yet, and would prefer it if nobody was told until after you marry – a few weeks after you marry, at least. We're a respectable family and we would rather people didn't talk.'

The look she gave me was one of reproach for having got myself so inconveniently pregnant.

'And we think that it would be better for you and for Gino to remain living here with us for the foreseeable future,' she continued. 'Although we will be able to offer a small amount of financial help you need time to save before you'll be ready to set up your own home. And there will be a lot of new challenges for you both with the arrival of the baby.'

I looked across at Gino, who didn't seem to be listening He was making patterns in his mashed potato with his fork.

'Did you hear what your mother said?' It was Gino's father. His voice was harsh.

Gino looked up immediately, like a startled rabbit.

'You'll be setting up your own home. You'll have responsibilities.'

'I know, Papá.'

'Well, you're going to have to do some growing up then, aren't you, son?'

Gino just looked back down at his mashed potato.

'The money you earn now isn't just yours to squander any more. You've got to start saving it, and when you do spend it, spend it wisely.'

'Of course Gino knows that,' said Gino's mother soothingly.

The big man made a grunting noise. 'Does he?' he said.

'Of course he does. Things will be different now.'

'They're going to have to be. And you can start off by not bailing him out all the time with money from your housekeeping. Don't think I don't know.'

Gino's mother opened her mouth as though to change the subject, but her husband would not let it go.

'And don't think that this excuses you from all the money you owe me for that motorcycle,' he said to his son.

Gino was sinking lower and lower into his chair. I reasoned that if his father carried on talking for much longer, his son's chin would touch the table and then he would disappear from view altogether.

'Haven't you got anything to say for yourself?'

Clearly Gino did not.

'He's got a lot on his mind,' his mother said. 'All this has been a big shock.' She waved her hand in my direction when she said 'all this'.

'Pah! No point telling you,' her husband said. 'He could set the church on fire and you'd still defend him.'

Gino's mother turned her attention back to me.

'We would like to keep the wedding small,' she said. 'We don't consider it necessary to have anything too costly. Just close family and friends and a few select business associates. I'm aware that you have family here, but Gino says you've never met any of them, so it seems pointless inviting them. What family do you have back in Lombardy?'

'My aunt is the only family I have left,' I replied.

'Oh good.' Signora Bianchi seemed relieved. 'Well, that makes things easier then,' she said, then added, 'But if your aunt is thinking of staying overnight she'll have to sort out her own accommodation. We can't be expected to pay for that too.'

The woman was silent for a moment before going on: 'Your aunt …' she began. 'She's not going to cause any problems, is she?'

'I don't understand.'

'Gino said she was deranged,' Signora Bianchi said, tapping her temple. 'And just to clarify, she's not a blood relation, is she?'

'No. She was married to my father's brother. Why?'

'Madness runs in families. It can be passed down,' she said, casting a suspicious glance in the direction of my belly, then carried on talking as though her vile words had not been in the least offensive.

Gino's sister arrived shortly after dinner. I was surprised. He had never mentioned that he had a sister.

Marina Bianchi was eleven years older than Gino and a very large woman, a sort of feminised version of her father. There was a defensiveness about her. Once the formalities of our introduction had been completed, she ignored me, diving straight into an argument with her mother about her choice of outfit for the wedding. Gino teased her about being fat, made an oinking noise and called her a pig. Shortly after that, she left.

My bedroom had previously been Marina's. It was a narrow, cell-like space. I could touch two opposite walls at once with my palms held flat. A single bed placed against the wall allowed just enough of a gap to squeeze past sideways to reach the window. Beyond it was a little wardrobe and a chair. A row of stuffed animals perched on a shelf above the door and a battered, one-eyed doll lay on the bed. The wardrobe was filled with Marina's old school books, all carefully packaged and labelled by year and subject.

I began to unpack my things. Although Zia Mina wanted me gone, she had conceded that my possessions, and specifically all the things which my mother had collected for me, could remain at Paradiso until Gino and I had our own home. It was just as well, I thought, as there was barely enough space to store the contents of my single suitcase.

My room was opposite the kitchen and smelled of boiled meat. I edged past the bed and opened the window to let in some fresh air, but the air here was anything but fresh. The atmosphere was dense and laced with the whiff of fumes and sun-baked concrete. Wafts of refuse blew my way as people went to deposit their rubbish in the communal bins in the street outside.

Beyond the bins a group of noisy boys were kicking a football against a small, windowless building, something to do with the electricity board. It made an intermittent buzzing noise. Beside some crudely drawn Communist graffiti somebody had painted GOD EXISTS in large letters. An arrow pointing upwards had been added in another colour, presumably in case anybody had trouble finding Him. A collage of peeling advertising posters had been stuck around it, beneath a large sign which gave the instruction that nothing should be pasted to the wall.

I sat at the window for a long time, surveying the great monoliths which surrounded me. They blocked out the sky. I couldn't see whether it was starry, or whether there was a moon. All I could see were people going about their business behind their lit-up windows, oblivious to what was happening above or below them or just a few centimetres away on the other side of a partition wall. A man in a bath-robe was cleaning his teeth. A few centimetres away, a woman stood at her sink washing up, facing the same wall.

Some apartments had balconies. Most were strung with washing and crammed with boxes, mops, buckets, brooms and bicycles. The one directly opposite me housed a kennel. An enormous dog emerged, sniffed the air, took a brief look at me and retired back to its quarters.

The distant wailing sound of scooter engines became louder and louder as they approached. A group of youths came to a stop outside. Moments later I heard the door of the apartment open and shut. Gino joined them and I watched as he got onto the back of somebody's Lambretta and the group rode off, yelling to one another and revving loudly.

When I climbed into my new bed I knew I was a long way from sleep.

There were footsteps just above my head, as though somebody was pacing their floor wearing wooden clogs. The muffled sounds of televisions and radios from elsewhere in the building vibrated through the walls and blended into an unintelligible booming and jingling. I could hear the echo of distant conversations, dogs barking and children crying, the constant sound of something dripping.

Gradually the noises around me died down. The footsteps above me stopped. Televisions and radios became silent. The lights in the windows around me were switched off one by one. Voices quietened. The world around me fell asleep, but I did not. I lay on my bed, staring open-eyed into the darkness. It was then that my baby kicked for the first time.

Reality came crashing down upon me. The reality of my situation, of my failure, of my wasted education, rolled over me in great waves, slamming the breath from me.

I wanted my mother. I wanted to go home. But all I had was everything I didn't want.

*

During the brief countdown to the wedding day Gino's mother rushed around and organised everything. My participation was not required. A dress arrived that was not my choice. It had been ordered from a catalogue simply on the grounds that it would cover me up sufficiently so as not to show the bulge of my belly. I was instructed not to stand sideways-on to the congregation during the wedding service.

Zia Mina did not want to travel to Pomazzo alone, so she didn't come. The only people at my wedding who were connected to me in any way were Giovanni and my mother's Cousin Ugo.

I was given away by Ugo. I had never met him before, only his friendly son Giovanni. He smelled of wine, trod on my skirt and I had to steady him as we weaved down the aisle.

The ceremony blared out over a shrieking loud-speaker system, which set my teeth on edge. The priest spoke about two lives becoming one, about two families uniting and about love being eternal. None of it seemed relevant. It felt as though I had mistakenly landed in the middle of someone else's wedding.

I thought about escaping. I pictured myself hitching up my nasty nylon lace skirt, flinging my flowers to the ground and fleeing from the church; running and running and running until I was far away.

But I didn't run. Instead I missed my cue when I was asked whether I wanted to take Gino as my lawful wedded husband. The priest mistakenly called me 'Grazia' twice. I wished with all my heart that whoever she was, Grazia would step forward and take my place.

By the end of the ceremony I was married. Graziella Ponti was gone. I was Graziella Bianchi – for ever.

Our wedding night was to be spent near Rimini, but finding the hotel took us a long time. The map we had was not very detailed and the combination of never having navigated from a map before, poor sign-posting and the dark meant that we were driving around in a circle for over two hours. Gino became increasingly frustrated.

'We'll run out of bloody petrol if you keep sending us in the wrong bloody direction!' he ranted.

Unfortunately the hotel had not been informed that we would be arriving late, so when we got there, it was closed. Gino banged on the door for a long time, until finally an angry man in pyjamas leaned out of the window and shouted at us, 'What do you think you're doing, making all that din in the middle of the night?'

'We've got a room booked!'

'The latest time for arrivals is half past nine. We're very clear about that.'

'But we've just got married!'

'That makes no difference to me. If you were going to be late, you should have called ahead to let us know.'

With that he shut the window. Gino was furious and began to hammer at the door again. Moments later the man reappeared.

'If you don't pack that in, I'll call the police!'

'Ah, fuck you!' spat Gino. 'We wouldn't stay in your shit hotel even if you paid us!'

We drove straight back to Pomazzo. The honeymoon was over.

CHAPTER 12

I did try to make the best of our marriage, but I didn't try very hard, or for very long.

Although my circumstances had changed immeasurably, marriage changed very little in Gino's day-to-day life. I didn't see much of him. He was at work all day at Bartocchi's Garage. Most evenings he went out with his friends, none of whom I was ever introduced to. I was an invisible wife.

I spent my days trying to be useful without getting in the way, although Gino's mother made it clear that I *was* in the way. My presence in her home was about as welcome as toothache.

As soon as we were married I moved into Gino's bedroom, not because I wanted to, but because it was expected. His room was plastered with posters of motorcycles and pictures of racing drivers. One wall was shelved and displayed a collection of model cars, trains and aeroplanes. An army of toy soldiers took up an entire shelf.

I conceded to sex to avoid confrontation, but it was a joyless experience, made worse by the creaking of the bed and the knocking of the headboard on the wall. All I could think of was Gino's parents, lying in their bed on the other side, listening to the noise from our room.

Most attempts were mercifully brief. At least I was not worried about falling pregnant. Sometimes I would count the toy soldiers on the shelf as a distraction. There were two hundred and thirty-two.

But once my belly swelled to the size of a watermelon, Gino lost interest anyway.

By the end of my pregnancy I felt so huge, hot and tired that I moved back into Marina's old room. I never returned into Gino's.

I tried to consult Gino about our baby's name. I had suggested Renzo for a boy and Lucia for a girl, like the characters in *The Betrothed*. I had found Marina's old school copy in the wardrobe and read it again, but Gino said he'd never read the book, then just shrugged and said, 'Call it what you like.'

According to the doctor's calculations I was due to give birth in mid to late January, but January came and went and there was no sign of the baby wanting to emerge. By the beginning of February I thought I would explode, but I was made to wait one more week. Lucia was born in hospital on 7 February 1957.

Gino had always maintained that he did not want to be in the room for the birth, something which was not unusual then anyway. Most prospective fathers were penned into a smoky waiting room at the end of the ward and were only called in when their wives had recovered sufficiently to be fit for viewing and the babies could be presented to their fathers washed and wrapped in clean blankets.

But as I sat up in my bed, exhausted, torn and dazed, it was not Gino who came into the room but his sister Marina.

'Where's Gino?' I asked.

'He went home.'

'Home?' Did he not want to see his new-born daughter, I thought, and to make sure that I was recovering?

'Yes, but I thought you'd want somebody here, so I stayed. I telephoned my mother to say everything was all right and she said that Gino would come back later.'

She cradled Lucia in her arms and clucked gently at her. 'She's so beautiful,' she murmured.

I did not know Marina well, since I only saw her when she came for lunch on Sundays. She worked in the family plumbing business and usually spent most of the meal discussing work with her father. Her mother criticised her frequently and needlessly. Gino had little to say to her, unless he was taunting her for being fat. When I had reproached him for it he told me to shut up because I was an only child and didn't understand jokes between brothers and sisters. Clearly for Marina it was no joke.

'I don't suppose I'll ever get married or have children,' she said to me, which surprised me as I had never heard her speak openly about anything, let alone a subject which was so personal.

'Would you like to?' I asked, but Marina shook her head in a very determined way.

'I'd need a husband first and that looks unlikely,' she said. 'Everyone seems to think it should bother me, but to be honest, it doesn't. I'm really quite content living by myself and only having myself to look after. And anyway, I have a responsibility to the family business and that responsibility will increase when my father retires. I can't see marriage or children fitting into that. It's different for men. A man can be out at work all day and barely spend any time at home, but a woman can't. I couldn't imagine myself being at home looking after children, or having a life like my mother's.'

She shuddered at the reference to a life like her mother's.

'It's funny really,' she said. 'It was always presumed that I would get married and have a family, and that Gino would take over the business. Even when we were children, I remember conversations where my parents would talk about Gino running the business one day. My participation wasn't even considered. A woman running a plumbing firm just seemed ludicrous to them. You know, even though I worked hard and did well at school and I knew from the age of about thirteen that I wanted to be an accountant of some sort, it seemed to by-pass my parents.'

An ironic smile twitched across Marina's expression.

'It wasn't until I finished my accountancy training that my father realised that I was the son he'd always wanted.'

Suddenly Marina looked uncomfortable, as though she felt she had said too much. The conversation ended there. I cannot say that we became friends in that moment, but we became friendly, and that was a start.

Marina stayed as long as she could and as she left she promised to call Zia Mina to tell her the news. Gino did not come until the following day. When I asked him why he had left, he said, 'Because I didn't want to spend hours stuck in a waiting room with my stupid sister.'

He held Lucia uncertainly in his arms, glanced at her briefly and handed her back.

'How long are they keeping you in?' he asked. 'Mamma wants to know whether there's any point in her coming to visit. She doesn't like sitting in traffic.'

The hospital kept me in for three more days. During that time Marina was my only visitor.

Signora Bianchi's expectations of me as a mother had been so low that it was not difficult to surpass them, but on finding herself unable to offer any credible criticism, she simply commented that I was welded to my child. She kept her interference to a minimum, making it clear that she could not be called upon if I needed any assistance. I was glad.

The lack of interest that Gino showed towards me was extended to Lucia. His invisible wife had given birth to an invisible daughter.

I cannot say that the first months of Lucia's life were easy. It was winter, and most of the time we were confined to our tiny room. I was wary of the baby waking the Bianchis during the night. But as the first winter gave way to spring in Pomazzo I was relieved to be able to go out. I pushed Lucia's perambulator for miles around town, until I had memorised every street.

The old centre of Pomazzo was pleasant, with traditional brick houses, some rendered in shades of red and yellow. The church was salmon pink. There was quite a variety of shops. I could distract myself for hours looking at their window displays, although I never bought anything as I didn't have any money.

The roads which radiated out from the piazza led to residential areas and new blocks of apartments, such as the one in which the Bianchis lived. Beyond the residential streets the outskirts were dominated by a huge ceramics factory, which spread out like a smouldering dragon across the landscape. It employed almost a quarter of Pomazzo's residents, either directly or through subsidiary industries. Smaller workshops and commercial units sprawled out around it. The Bianchis' business was housed in one such building. Several vans were lined up in front of it, each bearing the name *Pomazzo Plumbing*.

Pomazzo was my home, whether I liked it or not. I hoped that over time I would begin to feel some connection to it. True, I had family in the area, but no idea who they were, or where to find them. I hadn't seen Giovanni or Ugo since the wedding. My mother's first love, the chicken thief, had been from Pomazzo and I often found myself wondering whether our paths had crossed. I had never thought to ask his name.

The plan was that Gino and I would remain living with his parents until such a time that we had enough money to set up our own home, but as Lucia began to grow, to crawl and then to walk, the tiny room we shared and the crowded apartment seemed to shrink and the need to have our own place grew urgent.

On his father's orders Gino had opened a savings account and promised to save a good portion of his wages, but he didn't like to deny himself. He spent money on going out, on clothes, on things for the motorcycle. When I questioned his spending, he became irritable.

'I work bloody hard – I need a bit of leisure time,' he said. 'It's all right for you, sitting around at home all day whiling away your time. You're not going to be one of those wives who kicks off because her husband has a bit of time with his mates, are you?'

Just before Christmas 1957, when I presumed that we had enough to start looking for an apartment to rent, Gino informed me that he had spent most of the savings on new parts for the motorcycle. When I remonstrated, he became angry.

'How am I supposed to get to work if the Guzzi's not roadworthy? She needed work done and that work cost money. And it's not like *you've* been putting anything into the account, is it? It's *my* money that's been going in there – and if I want to spend my money, I'm entitled to do so. But don't tell my father.'

On Sundays after lunch Marina began accompanying me on a walk. Sunday lunches were uncomfortable, argumentative affairs; a time for family disunity. Once the food was eaten and the dishes were washed, Marina and I would escape together.

We took it in turns pushing the perambulator to the park and we would sit together on a bench, chatting about this and that.

Although Gino had said that his sister's involvement in the family business consisted of little more than typing a few letters for their father, nothing could have been further from the truth. Marina ran the business finances and was in charge of everything from purchases to payroll. No monetary decision was made without her approval. She was sharp and smart with a clever head for numbers.

Our friendship was tenuous, but it was precious to me. We were both aware of its limitations. I respected the fact that Marina was an intensely private person. There were certain subjects we only skirted around, namely Gino and her mother. Nevertheless, I looked forward to Sundays more than any other day because I looked forward to seeing Marina.

Gino did not approve of our friendship and objected to our after-lunch walks.

'I don't want my stupid sister bitching about me,' he said, although Marina offered surprisingly little criticism of him. She would just say, 'Well, you know what Gino's like,' or 'Well, Gino's used to getting his own way,' and move on to a different subject.

It was only after several weeks of walking and chatting in the park together that Marina said, 'Would you like to see where I live?' She pointed to one of the houses which overlooked the very spot where we were sitting. 'It's that house there. The one with the curly iron railings.'

We had been sitting on the same bench facing her house every week for over two months, but she had never mentioned it. I knew that inviting me to see it was a significant thing for her. It was her sign that our friendship meant something to her too.

I had expected Marina's home to be a quiet, dour place and could not have been more surprised when I found it to be quite the opposite. It was a bright, cheerful ground-floor apartment, with high ceilings and coving like lacework. The inside walls were painted in lively shades of yellow and apricot.

'I was thinking,' said Marina. 'I'd be happy for you to have a key to my apartment. If you're in the park and Lucia needs changing or feeding, or if it starts to rain – or even if you just need a bit of space to yourself – you're welcome to let yourself in, even if I'm at work. I do understand how hard it is for you living in my parents' flat and I especially understand how hard it is living in that little room. It always felt like a prison cell to me.'

I was so grateful that I flung my arms around her. She took my embrace stiffly, like someone unaccustomed to physical contact. When at last I let her go, the look on her face was one of pity for me.

Seeing Marina's home made me long for a place of my own. There was no shortage of newly-built apartments for rent, but I didn't want to feel imprisoned in some high-rise box. An apartment in the old centre of Pomazzo near the park, even a very small one, would be so much nicer. I had seen one for rent not far from Marina's at a very affordable price. It was a little shabby, but nothing that a lick of paint and a good clean couldn't put right. It even had a little courtyard garden with a plum tree. I tried to convince Gino to come and see it, but he said he didn't want an old place and he didn't want to live near his sister.

It was not long afterwards that he bounded into my room in an unusually excited state and exclaimed, 'Come and see this, Graziella!'

Parked outside was a small white car.

'What do you think?' He grinned. 'It's an Autobianchi Bianchina. We're called Bianchi and so is our car. Isn't that just perfect?'

'*Our* car?'

'Yes – our very own car.'

'Did you buy it?'

'Of course I bought it. People don't give them away for free, do they?'

'But why did you buy a car when we're saving to move out?'

'Because we need one! We can't take a baby on a motorcycle, can we? And we can't always borrow Papá's car if we have to go somewhere.'

'But we don't ever go anywhere.'

'Only because we haven't got a car.'

'It's only got two seats.'

'I know. I bought it from Bartocchi's fishing buddy. He had the back bench taken out so he could put his fishing gear in there, but it turned out it's not big enough for his equipment. That's why he wanted to sell it. It's not a problem though. We can get a replacement seat, and in the meantime Lucia can sit on your lap.'

Once again, I learned, Gino had emptied the savings account.

'Why did you spend all our moving-out money,' I asked angrily, 'and why didn't you ask me before buying a car?'

'Because you don't know anything about cars.'

I turned and went back upstairs, but he followed me and yelled, 'Why are you being such a bitch?'

'Because you've spent the savings without telling me. And now we're stuck here for months on end again!'

'What do you mean, *stuck* here? You are so ungrateful, do you realise that? My parents are really putting themselves out having you here with a kid.'

'Lucia is their grandchild! Right, you can sell the motorcycle to get the money back,' I said.

'No way.' His voice rose. 'I'm never, ever selling it! It's got too many good memories attached to it.'

We were having a big row in the stairwell. Our accusations and recriminations echoed all the way up to the sixth floor. People opened their doors and leaned over the banisters to watch the spectacle and to hear us tear each other apart.

It was impossible to reason with Gino, so I yelled and I screamed. I didn't care whether what I said made sense to him, but when I called him 'useless' it unleashed such a surge of anger in him that he raised his hand to strike me. Had I not side-stepped his fist, I would have gone flying down the stairs.

The result of our fight was that not a single lira was ever put back into the savings account and the plan of moving into our own place was scrapped.

CHAPTER 13

1958 rolled into 1959, which then rolled on into 1960. The new decade dawned with the promise of ever-increasing change and technological advancement, but apart from the fact that Lucia was growing, my own life remained stuck in the same dreary routine.

I focused on my three-year-old daughter, ignoring the fact that I was unhappy, sometimes to the point of desperation. I was treading water, frantically trying not to sink beneath the surface.

My only solace, apart from Lucia, was reading. There was a little library in Pomazzo where I would take out several books every week. I didn't care what they were about. I read anything and everything. At least when I was reading my mind was occupied.

I would remind myself to be grateful for what I had. Lucia and I had a roof over our heads. We were fed. We had all the basic necessities for survival. Things could be worse.

Graziella, the cheerful, optimistic girl with plans and ambitions, felt like some distant acquaintance. I tried not to think about my life as it would have been if I had not married Gino. Perhaps one day Italy would drag itself into the twentieth century and allow divorce, but until it did so, Gino and I would remain trapped in our pointless purgatory.

Sometimes I thought about Gianfrancesco, wondering what married life was like for him. I did not doubt that his wife, Anna, was living a life very different to mine.

The thought of leaving was constantly in my mind, but it was not as easy as that. I had no means to leave Pomazzo and I was not welcome back home. I still thought of Paradiso as home.

Lucia was a bright and inquisitive child. I took some comfort in the fact that my years spent at the Istituto Magistrale had not been entirely wasted. By the time she was four, Lucia could read as fluently as an eight year old. The time would come all too soon when she would start nursery school. Without her, my days would be empty and the joy of teaching her would be somebody else's. When I suggested to Gino that I could resume my studies when Lucia started school he told me not to be so stupid.

I returned to Pieve Santa Clara only once during that time, and only for the day. Zia Mina had aged quickly, but seemed in good health – physically, at least. But she was remote. I felt like a stranger. Since moving to Pomazzo I had telephoned her regularly, or tried to. She didn't often answer. Sometimes I would call the Pozzettis instead to ask if she was all right. The answer was always the same. Zia Mina was well, but she preferred to keep her own company.

I had wanted to visit Signora Grassi but Gino, who had been reluctant to make the trip in the first place, was in a hurry to leave.

The visit weighed heavily in my heart. I missed my home and having gone back, even briefly, made me miss it all the more.

It had been a cold, interminably drizzly winter. The smell of damp concrete oozed into the flat and the central heating gave me a thick head. Lucia and I had been passing each other the same cold back and forth since before Christmas, and I hadn't had a proper conversation with Marina for months as it was always too wet to walk Lucia back home. Apart from Marina I did not know anybody in Pomazzo.

Until then I had coped with life in the Bianchi household – sometimes only just, but I had coped. But following my visit to Pieve Santa Clara and the seemingly endless winter, I sank. I grew listless and absent-minded and it seemed impossible to hold on to any thought. Looking after Lucia's day-to-day needs took all my strength. I couldn't even find the energy to read.

156

As my state of mind deteriorated, my physical state did too. I couldn't be bothered with my appearance. My clothes hung on me. I struggled to eat. Gino's mother was offended that I didn't finish my meals and the less hungry I was, the more she piled my plate high with repulsively rich food.

All I could think of was Paradiso. Homesickness consumed me with such force that I felt it as a painful physical affliction. I would sit immobile on the edge of my bed for hours, staring at the wall, with my arms wrapped around myself, as though I was somehow trying to hold myself together.

I often spent time at Marina's when she was at work. At first I had found her cheerful home a sanctuary, but as I sat on her couch I felt such a pitiful heartsickness that I knew that if I did not go back home, I would die of melancholy. I called Zia Mina from Marina's telephone and surprisingly, she answered.

'I want to come home for a little while, Zia Mina. To spend some time with you, and you could spend some time with Lucia,' I began, but my aunt interrupted me.

'What do you want to come back here for?' she said irritably. 'And what about your husband? You've got responsibilities. I don't suppose Gino wants you swanning off for a holiday. Anyway, I'm busy. It wouldn't be convenient.'

Her blunt rejection devastated me. It made me wonder how I could ever have felt any love for Zia Mina. I had made so many excuses to myself about her sorrow making her unwell, but the more I thought about her, the more I concluded that she was not grief-crazed. She was just a horrid old woman.

*

When I returned from my walk the next day, Gino's mother said that there had been a telephone call for me.

'It was from a Signora Pozzetti. She said it was urgent.'

The telephone rang only three times before Ada Pozzetti answered.

'I'm very sorry but I have some bad news, Graziella,' she said. 'It's your aunt. I'm afraid she's passed away.'

'When? I only spoke to her yesterday afternoon.'

'Did you? I'm glad of that. You were probably the last person to speak to her then. We can't be sure exactly what time she passed. The doctor thought it was some point late yesterday afternoon or early evening.' Ada Pozzetti sighed. 'It was me who found her this morning. But it looked as though she'd gone very peacefully, as though she hadn't suffered at all. The doctor said it was a stroke. I'm so sorry, Graziella.'

'I'll come down,' I said. 'I'll have to organise things.'

'If it's any help, Mina left a file of documents on the table. I hope you don't mind, but I had a look through them. She seems to have organised a lot of things already. There doesn't appear to be much to arrange, apart from booking the church. By the looks of it, she's paid for everything too.'

Gino drove me to Pieve Santa Clara the next day. The stench of old fish made me feel sick. The car began to make a whining noise not long after we left, and just outside Cremona the smell of fish gave way to a stench of burning – which was followed by a grating noise. Gino wrestled with the gearstick for a few moments and pumped the pedals, then pulled over.

'Shit!' he said, beating his fist on the steering wheel. 'The clutch has gone!'

I had to telephone Pozzetti, who came to fetch us in his old yellow truck. He towed the broken car to a new garage which had opened in Mazzolo. Our breakdown had caused Gino to be in a foul mood and I was relieved when he said he wanted to stay with the car.

'I don't trust these country mechanics,' he said loudly.

I travelled back to Pieve Santa Clara alone with Pozzetti.

158

'It's lovely to see you after all this time, Graziella,' said Ada Pozzetti, hugging me and holding me for a long time. 'But it's sad that it has to be in these circumstances.'

She repeated what she had told me on the telephone, that they had been seeing less and less of Zia Mina.

'We've been trying to keep an eye on her, but she kept herself to herself. Didn't want company. We've never known her not to tend her garden, and yet this year she's grown nothing at all, not even tomatoes for Salvatore. She spent her days shut away in the house praying, and she made it very clear that she didn't want to be disturbed.'

'I shouldn't have left her,' I said.

'Graziella, your aunt wanted you to go and start a new life. She was pleased about it. She was relieved that you'd found a good husband and that you were settled and happy. You're young and you've done what all young people do. You've gone out into the world and made a life for yourself. And if it helps, the doctor said it was a stroke that took her, so even if you'd been there, you couldn't have stopped it.'

'But she was very unhappy.'

There was a moment of silence, and then: 'It's no secret that Mina had periods of deep unhappiness throughout her life,' Ada Pozzetti said carefully. 'I knew her over thirty years and we weren't just neighbours, we were friends through happy times and sad times. She had a tough life, Graziella, and she experienced so many losses. It's hardly surprising that sometimes it all overwhelmed her.'

'She thought she was cursed,' I said. 'And that Paradiso was cursed.'

'I suppose it was her way of trying to make sense of losing everybody. I did speak to her about it many times, saying that I didn't think it was anything like that, but it made no difference: she believed it very strongly. Not even Don Ambrogio could

159

convince her otherwise. In fact, the past year she didn't want to see him either. They'd fallen out about it. He called by many times, but she wouldn't open her door to him. Mind, right at the end she wouldn't even open the door for me. She just locked herself in.'

'But the door wasn't locked when you found her?'

Ada Pozzetti looked down at the table for a moment. 'No,' she replied heavily. 'It was open.'

'Where was she when you found her?'

'She was lying on the bed in the little bedroom. She was fully dressed and it looked as though she'd just gone for a lie-down.'

'The little bedroom? Ernesto's room?'

'Yes.'

*

As Ada Pozzetti had said on the telephone, there was very little for me to organise. My aunt had left instructions for a simple funeral and had paid for everything in advance. There was an envelope of money in the file to give to Pozzetti for her coffin. It was enough to pay for quite an elaborate casket, but her note specified that she wanted the simplest and cheapest coffin possible and that Pozzetti was to keep any excess and give it to his children. Pozzetti said he would provide a good quality casket and would charge nothing. I went to see it as a work in progress. It was the longest, thinnest coffin I had ever seen. It looked like an enormous cigar.

As I stood in the workshop with Pozzetti, a stonemason arrived.

'I'm sorry for your loss,' he said. 'I have the slab ready.'

'Already?' That seemed odd.

'Yes. Signora Ponti came to order it several months ago.'

'Several months ago?' I echoed, taken aback.

'Well, it was rather unusual.' The man frowned. 'She requested that I should engrave both her year of birth and year of death on the slab. I did say that putting the year of death was a bit premature, but she insisted and said that if I didn't do it, she would find somebody else who would. It's been ready for five months.'

The mason left the slab in Pozzetti's workshop. It was plain, without ornamentation, and simply read *Gelsomina Ponti 1901 – 1962*. There was no frame for a photograph, or bracket to hold a vase, or any mention about eternal peace. It was just a simple marble label, with the span of Zia Mina's life, all its experiences, all its moments of joy and all its tragedies reduced to a hyphen between two dates.

The circumstances surrounding my aunt's death troubled me deeply. The way she had left her funeral arrangements in full view on the kitchen table was like a suicide note.

'Do you think Zia Mina killed herself?' I said at last. 'Could she have taken poison?'

Pozzetti scratched his chin and shifted uneasily. The question was obviously not a surprise.

'I don't know, Graziella,' he said. 'Mina wasn't well in her mind. She had no appetite for life any more. But the doctor said it was a stroke and I don't think we should look beyond that.'

'But what if the doctor's wrong? He was wrong about my mother's brain tumour. He said it was eyestrain. I think we should ask another doctor what he thinks.'

A cloud passed over Pozzetti's kind face.

'It's possible to ask for an investigation,' he said, 'but if it was found that Mina did something to help herself along, well, for a start she couldn't have a Christian burial and be laid to rest in the cemetery. Suicides can't be placed on consecrated ground. And the thing is, everyone she lost is there in the cemetery. Your uncle, your father, your mother – and of course, all of Mina's children. They're all there. And it would be tragic if she couldn't be with them.'

He put his arm gently around my shoulder and pressed his prickly cheek against mine. For a moment I was reminded of being held in his arms, looking down at my father in his coffin.

'I know it's incredibly difficult, Graziella, but I think that we

161

should take some comfort in the fact that whatever the circumstances might have been, Mina's at peace now,' he said.

*

On the morning of the funeral I stood in the yard, looking at Paradiso. The vines had not been pruned, and most of the vegetable garden had been covered in black polythene to choke away the weeds. But despite its shabby state, the old house still had a simple, solid beauty, which seemed to pull me in.

'So who gets this place now?' demanded Gino, breaking into my reverie.

'I don't know.'

'Did your aunt have any other relatives?'

'Not as far as I know.'

'So it should be yours then?'

'Maybe.'

'Didn't the woman ever talk about it? She seems to have arranged everything else.'

'No. She never talked about it and I don't want to talk about it now either.'

'But what's a place like this worth?' he persisted.

'I don't know.'

'Probably not much. But it's worth something. Probably enough for us to buy something.'

'I wouldn't sell it.'

'What?' he scoffed. 'Don't give me that. What would *you* do with it?'

'Live in it.'

'No! Absolutely not! This place is the arsehole of the world. There's no way I would live here.'

I walked away. No, you wouldn't live here, I thought. You most definitely wouldn't live here.

162

As I stood in the yard looking at the empty house and forlorn garden it was not just Zia Mina I felt grief for, but also my parents. Being back at Paradiso had unleashed pangs of intense yearning for them and spasms of deep distress. I wanted to touch everything I knew they had touched. I could see them everywhere I looked: my father sitting on the bench by the door with his newspaper; my mother at her workspace by the window, sewing. I could hear the echoes of their voices. I felt a dark, bitter emptiness. I missed them more than I could express.

A raging grief consumed me. I needed to come back home.

*

The car was fixed on the day after the funeral. I sat in silence during our journey back to Pomazzo, emotionally spent, lost in my thoughts and trying to ignore the smell of fish.

After our return Gino talked incessantly about my possible inheritance, as did his mother.

'Well, let's hope her aunt had the good sense to make a will, or the government will help themselves to it,' I heard his mother say. They were in the kitchen discussing money. I could almost hear them rubbing their hands in anticipation.

The chance that I might soon be in receipt of Paradiso changed Gino's attitude towards me entirely, but I was not receptive to his newly amenable state. His attentions made my flesh crawl.

I refused to join in any conversation concerning my potential inheritance, but secretly my mind was racing, awakened to the fact that if indeed Zia Mina had bequeathed Paradiso to me, I could go home. Suddenly I felt something I had not felt since my arrival in Pomazzo. I felt a sense of hope.

A week later I received a letter from a notary in Cremona by the name of Avvocato Furboni, expressing his sympathies at the news of my aunt's passing and informing me that I was her sole heir. The letter went on to tell me that my aunt had made arrangements for Paradiso to be sold upon her death and for the money to be given to me. A signed contract was already in place. Once all taxes and death duties had been deducted, I would be in receipt of 18 million lire.

I read the paragraph several times in disbelief and several more times in horror. I did not want to sell Paradiso – not for 18 million, not even for 80 million.

Gino was so ecstatic that he could barely keep still. He even suggested that we should go out to dinner to celebrate. We didn't.

'Eighteen million!' he grinned, kissing me loudly on the lips. 'We can do so much with that. What a stroke of luck that your aunt's died just as Bartocchi is ready to retire. He told me he's going to sell the garage and buy a house on the coast and a boat. Says he intends to spend his retirement fishing. It's all he talks about. The timing couldn't be better.'

I kept quiet, but Gino was suspicious. He guessed what my intentions were.

'We need time to think about what we should do,' I said, keeping my tone calm and placatory. 'It would be foolish to rush into any purchase.'

'We wouldn't be rushing,' he replied irritably. 'It's something I've wanted since I started working there. My own garage with my name above the workshop door. Don't act like you don't know that, Graziella. And Bartocchi's would be perfect. You should see the size of his apartment on the first floor – it's huge. You keep going on about how we need to have our own place.'

We had been married almost six years and during that time Gino had never taken me to see where he worked.

'Come on. Come and see it,' he said.

I conceded, just to keep the peace. We drove four kilometres out of town, past the vast ceramics factory to a scrubby industrial estate.

Bartocchi's Garage was situated on an awkward, spoon-shaped piece of land, trapped between three large factory units. One was a metalworks. The other was a shoe factory. Towering behind it was a leather-processing plant. The building was not small, but it was dwarfed by those which surrounded it. It was still a work in progress, although clearly progress had been slow. A greenish lichen stained the unfinished walls. The huge edifices which encircled it blocked out the light and any hope of sunshine.

I could not imagine how anybody would choose to live there. I certainly could not see myself living there, let alone with a small child who needed safe space to play.

The ground floor was entirely taken up by the workshop. A steep external staircase on the side led up to the apartment which had two balconies, although neither had railings. The windowpanes were filthy and the frames were suffering from rot.

Above the workshop door, a simple metal sign, showing signs of age and rust, read *Bartocchi – All Mechanical Repairs and Bodywork*.

I shuddered. 'It would be a horrible place to live,' I said.

'What? It's only five minutes' drive to the centre of town.'

'I don't drive.'

'No, but I can give you lifts.'

'Nobody else lives here. It's got factories around it.'

'What do you want? Fields?' Gino sneered.

Yes, I did want fields. I wanted them more than I had the words to express. I wanted the scent of sun-warmed soil and newly-mown meadows, not the stench of burning oil and rubber; although like it or not, I knew in my heart that very soon that is what I would have.

CHAPTER 14

It was a beautiful, warm afternoon in mid-May when I alighted at Mazzolo. I was alone, of course. Gino had kept Lucia as his insurance policy, just in case she and I did not come back – or rather, just in case we did not come back with any money. I had not put up any resistance, but I had insisted that Lucia should stay with Marina during my absence.

I had absolutely no intention of selling Paradiso. I would pull out of the contract my aunt had signed. Once I had done that, I would return to Pomazzo to collect Lucia and bring her home, even if we had to escape in the middle of the night.

Gino would protest, of course. He would threaten me. He would demand money, but there would be none. He couldn't sell the house without my consent. I knew that because I had looked it up in the library. I had spent days poring over law books and studying the relevant chapters.

A taxi took me down the North Road, past the gateposts at the end of the Marchesini driveway and finally stopped in front of Paradiso. As I opened the car door I heard the familiar sound of a circular saw from Pozzetti's workshop and felt such a sensation of relief that I had to stand still for a moment to gather myself.

I looked back up the North Road towards Mazzolo, south in the direction of Pieve Santa Clara, west at Pozzetti's and finally east at Paradiso, and breathed in the clean, spring-infused air. I was home.

The Pozzettis welcomed me warmly and offered me a bed in their house, but I wanted to stay at Paradiso. I was filled with a sense of urgency to be back within the walls I knew.

Paradiso reminded me of the Marchesini house after Amilcare Marchesini's death, with its closed shutters and untended land. The vines trailed so low that they almost touched the ground. Zia Mina's garden was overgrown with rough grasses. Some had even pierced through the polythene. But the chestnut tree was in full spring bloom, laden with great sugarloaf cones of white blossom. A heron had made its nest on the branch where the swing had once hung.

I stood in the yard for long time, absorbing the familiarity of my surroundings. Even in its unkempt state, Paradiso was beautiful. Its pale walls glinted against the blue of the sky.

A spare key was where it had always been, exactly where my mother had always kept it, under a pot in the barn. She was probably the last person to have touched it.

The annexe had been partially emptied of its contents. Our kitchen chairs were stacked in the corner, along with a wheelbarrow, a sack of mulch and a long-handled spade. I walked through the laundry room, past the oven built by my father, past the old stone sinks and the washing machine. I listened to the hollow echo of my footsteps on the terracotta floor and breathed in the scent of the plaster imbued with starch and soap.

The gentle glow of the spring sun flowed in as I opened the shutters in Zia Mina's kitchen. Everything was exactly as she had left it. The little shrine was still in its place. Strings of shiny brown onions hung from the ceiling. Two washed saucepans and my aunt's metal bowl sat upturned on the draining board.

The circumstances of Zia Mina's death still troubled me and something about the kitchen didn't feel quite right. I felt it was overly tidy, as though it had been prepared for inspection – but then I thought about what Pozzetti had said, that it was easier not to question the doctor's conclusion that she had died of a stroke. That she was at peace, resting for eternity with all those she missed. I hoped that was true, and that the God in whom she believed so absolutely had taken into account the good things she had done. I hoped that her many acts of kindness had been enough to cancel out the poisoning of the soldiers, who had drunk their deaths at the same kitchen table where I was sitting.

I sat for a long while, listening to the beautiful silence. No noisy neighbours scraping their chairs or shouting. No Bianchis arguing. No car horns outside. No banging dustbin lids.

If I closed my eyes I could imagine Lucia playing on the steps, or hiding in the garden and calling out for me to come and find her. She would have a new swing hanging from the chestnut tree. I imagined her older, riding her bicycle down to the village, just as I had done.

Thoughts of making my own life here, of achieving a simple serenity, of a life without the Bianchis, without arguments but with the simple pleasures of eating food grown in the garden, of picking fat, ripe peaches from the trees, infused me with a glorious comfort and a resolute determination.

I remained lost in my thoughts until the light began to fade, the setting sun streaking the sky with flashes of orange and lilac then darkening to a deep, crepuscular blue. I could see a vague luminous haze hovering above the village and blobs of light from the newly-installed lamp posts.

Just like the kitchen, Zia Mina's bedroom seemed overly tidy. The bed had been made with fresh sheets, but never slept in. Don Ambrogio's bottle of holy water was on the bedside table. Everything else had been put away.

Tucked into a drawer, under some very old-fashioned underwear, was a large brown envelope. It contained the birth and death certificates of all my aunt's children, all my little dead cousins. Folded into a sheet of writing paper were four tiny wisps of baby hair, each bound with thread and each labelled – Odetta, Oreste, Saverio, Marta – and half a dozen milk teeth, which must have been Ernesto's.

There were also photographs. The first was relatively recent and I already owned a copy. Salvatore had taken a picture of my mother and my aunt sitting at the table under the vines. Zia Mina had insisted that it should be taken there and that they should both be seated. Even in her later life she had never come to terms with her height.

The next photograph was also familiar, although I had not seen it for a long time. It was the picture of the rice workers in their wide-brimmed hats with my aunt standing head and shoulders above any of them.

The third photograph was new to me. It was of a young man, whom I assumed to be my uncle, Augusto, at a guess aged around twenty, but when I turned it over I found a dedication: *To Teresa, my true love. I am counting the days until we see each other again. Your Luigi.* Beneath the words, two little caricature figures of a man and a woman holding hands were sketched in the corner, framed within a heart.

I turned the photograph over again and stared at the young man, then turned it back again and re-read the dedication. It was not Zio Augusto. It was my father.

The photograph was posed as though he was holding his breath and his hair was so carefully parted that I could see the tracks left by the comb. It was definitely Papá, but in best formal pose. This was the picture my mother had lost but couldn't think how.

Looking into my father's face for the first time since his death made my heart swell with a mixture of deep loss and joyous reconnection. When I looked at him, I saw myself and Lucia. I gazed at him for a long, long time, then laughed suddenly. There was something funny about the fact that my Papá had been hidden under Zia Mina's bloomers for so many years. He would have thought it a great joke. I kissed the picture and tucked it into my brassiere so that it would be close to my heart, just like the cherry blossom handkerchief which he had taken to his grave.

The mattress on Ernesto's bed, on which my aunt's body had been found, had been removed, but apart from that, nothing had changed in Ernesto's room since his death. His clothes were still folded in the chest of drawers. I had ambivalent feelings towards the room, which had been kept in a shrine-like state for so long. The ceiling was still marked with soot from the oil-soaked rags we'd used when the candles ran out as we watched over him on the eve of his burial.

I decided that when I moved back to Paradiso I would take over the room with the wardrobe. It was larger than Ernesto's and not quite as large as Zia Mina's, but the mirrored wardrobe made it look twice the size. It also had a lovely, endlessly rolling view to the east.

That night I fell asleep to the gentle pattering of spring rain and awoke to the sound of the dawn chorus. Fingers of light slipped in through the gaps in the louvres, beckoning me to push them open. A light spring mist lay knee-high across the fields before me. Spiders' webs, bejewelled with drops of dew, shimmered between the rails of the fence as they caught the early sunlight.

I breathed in the scent of the morning and the fragrance of the dew, and was so filled with relief that my head felt light. Only holding Lucia in my arms would have made that moment even better – and that moment was tangibly close.

I took the train to Cremona. I had an appointment to see the notary at ten. Avvocato Furboni's practice was situated in an old building near the cathedral. Every available space in his labyrinth of rooms was stacked with files; even the corridors were shelved on either side, making it impossible to walk down them in anything other than single file.

Furboni was ancient. He smelled of books and pipe smoke and wore a suit which was probably considerably older than me. He stood hunched with his neck bent forwards, as though his frame had moulded into the position of sitting at a desk for fifty years. What was left of his grey hair stuck upwards and formed a point, like a reflection of his goatee beard. Corresponding tufts grew from his ears. His eyebrows were so bushy that they caught on the top rim of his spectacles, causing them to rise and fall as he spoke. The only hair which seemed in any way managed was his moustache, which was waxed and curled at each end, like the curved prow of a gondola.

Despite his advanced years, there was a sharpness about him. He scurried like a mouse between the piles of papers and files, greeted me warmly, offered his condolences and directed me graciously to his office, which was so piled with paperwork that there seemed to be nowhere for me to sit.

'Please take a seat, Signora Bianchi,' he said, moving a stack of papers from the only available chair. 'This is just a formality, so I won't keep you long. I need to read your aunt's will to you and there are documents which I need to witness you signing in front of me before I can release the funds to you.'

Before I could tell him about my decision not to sell, he had begun to read.

'*This is the last will and testament of Gelsomina Ponti, born Gelsomina Marchesini, on the third of July 1901.*'

'Gelsomina Marchesini? No, that's not right,' I interrupted. 'My aunt's maiden name was Ogli. I don't know where you got Marchesini from.'

The lawyer frowned. 'No, Signora Bianchi. Your aunt was born Gelsomina Marchesini.'

'I think you need to check that.'

The lawyer pushed his glasses up on the bridge of his nose and began to rifle through the documents on his desk.

'Here,' he said after a while. 'This is your aunt's birth and baptism record. Marchesini *is* correct. Her maiden name was definitely Marchesini. Ogli was the name of the family by whom

171

she was fostered. It's a name she might well have been known by, but legally, she was Marchesini.'

Furboni waved the documents at me briefly and continued to read Zia Mina's will, but once again I interrupted him.

'I don't want to sell,' I said.

The lawyer raised his eyebrows, which took his spectacles with them. They remained wedged against his forehead.

'Signora Bianchi,' he said, 'with all due respect, it's not your decision. It was your aunt's wish that on her death the property should be sold. There is a contract in place.'

'No money has exchanged hands.'

'The money is in my escrow account and has been for over a week, but that's not the point. The point is that your aunt signed a contract and you, as the sole heir, are bound by that contract. My client made her wishes extremely clear.'

'But what if I don't agree? I don't think my aunt was in any state to make any rational decisions at the end of her life.'

Furboni pushed his glasses back into position before uttering solemnly, 'Contesting a will is a long and complex procedure, Signora Bianchi. And not one I would advise under these circumstances. Even if the buyer did agree to renounce the contract, which is extremely unlikely, breaking it would involve serious financial penalties. You have a young family, Signora Bianchi. I would imagine that the receipt of this money would be very useful to you.'

'It's not the money I want, Avvocato Furboni, or the land. It's the house. There must be something you can do.'

'Signora Bianchi, we are talking about a legally binding document.'

'But could you ask the buyer, just in case?' I said desperately. 'He signed for the purchase almost a year ago. His circumstances might have changed – he might have seen something else he'd rather buy and might be glad to get out of the contract.' I could hear myself begging. 'Please understand, Avvocato, that Paradiso is very important to me. It's the house in which I was born and brought up, and which I still think of as my home. It was my father who restored it. Every memory I have is linked to it in some way. If my aunt hadn't decided on this crazy arrangement, there is no way I would have sold it. Who is the buyer, anyway?'

'A property developer from Cremona. He has already purchased several properties in the village. You see, Pieve Santa Clara is becoming increasingly desirable. The easy access to the station in Mazzolo and—'

'A property developer? What will he do with Paradiso?'

'I don't know, Signora Bianchi. If he chooses to leave it standing, I expect he will modernise the place. I understand that it remains in quite a rustic state.'

The thought of a property developer tearing down my father's work, or maybe even the whole house, was unimaginably dreadful.

'*Please*, Avvocato Furboni. Please just ask him. Please tell him what it means to me.'

The lawyer sighed, and then tweaked his moustache.

'Very well,' he said. 'I can see it is truly important to you. I'll do what I can, but I can't make you any promises. Come and see me again tomorrow and I'll let you know.'

I left the office with a sick feeling in my stomach. As I waited for my train I took out my father's photograph, traced my finger around the outline of his face and said, 'Help me, Papá.'

The bus bound for Pieve Santa Clara pulled up the instant I stepped out of the station and took me down the North Road, but the driver forgot to stop at Paradiso, as I had requested. I didn't object. I rode all the way to the village, where I purchased a bunch of spring flowers from the greengrocer's and headed to the cemetery.

I did the rounds, sharing out my flowers – some for my

grandparents, some for my little cousins, some for my Uncle Augusto, some for Ernesto, some for my father, some for my mother. I hesitated, then left some for Zia Mina too. *Gelsomina Ponti 1901 – 1962.*

A gnawing curiosity about my aunt's maiden name troubled me. If it had been any name other than Marchesini, I don't suppose I would have given it much thought. I looked up and down every wall trying to chance upon other Marchesinis – but the only ones I could find were those in the mausoleum.

I had not been inside the mausoleum since I had visited it with my father, and judging by the moss and sprigs of wild chamomile which had seeded around the steps and across the threshold, nobody else had been there for a long time either.

I placed the remainder of my flowers on Amilcare Marchesini's tomb and stood looking at his photograph for a while. He was very handsome, in an old-fashioned kind of way. His hair was so rigidly set that it looked as though it had been sculpted with a chisel, a bit like my own father's photograph, which I realised I was still holding in my hand.

As I looked from my father to Amilcare Marchesini, the strangest feeling overcame me. It was as though my feet were not quite touching the ground. I looked down to check that they were, and as I did so, the words engraved into the floor seemed to rise up.

In Paradisum Deducant te Angeli – may angels lead you to Paradise.

I read the words again and again, and the more I stared at the writing, the more a single word stood out – *Paradisum*. The writing around it melted out of focus and *Paradisum* became Paradiso. *Paradisum*, Paradiso …

I had to steady myself against the wall. The coldness of the marble against my hand brought me back to my senses. I became conscious that I had been holding my breath for a long time. I kissed my father, then I traced my fingers over Amilcare Marchesini's name and kissed his photograph too, leaving the imprint of my lips against the glass.

'Help me,' I said again.

When the door opened behind me I was so startled that I squealed – which in turn startled the man who stepped through it carrying a bunch of flowers identical to the one I had just bought.

'Graziella!' he gasped.

We stood and stared at each other. The look on his face was one of astonishment, but I would imagine that the look on my face was no different. It was Gianfrancesco. He stared at me for a while, then seemed to pull himself together.

'I'm so sorry,' he said, taking my hand and kissing my cheek. 'I'm forgetting my manners. I'm just so surprised to see you – and to see you in here of all places. How are you?'

'I'm well,' I said. 'And you?'

'I can't complain,' he replied, taking his flowers and placing them with mine before kissing his fingertips and smoothing them across his father's photograph. The imprint of my lips left a pale pink trace on his fingertips.

'Is that lipstick? Did you just kiss my father?'

'I did.'

Gianfrancesco grinned and said, 'He'd have been thrilled,' then added, 'I was so very sorry to hear about your mother. I would have come to the funeral, but I wasn't told that she had passed away – I wasn't even aware she'd been ill. It was such a shock because she was so young. By the time I found out, you'd moved away.' He cleared his throat. 'Not much news of the village filters back to me, I'm afraid. And I've just been told about your aunt.'

'Thank you. My father used to say that he knew so many people in this cemetery that he'd never be short of company in heaven. I think I feel the same way now.'

I held up the photograph of my father for Gianfrancesco to see.

'I found him,' I said. 'After all those years of wishing I had a picture to remember his face.'

'Is he as you remember him?'

'Yes, he is. He's just younger.'

'Well, you have something to hold and to look at now,' said Gianfrancesco. 'But the rest is in your head and in your memories. And that's where all the really precious stuff lives.'

I had been thinking exactly the same, except it wasn't just in my head. It was also in Paradiso.

We sat together on the steps of the mausoleum with the sun on our faces. Sparrows chattered and danced around our feet.

Almost eight years had passed since I had last seen Gianfrancesco. He had grown into a fine, urbane gentleman. He was dressed in a light linen suit and Panama hat.

'I hear you're married now,' he said.

'Yes. I have a little daughter, Lucia. And you – do you have children?'

'Me? No, no. No children. I'm not married yet.'

'You're not?'

'I'm getting married this coming July. So, where are you living now?'

'A place called Pomazzo. It's in the province of Bologna.'

'And what brings you back to Pieve Santa Clara?'

'I'm here to sell Paradiso,' I said sadly.

'Really? What a coincidence. I'm here because I'm selling my house too.'

'You're selling Cascina Marchesini?'

'Yes. Finally. The place has fallen into an appalling state of disrepair. The chapel roof caved in last spring and the damp problems are out of control. I don't have the money to maintain it and even if I were to spend every lira I earn on its upkeep, it would be like trying to empty a well with a sieve.'

'But that's terrible! Centuries of your family history are in that house.'

'I know. But it was inevitable.' Gianfrancesco sighed. 'It had been in decline for so long. My grandfather left everything in a pitiful state. My father used to say that he wasn't born with a silver spoon in his mouth, but with a silver knife to his throat. He borrowed a lot of money to get the farm up and running again. If he had lived, I'm sure it would have been a success eventually, but it was a work in progress. When he died, all that was left was the debt. At least selling up will clear the last of it.'

'Will you buy something else here?'

Gianfrancesco shook his head. 'No,' he said flatly. 'After the debts are paid I'm giving a large portion of the money to my mother so that she'll be financially comfortable for the rest of her life. Then I'll buy something in Milan. That's where my life is now.'

'So that's it. The end of the Marchesinis in Pieve Santa Clara, and maybe the end of the Pontis too.'

'It pains me to think that,' said Gianfrancesco. His words were like sighs.

'Who's buying Cascina Marchesini?'

'An industrialist from Parma. Who's buying Paradiso?'

'A property developer from Cremona.'

There was a moment of shared, regretful silence.

'I suppose it's the way of all things,' said Gianfrancesco at last. 'Nothing stays the same for ever. All that will be left for us is memories. I still think of all those lovely times we had there together. What glorious times those were. Yes, I still think of them often.'

'Me too.'

'We didn't realise how free we were, did we? I was so impatient to grow up. When your daughter is the age we were then, tell her not to be in a hurry.' His words stopped suddenly. 'Graziella, are you crying?'

I looked down at the cracks on the steps and picked at the little sprigs of wild chamomile. I could have poured out my heart, but I knew that if I began, I would disintegrate.

'I've never really settled in Pomazzo,' I said. 'I never wanted to leave here.'

Gianfrancesco passed me his handkerchief and placed his hand on my shoulder.

'It's natural. This is where you were born and raised, and selling Paradiso is like tearing out your roots. I feel the same thing. Milan was a wonderland at first. So many interesting people. So much going on. But the truth is that living there is exhausting. I would give anything to be able to make my life back here in my family home. I can't pretend I haven't shed a few tears too.'

I finished wiping my eyes and then looked at the handkerchief. 'Is this the one I made for you?' I asked disbelievingly.

'Yes, the very one. It's a bit thin now and it's got a hole in it. It must have been washed a thousand times but your embroidery's still there. The herons still look like ducks with their legs on backwards, but that's part of its charm. It's always been my favourite handkerchief.'

I looked at my amateurish design and for a moment I was fourteen again, sitting on the kitchen step, with Gianfrancesco telling me he would think about me every time he blew his nose. I wondered whether he had.

'I asked the lawyer if I could get out of the contract,' I said, 'but he told me there would be a lot of penalties.'

'Who's the lawyer?'

'Avvocato Furboni. He has a practice in Cremona.'

'I know Furboni. My family have used his family's firm since my grandfather's day. He's dealing with the sale of my house too. Do you want me to have a look at the contract?'

'If you like. The papers are back at the house.'

'Are you selling the land as well?'

'Yes.'

'The land that runs alongside the road? The fields that your aunt used to rent out?'

'Yes.'

'Do you know that the regional council is going to award building permission on land with direct road access?'

'No.'

'Well, it's not surprising that a property developer wants to buy it considering there's so much constructible land with it. More and more people are looking to live outside Cremona. It's become an expensive place to buy property and Pieve Santa Clara has easy access to the railway.'

'That's what Furboni said.' I paused. 'There's something else though.'

'What?'

'It's probably nothing, but it's odd. I always thought that my aunt's maiden name was Ogli, but the notary insists that her maiden name was Marchesini. Apparently, Ogli was just the name of the family who fostered her.'

'Well, we're not the only Marchesinis in Italy.'

'I know. It just surprised me. As I said, it's probably nothing, but I've just had a look around to see if there were any other Marchesinis here apart from in your mausoleum and I couldn't find any.'

'There aren't any others in the village. There are a few Marchesini families in and around Cremona, but nobody directly related to us. Who was your aunt's father? Where was he from?'

'I don't know. All I know is that Zia Mina was illegitimate. Her mother died giving birth and so Zia Mina was entrusted to Immacolata Ogli.'

'What was her mother's name?'

'I don't know that either. It seems terrible now, not knowing something like that, but Zia Mina didn't talk about it. Immacolata never told me and it's too late to ask her now. I heard she passed away last year.'

'There are many things we don't think to ask until it's too late,' Gianfrancesco said. 'But if your aunt's mother did work for my family, her name would be in the records. We might have had employees called Marchesini. It would be coincidental, but certainly not impossible. Do you want me to look?'

'You don't have to. I expect you have more than enough to do already. It probably doesn't mean anything at all,' I decided. 'It's just … it's strange that in all this time I never knew her name was Marchesini.'

We sat in the sunshine, chatting and catching up, but every time the conversation turned to matters pertaining to my life, I changed the subject.

'I finished my studies,' Gianfrancesco informed me. 'First I did my degree in Classics, then I changed to Literature. I've just completed my doctorate.' He scratched his head. 'I was a bit sick of it all by the end.'

'So you're Dottor Gianfrancesco Marchesini now?'

'Yes,' he replied, 'but not a doctor of anything useful. To be honest, I feel as though I've studied a great deal and learned nothing. Nothing that does much good to anyone in the real world, anyway. ' He turned to look at me. 'You were right.'

'Right about what?'

'When I told you my plans to go to university to study Classics you asked me whether studying agriculture wouldn't be a better idea. You were right: it would have been a far better idea. And it wouldn't have taken so long. I might not have been able to save the house, but I might have been able to save the farm. Instead, all I have to show for all my years of study is a clerical job with the Ministry of Education.'

Gianfrancesco bowed his head and clasped his hands between his knees.

'I wish I had my father's life,' he said. 'I know he had his worries and his problems, and some of them were serious, but he loved spending his days outside, working. And his identity as a Marchesini was really important to him: being one of so many generations born of this land and being the keeper of a place to pass down to future generations. It's in our blood. One of the reasons I haven't been here to see him for so long is that I'm ashamed.' Gianfrancesco reached up and touched the picture of Amilcare Marchesini. 'My father would be devastated to know the house was being sold. He himself would never have allowed it to happen. I'm certain he would have done *something* – have found some way to prevent it. But the thing is, I can't seem to find a way through.'

*

The afternoon passed so quickly that when we both heard the church clock strike six we looked at each other in astonishment. We had been talking for over four hours.

We left the cemetery and made our way back up the North Road, wheeling Amilcare Marchesini's enormous bicycle between us.

'How long are you going to be here?' asked Gianfrancesco as we neared Paradiso.

'A few days, if everything is dealt with as my aunt wished. I know I need to sort through her things, but I'm praying that tomorrow when I see Furboni he'll say that the buyer doesn't want to purchase it any more.'

'I'll pray for that too.'

'You'll *pray*? So what happened to being an agnostic?'

Gianfrancesco grinned. 'That's the beauty of agnosticism. It leaves all options open!'

We stopped outside the gate and he took a long look at Paradiso.

'It's sad to see the place unlived in,' he said. 'It was always such a vibrant house. There were always people around and things going on.'

'I hope that one day, I can make it that way again.'

'What's that in the chestnut tree?'

'It's a heron's nest, I think.'

'How strange. I've never seen one on its own. Herons are colonising birds.'

I would have quite happily spent hours standing at the gate chatting about herons, their nesting habits or absolutely anything else, but finally Gianfrancesco said, 'I'll have a look through a few documents and maybe I could stop by tomorrow if I find something which has your aunt's name on it.'

'You can stop by anyway, documents or no documents,' I said as he kissed my cheek. 'See you tomorrow.'

I watched as he wheeled off down the road. My heart was beating fast, as though it was trying to break its way out of my chest and chase after Gianfrancesco as he pedalled away. I clasped my hand to my breast to hold it in.

'If I had waited for you, would you have come back for me?' I said quietly as he shrank into a dot on the horizon.

*

That evening, I called Marina from the Pozzettis' telephone.

'We've had a lovely day,' she said. 'We went to the park and Lucia played herself to exhaustion. Then we came home, had supper and she fell asleep on the couch. She's in my bed now, snoring her little head off.'

I didn't call Gino. I had nothing to say to him.

I could have joined the Pozzettis for supper that night, but I knew that they would want my news and I had no appetite to speak about my life in Pomazzo. Instead, I sat on the kitchen step eating Zia Mina's preserved cherries straight from the jar.

Despite the bad news from the lawyer that morning, my afternoon spent with Gianfrancesco had lifted me to a serene state. All the heartbreak and anger I had felt when he had left me seemed inconsequential. All I felt was the joyful warmth of the friendship we had shared.

I was looking forward to seeing him the following day more than I had looked forward to anything for a very long time. However, I was not obliged to wait until the next day, for Gianfrancesco turned up at about half past eight that same evening, carrying a satchel of documents.

'I've done a bit of digging,' he announced. 'I've found your aunt and her mother.'

'That was quick.'

'You know me, I always liked a project. And if it involves rooting around old documents, I can't resist.'

He took out a leather-bound ledger and laid it on the table. As he opened it, the musty smell of Signor Marchesini's library burst out from it.

'This book is the census that used to be taken every year of the farm employees. Your aunt is shown here: Gelsomina Marchesini born third of July 1901 to Odetta Colombino. Odetta Colombino was a silk-worker. Her date of death is also the third of July 1901, so she died in childbirth and her baby, your aunt, was entrusted to Immacolata Ogli very shortly afterwards.'

Apart from Zia Mina's mother's name, none of the information was new.

'Does it mention Zia Mina's father?'

'No. The space has been left blank. And I couldn't find any employees called Marchesini. But I do have more information on Odetta Colombino.'

Gianfrancesco turned back several pages and ran his finger down a long list of names.

'Odetta Colombino was a foundling. There's no mention of

her parents or of where she came from. She was left on our farm as a new-born infant, apparently, and she too was entrusted to Immacolata Ogli.'

This didn't make sense. 'How can that be possible? Immacolata wouldn't have been old enough.'

Gianfrancesco looked up from the old book with a solemn expression and said, 'Odetta Colombino was left on our farm in 1889. That means she was only twelve years old when she gave birth to your aunt.'

'Twelve years old?'

Suddenly Immacolata's words about the guilt she carried at not knowing that Odetta was with child made painful sense. My heart broke for little frightened Odetta, just a few years older than Lucia, taking herself off to give birth in a mulberry field all alone; and for Zia Mina, for the burden of shame which was no fault of hers.

We sat in silence, staring at the ledger and thinking the same thoughts separately.

'You know it was your grandfather who named my aunt Gelsomina?' I said after a while.

'No, I didn't. How do you know that?'

'Immacolata told me.'

'It makes sense. Gelsomina is an old word for mulberry.'

'She also said your grandfather was kind to Zia Mina.'

'Really? That's the first good thing I've ever heard anyone say about him.'

Gianfrancesco stayed long after it was dark. He took a look at the contract Zia Mina had signed for the sale of Paradiso and reiterated what Furboni had said about the penalties.

'I'll come and see you tomorrow,' he said, kissing my cheek and squeezing my hand. 'By then, I hope you'll have some good news.'

I watched him disappear into the darkness. I only closed the door once the sound of his footsteps had faded away.

I began to look through my aunt's documents, trying to find something useful, or something in the name of Marchesini, but the papers mainly consisted of household bills – and everything was in my aunt's married name, Ponti.

Suddenly a thought struck me. If my aunt was the illegitimate issue of a foundling silk-worker who died at the age of twelve, from whom did she inherit Paradiso?

CHAPTER 15

Avvocato Furboni had bad news: he informed me that the buyer did not wish to renounce the contract under any circumstances – not even if he was offered the compensation I could not possibly afford to pay him. I felt my prayers and my future crumble around me.

'Did you tell him what the property means to me?'

'Of course, Signora Bianchi. But the buyer is a businessman. I'm afraid that sentimental value was not a potent enough argument for him.'

I blinked away my tears and gripped Gianfrancesco's handkerchief in my hand.

'Could I buy it back from him? I don't need all the land that runs alongside the road. Just the house and garden.'

Furboni stroked his beard and said, 'I had a feeling you might ask me that.'

'But I could, couldn't I?'

'If you have twenty-five million lire at your disposal, yes.'

'Twenty-five million? Just for the house and garden?'

The lawyer nodded. 'Correct. That is the re-sale price he requires. Plus all legal and conveyancing fees to be paid. Sadly for you, the buyer is not a man known for his charity.'

I seethed, furious at the buyer's greed and how to him Paradiso was just a commodity, just a means of making a profit; and I was also furious with Zia Mina who had sold my birthright so cheaply.

'I'm very sorry, Signora Bianchi, truly I am. If I had known what the property meant to you I would have tried to discourage your aunt. But I do know of other properties in and around Pieve

Santa Clara which are for sale and well within your budget. I would be more than happy to draw up a list for you.'

I thanked him, but it was empty gratitude. It was not some other house I wanted, it was Paradiso.

'Signora Bianchi, I really do have to ask you to sign these documents now,' said Furboni with an apologetic smile as he pushed a sheaf of papers across the desk.

'Before I do,' I said, 'could I ask you something else? Do you have any documents pertaining to my aunt's inheritance of the property?'

The lawyer removed his spectacles and pinched the bridge of his nose between his fingers.

'I assure you everything is in order, Signora Bianchi,' he said wearily. 'Your aunt was the legal owner.'

'I'm not disputing that. I just want some information about how she came to inherit it, that's all.'

'I don't see how this is relevant, Signora Bianchi.'

'I'm trying to fill in some gaps in my family history, Avvocato Furboni.'

'It was a perfectly straightforward succession.'

'A succession from whom?'

Avvocato Furboni wiped his spectacles with his handkerchief and pushed them back onto his nose.

'From her mother,' he said reluctantly.

'From Odetta Colombino?'

'Yes. And as I said, it was all perfectly straightforward.'

'But Odetta Colombino was only twelve when she died giving birth to my aunt. She was a foundling who had lived on the Marchesini farm all her life with a foster family. How on earth did she come to be the owner of Paradiso?'

'Please understand that I am bound by rules pertaining to client confidentiality,' Avvocato Furboni said, shifting uncomfortably.

'Even if the clients are dead?'

'Yes, Signora Bianchi. Even if the clients are dead.'

'That's ridiculous.'

'Be that as it may, Signora Bianchi. It is the law.' He slid the paperwork towards me once more. I pushed it back.

'I won't sign anything unless you tell me,' I said.

The lawyer gave a despairing sigh, rested his elbows on his desk and rubbed his temples.

'Do I have your assurance that if I tell you, everything I say will remain strictly between us, Signora Bianchi?'

'Of course.'

Furboni lowered his voice, as though what he was about to divulge was so secret that not even the piles of paperwork which surrounded us should be party to it.

'Paradiso was gifted to Odetta Colombino by her benefactor, Carlo Marchesini,' he said, clasping his hands together, seemingly praying for forgiveness for his transgression.

'Carlo Marchesini? Why would he gift a house to a twelve-year-old silk-worker?' But as I asked the question, I already knew the answer.

'Carlo Marchesini was your aunt's father,' Furboni stated heavily. 'Hence your aunt was born Gelsomina Marchesini. But Signora Bianchi, please appreciate how delicate the matter was, both in view of Carlo Marchesini's status and Odetta Colombino's young age.'

'How old was Carlo Marchesini at the time?'

'I couldn't say precisely without looking it up. But certainly he was somewhere in his fifties. So you understand, Signora Bianchi, how keen he was to keep the scandal quiet.'

'So he gave Odetta Colombino the house to buy her silence?'

'Well, in part, yes,' the lawyer conceded. 'Carlo Marchesini had led a life which most would consider headstrong and outrageous. His fondness for gambling, for drinking and his penchant for young girls was not exactly a secret. I do not suppose that anybody envied his poor wife. However, when he learned that Odetta Colombino was carrying his child, he feared that the scandal would destroy him and cause irreparable damage to the Marchesini name.'

Furboni sat back with his hands still clasped.

'By gifting the property to Odetta Colombino and giving her a home in which to raise his child, this was Carlo Marchesini's attempt at making amends. Tragically, the young girl did not live long enough for that to happen. Her death, for which Carlo Marchesini knew he was ultimately responsible, changed everything. He put aside his reckless habits and became a pious man. In his will he bequeathed a considerable sum of money to the Church.'

'And he thought that would make it all better?'

'It's not my place to conjecture, Signora Bianchi.'

'Did his son, Amilcare, know about my aunt? She would have been his half-sister. Did he know about Paradiso?'

'The transaction was carried out in the strictest confidence, with the understanding that Carlo Marchesini's wife and son should never find out, either about the house or the child. If Amilcare Marchesini did know anything, he never made any mention of it to me, or to my father, who was the notary who dealt with the original matter.'

'And my aunt? What did she know?'

'For years your aunt knew absolutely nothing, apart from the fact that her mother had been very young. She knew nothing of her father's identity. Following Odetta Colombino's death, Carlo Marchesini ordered that the property should be placed in a trust and that it should remain so until your aunt came of age. Hence the house remained empty for over twenty years.'

'So my aunt had no idea about any of this until she came of age?'

'That is correct. And by that time both Carlo Marchesini and

189

his wife had passed away. Your aunt was also keen that the circumstances surrounding her ownership of Paradiso should be kept confidential, once she learned who her father was.'

We sat in silence for a few moments, until Furboni said, 'Signora Bianchi, I have broken the law by divulging all this to you. And I have told you absolutely everything that I know. So please, now I *must* ask you to sign.' He gestured to the papers.

And so, with Avvocato Furboni's gold fountain pen in my hand, I signed away my beloved Paradiso, all its memories and all its history, and passed its ownership to a man I had never met and who cared nothing for any of that.

CHAPTER 16

When I arrived back at Paradiso, Gianfrancesco was sitting waiting for me on the steps.

'Well?' he prompted with a hopeful smile. Then, on seeing my expression: 'Oh Graziella, I'm so sorry.' He wrapped his arms around me and planted a kiss on my head.

'Looks like we didn't pray hard enough,' I said.

'How long before the property developer takes ownership?'

'He already has. He's given me two days to clear the furniture out. Pozzetti's going to store it until I have somewhere to put it.'

It was hard to believe that it had happened. I didn't have a sack of gold coins, or a pile of banknotes to show for it. Avvocato Furboni had arranged for a banker's draft to be delivered to my address in Pomazzo by secure courier. All I had was a receipt. To me, it just felt as though I had sold my soul for a small piece of paper.

I sat down heavily on the step beside Gianfrancesco, trying to decide how I should start explaining what Avvocato Furboni had just told me, but it was Gianfrancesco who spoke first.

'I had a look for some more information, but I didn't find anything useful. The mystery of your aunt's name remains just that – a mystery.'

'Well, I found out quite a lot,' I replied.

When I told Gianfrancesco everything that Furboni had just imparted to me, the colour drained from his face. He asked me to repeat it all again twice, then fell utterly silent.

'I can't find the words to express how awful I feel,' he said after a while. 'That poor girl! How could any decent man do that to a child?

Whether my father knew or not about Odetta Colombino and about Zia Mina, I'm glad he hated his father so much. My grandfather was not deserving of anybody's love.' He clenched his fists. 'I feel like going back to the house and setting fire to his portrait. Having his blood running through my veins makes me feel tarnished.'

'What your grandfather did doesn't reflect on you or on your father in any way,' I said. 'Your father was a good man. You are a good man. Carlo Marchesini wasn't, but that's just the way it is. Some people are just bad people and they do bad things.'

'I suppose. At least Zia Mina and you and your parents had a lovely place to live in.'

'Had,' I sighed. 'Not any more though.'

I looked out across the overgrown garden. Several rogue tomato plants were poking through the grass.

'Giving up this place feels so wrong,' I told Gianfrancesco. 'And now, knowing the connection it has to your family, just makes it feel even worse.'

Gianfrancesco squeezed my hand in his.

'I don't know what to say, Graziella., but if you would like me to, I'll help you to pack up. We should get everything done in a couple of days and you can go back to your family and look forward to a new start. You're a woman of means now. Think of the lovely new home you will be able to buy. You can make your own new family history there. A fresh start.' He cleared his throat. 'Your husband must be keen for you to have your own place too.'

I looked away and did not respond.

'Graziella? By all means tell me to mind my own business, but you seem so terribly sad, and I don't think it's just because of Paradiso being sold. What's the matter? You've told me all about Lucia, but every time I mention your husband you change the subject.'

I didn't need to answer. The look on my face must have said it all.

'What about you?' I said. 'You're getting married in July, but you've barely mentioned it. And you haven't told me anything about your fiancée.'

It was Gianfrancesco's turn to look away. 'Her name's Isabella,' he said.

'I thought you were already married. I was told you were getting married several years ago.'

'Several years ago? No. That's just village gossip. Apparently someone said I'd gone to Africa to work as a missionary too. Who told you I was getting married?'

'Your mother.'

'What? Are you sure?'

'Absolutely. She said you were engaged to be married to a girl called Anna.'

Gianfrancesco frowned. 'I don't believe I know anyone called Anna. I've certainly never been engaged to anyone called Anna. When did my mother tell you I was getting married?'

'At the end of the summer in 1955.'

'But that makes absolutely no sense. Are you sure?'

'I couldn't be any surer. Your mother commissioned my mother to embroider a set of silk wedding sheets as your wedding present.'

'My mother's behaviour could be rather bizarre sometimes back then. She was still taking a lot of pills. But I don't know why she would say something like that.'

'She was just warning me to keep away from you,' I said. 'I didn't realise it at the time, but I can see it now. We didn't exactly have her blessing, did we?'

'Not exactly.'

'Your mother did what she thought was right. She didn't want you wasting your life with some uneducated country girl like me.'

'Oh Graziella, don't say that!'

'It couldn't have worked though, could it? Even Zia Mina warned me. She said that men of your social standing didn't marry girls like me.'

Gianfrancesco took my hand, saying, 'That's the past, Graziella. All those old constraints of class and social standing don't make sense any more. We were very young, true, but the love we shared was real. I should have stood up to my mother and I completely understand why you never replied to my letters.'

'Your letters? Which letters are you talking about?'

'The ones I wrote from Milan.'

'I never received any letters.'

'I wrote you two dozen at least which I posted and a dozen more which I didn't have the courage to post. That time you came to see me after summer school I left too many things unexplained. My mother was there just behind the door listening to every word we said. I was a coward and I felt awful. My mother said that if I didn't end things with you, she would tell your mother that we'd been intimate. I didn't want you to get into any trouble so I obeyed her. But I explained all this to you in my letters.'

'I had no news from you. You and your mother just vanished. Nobody knew where you'd gone.'

'We went to live in Milan. My mother couldn't face another winter in the house and she was afraid I would throw away my education and my future to be with you. So I did my final year of Liceo Classico in Milan and then went to university there. I hardly came back after that.'

'Signora Grassi saw you once, passing in the car with your mother. I hoped you'd come to see me, but as you didn't I assumed you didn't want anything more to do with me.'

'The only reason I didn't come to see you was that you hadn't replied to my letters. So I assumed *you* didn't want anything to do with *me*. But I did come to find you the following summer.'

'You did?'

'It took a few attempts. I set off from home several times but on the way here I'd convince myself that you wouldn't want to see me. I hoped that even if you were too angry with me for things

194

to go back to the way they were, we could still be friends. I even saw you in the village wearing a pretty pink dress and you looked so incredibly lovely, but I didn't have the courage to come and say hello. And then I saw you again a week or so later riding on the back of a motorcycle. Then my mother saw you too. I knew I'd missed my chance, but I thought I would give it one last try and I came here to talk to you, but Zia Mina told me in no uncertain terms to leave you alone because you were with Gino. And she ordered me to stop writing to you.'

'Zia Mina knew you'd been writing to me?'

'Oh yes. I expect my letters were delivered straight into the firebox of her stove.'

His words hit me like punches. In that moment I could have screamed. I could have torn out my hair in rage. I could have cried and sobbed and gnashed my teeth, but instead I took a deep breath and said, 'I'm sorry.'

'You have nothing to be sorry about,' Gianfrancesco said. 'It's all my fault.'

'It's not an apology. It's a regret. I'm sorry that things have turned out like this. And that we lost sight of each other in the way we did.'

'But now we've found each other again. It's not too late. We can still be friends, can't we?'

He placed his arm around my shoulder and pressed his cheek against mine.

'We have history, Graziella, and that means we'll always be connected in one way or the other, no matter what path our lives take. So let's use it. Let's be friends and help each other with a listening ear, or a word of advice from time to time. I want you to know that you can always call on me, and that if you ever need help, I will do everything I can. I know your situation's different from mine and I don't expect you to say the same to me, but I absolutely mean it when I say that I will always be here for you.

I've missed you more than I can express. I've felt dull and hollow without you.'

We sat leaning against one another for a long time, until Gianfrancesco nudged me gently with his elbow.

'Come along, my dearest friend. We can't sit here chatting all day. We have a lot to do,' he said, pulling me up off the step. In that moment, I could have fallen into his arms.

We placed Salvatore's old blackboard on the verge outside the gate to advertise items for sale. There were things I would never need – garden tools, the market barrow, items of furniture. Word spread quickly and before long people arrived to view the items for sale in the yard.

My dowry was still exactly as I had left it, stuffed haphazardly into the wardrobe. I began to fold up all the embroidered linens: everything was terribly creased. My mother would have been most unhappy about it.

'Would you like to see your wedding sheets?' I asked Gianfrancesco.

'You've still got them?'

'Yes. Your mother never came back for them.'

I heaved the brown-paper package off its shelf, then spread the sheets across the bed. They were the only things I had bothered to fold and they were even more beautiful than I remembered.

'You can have them now,' I said, but Gianfrancesco shook his head .

'I couldn't.'

'But they were made for you – except that the monograms are wrong now.'

'G.A.M.? But those are my initials. Gianfrancesco Amilcare Marchesini. I have my father's name as my middle name. My mother didn't after all constrain me to marrying a woman whose name begins with A.'

'I'll wrap them back up and you can take them,' I said.

'No,' he replied firmly.

'Why not?'

'I couldn't honeymoon on sheets that you had embroidered. It would feel very strange and very wrong. You keep them.'

We both stared at the beautiful sheets that neither of us wanted. Gianfrancesco seemed distant. After a long silence he ran his hand through his hair and sighed.

'What should I do, Graziella?' he said. 'I lie awake at night wondering whether I'm doing the right thing by getting married.'

'Do you love Isabella?'

'She's a lovely, sweet girl,' he replied, which was not the answer to the question I had asked.

'If you're not sure, why are you getting married? Is Isabella pregnant?'

'Good Lord, no!' exclaimed Gianfrancesco. 'There's absolutely no chance of that.' He rested his chin on his hands and said flatly, 'We met two years ago. There had been nobody in my life since you.'

'What – nobody?'

'Nobody at all. I'd become very serious, very bookish, just focused on my studies – not exactly the type any girl would want as a boyfriend. Then I met Isabella and it was nice. I mean, it *is* nice. She's lovely. She made my life feel brighter. But she's from a very traditional and very conservative background. The time we're permitted to spend together is limited by her parents. It's hard to get to know somebody well under those constraints.'

'So why the decision to marry if you feel like that?'

'I hadn't really been considering marriage, but her father started breathing down my neck about it.' Gianfrancesco rubbed his neck, as though in that moment he could feel his future father-in-law's presence.

'One evening over dinner just before Christmas her father asked about my intentions and by the time we were drinking our coffee, Isabella and I were officially engaged. And as soon as we were, even before I could think about what I'd just committed to, wedding preparations were being made. The church was booked within days. She's already had her dress made. Her mother's sent out the invitations. And all this has happened at the same time as the house being sold, so Isabella and her mother have been looking at homes for sale in Milan. I always intended to buy a place there, but I imagined I'd purchase a small apartment for myself once I'd given my mother some money. But Isabella and her mother have been looking at family houses with a view to us having children. If we go for the sort of properties they've got in mind, I'll end up penniless. Property is really expensive in Milan. But Isabella's so excited about it. I feel awful, but I don't share her enthusiasm. '

Each lost in our thoughts, we carried on sorting through the wardrobe in silence. It was oddly comforting to know that he was thinking the same thing as me – that we had missed our chance and that we both regretted it. After a while he looked up from behind a pile of linens and said, 'Graziella, you need to see this.' He was holding a tin box. I opened it expecting to find more household items, but instead It was full of money.

'Could it be Zia Mina's savings?' I wondered.

Tucked in beside the money was a little red accounts book. I leafed through it, looking at dates, references and precise columns of figures on each page, but the writing was not Zia Mina's. It was unmistakably my mother's.

Each roll of notes contained 10,000 lire. There were eleven rolls plus a few loose notes. The accounts book showed that my mother had put money aside for over ten years, right up until the week before she went into hospital. She had saved some of her earnings every single week, sometimes as little as 50 lire, other times as much as 1,000. In addition, she had saved all the money I had given her from my wages with Signora Grassi. The mystery of the missing 15,000 lire was solved. It was the last and the largest sum she had put in the box.

My mother's delirious talk about there being enough money in her box to see me through my last year of school had not been a drug-induced delusion. I had simply been looking in the wrong box. I buried my head in my hands and sobbed.

*

That evening, I telephoned Gino from the Pozzettis'. I had not spoken to him since I had left and he was annoyed.

'You were supposed to tell me when you'd signed,' he said. 'Why didn't you tell me a courier was coming to the house with the cheque? I had to come home from work early to take it to the bank. When are you coming back?'

'Tomorrow. But I'm catching the last train and won't be home until late evening. There's a lot to sort out. The buyer wants the house completely empty.'

'You'd have been better off just leaving it all in the house for him to deal with. That old shit's no good to us.'

I felt as though he was about to say something else, but then changed his mind. Finally he said, 'All right then. I'll come to fetch you at the station tomorrow evening. Wait for me on the platform. I don't want to have to go looking all over the station for you.'

I went back to Paradiso where Gianfrancesco was finishing sorting through tools in the barn.

'Are you all right?' he asked.

I nodded, but he could see that I was upset. The thought of returning to Pomazzo and the battle I knew I would have to fight with Gino filled me with dread. I could feel it aching through my bones.

'I was thinking,' said Gianfrancesco. ,'we've done pretty much all we can now. Perhaps in the morning we could go and look at some of the houses Furboni spoke to you about.'

'Yes, perhaps,' I replied, but with no enthusiasm.

Since being reunited we had kissed hello and goodbye numerous times. Gianfrancesco had put his arms around me to comfort me. We had sat on the steps with our heads close together. Any one of those small instances of intimacy could have been transformed into something more if we had let ourselves be drawn in – but in the end it was his hand, gently placed against the small of my back as we walked through the barn door which made me turn, take his face in my hands and press my lips against his. There was no hesitation on his part. A sudden fearsome, absolute passion tore the breath from our bodies, like a high-speed collision.

We didn't ask whether it was right. I was married. Gianfrancesco was soon to be. In that moment and all through that night none of that mattered. We consumed each other passionately, euphorically, tenderly and lovingly on the silk wedding sheets.

As dawn broke and slivers of light slipped through the shutters we lay entwined, surrounded by embroidered hyacinths, peonies and orange blossoms.

'Graziella,' he said. I could feel the warmth of his breath in my hair as I nuzzled against him. 'We can never just be friends, can we?'

*

I took my mother's money to the bank in Pieve Santa Clara and opened a savings account. It was for Lucia, a little nest-egg for her; a gift from my mother. I could feel Mamma smiling down on me as I handed the teller the rolls of notes.

I walked slowly back up the North Road in time to see Pozzetti and his sons shifting the last of the furniture. I watched as pieces of Zia Mina's big old wardrobe were carried across the road. By lunchtime Paradiso was empty.

Gianfrancesco took the bus with me to the station, where we waited side by side on a bench for my train. Although there were so many things to say, there was a silence between us. Minutes before my train was due, he took a package from his bag. Inside it was a red velvet case, embroidered with a golden shield.

'I would like your little daughter Lucia to have this,' he said.

It was Amilcare Marchesini's illustrated limited edition of Alessandro Manzoni's book *The Betrothed*, the very copy we had studied together as children.

'But it's so valuable and it was your father's. Are you sure?' I asked, tracing my finger over the silver embossed cover.

'Yes,' said Gianfrancesco, stroking my hand. 'It would give me great pleasure for Lucia to have it, particularly as you named her after the character in the book. And I'm certain my father would have liked her to have it too. Although obviously it will be a few years before she is able to read it.'

'Thank you,' I said, then kissed his lips gently. We remained with our noses pressed together until a whistle signalled the train's approach.

'Thank you,' I said again. 'Thank you for everything.'

'There's something else.' He hesitated for a moment, then reached back into his bag again and took out a handful of papers. 'You're under no obligation to read them and you can burn them if you want,' he said, 'but these are the letters I wrote to you and never sent. And I meant every word I wrote.'

There were twelve letters, starting in August of 1955, just days before I met Gino, and continuing up until Christmas of 1956. Each letter became more open and more passionate, perhaps because he knew he would never send them. I read loving words, lustful words, beautiful words, pained, regretful and lonely words.

I read words which expressed the very same things I had been feeling at the very same time.

In his final letter, dated December 1956, in words which were both sweet and bitter, Gianfrancesco congratulated me on the news of my marriage and wished me all the best.

I spent the entire journey reading and re-reading his thoughts and his confessions. He repeated again and again what a coward he had been. I had thought him a coward too, but handing me his letters, which was like handing me his heart on a plate, was brave.

In addition to the letters, he had given me a telephone number. It was his office number. He said I could call him whenever I wanted, and that as soon as the sale of Cascina Marchesini had gone through and he had bought a home in Milan, he would give me his new home number too.

I read the number so many times that I memorised it, but I knew that keeping in touch as friends, as we had first promised, would be impossible. As Gianfrancesco had said, we could never be just friends.

CHAPTER 17

The platform was packed with people weaving in different directions. I looked up and down through the chaos until finally I saw Gino, standing by a billboard smoking a cigarette. Clutching my bag containing Amilcare Marchesini's book and Gianfrancesco's letters close, I began to pick my way through the crowd towards him.

'You're pale,' he said, and I wondered whether my infidelity was written in my pallor. I was certain that he would discern something in my expression. My heart nearly stopped when he took my bag.

'Hurry up. I've parked in a restricted space,' he said, leading me quickly through the mass of travellers to the exit.

I sat in silence as Gino swerved his way through the traffic, cursing other drivers and hooting at pedestrians. He seemed agitated, but I was relieved that he was not asking questions about my trip. As we left the snarl of the centre of town, Gino broke the silence.

'Did you get everything done?' he asked.

'Yes.'

'Did you manage to sell the stuff we're not keeping?'

'Some of it. I've left the rest with Pozzetti.'

'Get much money for it?'

'About fifty thousand.'

'Is that it? You should have sold the lot. It's going to cost us more than that to have all that old shit brought here.'

I sat with my face turned away from Gino. The reality of being back weighed down heavily, as though my body and brain had turned to lead. I knew I had a fight ahead of me, but I seemed to have left all my strength back in Pieve Santa Clara.

Just before we reached Pomazzo, Gino pulled over.

'Why are we stopping?' I asked.

He grinned, reached across, grabbed my face and kissed my mouth hard, crushing my lips against my teeth.

'I've got some great news!' he exclaimed, barely able to control his excitement. 'I didn't want to tell you while you were away – I wanted to save the surprise. Bartocchi lowered his price for me!'

Gino's mouth was close to mine. I could feel the punch of his cigarette breath. He was looking directly into my eyes.

'And so today I signed the purchase documents for the workshop and the flat and the business. I was going to wait until you were back, but Bartocchi was in such a good mood that I didn't want to miss the opportunity. Graziella, the place is finally going to be ours!'

'You did what? For how much?'

'It was twenty-six million lire,' he said excitedly. 'I told Bartocchi we only had eighteen million now, and he agreed that we could pay the rest in instalments over the next year. He wants another ten million for the business and all the equipment, including the tow truck. We're going to have to ask my father for a loan for that, but he can't possibly refuse and we'll pay that back easily with the income from the garage. Isn't it wonderful? We'll finally have our own home now and a great business.'

'No!' I screamed. 'I don't want to live there! You can't have Zia Mina's money to buy Bartocchi's!'

'It's already done. Bartocchi's got the money.'

'What?'

'I couldn't sign the documents without paying a deposit, could I?'

My mind disintegrated, as though my head had been cracked open and all my thoughts and feelings spilled out in a chaos of anger and disbelief and horror. My heart beat so fast so suddenly that my throat clenched and I gasped to breathe.

'You did what? How could you? Why did you do that without telling me?'

'What do you mean, without telling you? Don't pretend you didn't know that's what I wanted to do! I took you there just before you went away. It's not like I haven't been clear about what I want to do.' He paused for a moment, then added sulkily, 'Anyway, it was the only way. I knew you'd do this. I knew you'd make some stupid, crazy fuss.' He tapped his finger on his temple, just as he did every time he spoke about Zia Mina. 'If you knew anything about business you'd realise that I've made the best possible investment of our money. You're behaving as though I've lost the lot on the horses.'

'No!' I screamed again, beating his shoulder with my fists. 'No! No! You've stolen my money! Not our money, *my* money! How could you do that? Get it back! Get my money back!'

He grabbed my wrists hard and shoved me back against the seat.

'Shut up and stop shrieking!' he yelled. 'Shut your stupid mouth right now and calm down or I'll shut you up myself! I'm doing this for us, aren't I? We're going to tell my parents and ask for a loan at lunch tomorrow. I expect your full support.'

'They don't know?'

'No, not yet. I wanted you to be there when I broke the news. So don't fucking spoil it with your fucking whining!'

Gino had taken my money, although legally, he had not stolen it. In the eyes of the law, there was no concept of theft between spouses. His actions, although underhand, were not illegal. I had read about it in the library. I should have known. I should have guessed. I shouldn't have been so stupid. Stupid. Stupid. Stupid. *Stupid.*

As Sunday lunch was served, Gino was so excited that he could not sit still. I could feel him tapping his foot under the table as his mother served up piles of cannelloni.

'We've got an amazing announcement to make,' he said, grinning.

Everybody turned and looked straight at me.

'Another baby?' asked Marina.

'What? God, no. That wouldn't be amazing, would it?' said Gino. I looked at my little Lucia and was glad that she was too concerned with her cannelloni to have heard or understood.

'I'm buying Bartocchi's Garage,' he announced proudly.

Marina glanced over to her father, who frowned and pushed away his food.

'You are?' he said.

'Yes! It won't be Bartocchi's Garage any more. It will be Bianchi's Garage. *Gino Bianchi – All Bodywork and Mechanical Repairs.* I'm going to get the new sign made straight away. A big one, with lights.'

Gino's father sat back with his knees wide apart and folded his arms.

'How exactly are you buying it? The last I heard, Bartocchi wanted a significant amount of money for that place.'

'I negotiated, Papá,' Gino boasted. 'I managed to get him down from forty million to thirty-six million all in for the workshop, the flat, the business, the equipment, tools, even the tow truck – the lot.'

'And how do you propose to pay for it?'

'Well, we've been able to give him eighteen million already. I've promised to pay another eight million over the next year in instalments.' He smiled sweetly, reached across and rested his hand on my arm. My skin prickled to his touch. 'And Graziella and I wanted to ask you if you would lend us the rest. Please.'

His father's frown deepened. 'I'm in no position to lend you ten million lire,' he said. 'What on earth makes you think I have that sort of money to hand? What's more, why do you think I would lend you such a large sum when you didn't even have the courtesy to consult me on the purchase? I would have expected you to ask me *before* you signed your name to anything. And if you had, I would have told you that I have serious reservations as to whether that property and that business are worth anything like what you've agreed to pay.'

Gino's grip on my arm tightened, his fingers denting my flesh.

'Can't you help with s-some of it?' he stuttered. There was panic in his voice. 'I thought the family business was sound.'

Gino's father's face turned instantly purple and the veins in his temples swelled to the size of cables.

'The family business *is* sound! Very sound!' he bellowed. 'Which is why I was able to go to the bank eight years ago and get a loan to build the new unit so I could expand. But whilst I'm still repaying that loan I have to run a very tight ship. I have suppliers to pay and staff to pay as well as the bank every month. And don't get me started on the taxes! If you had ever shown any interest in the family business, you would know that. I can't help you, Gino.'

'But if I can't complete the sale Bartocchi will just keep the money I've given him and I'll look like an idiot and I'll probably lose my job,' wailed Gino.

'Yes,' said his father. 'It's a fine mess you've got yourself into, son.'

'Did you know about this?' asked Marina, turning to me. And seeing my wretched expression: 'What? Gino gave all your money to Bartocchi without asking you?'

I nodded and screwed my eyes up tightly, sealing in my tears. I felt Gino's glare bore through me. Marina rounded on her brother.

'You arsehole! What a bastard thing to do!' she exclaimed.

'Marina!' snapped her mother. 'There's no need for language like that.'

'I think there *is* need for language like that, and far worse, Mamma,' replied Marina. 'Gino's helped himself to all of Graziella's money without her agreement, and he's put the whole lot at risk! A deposit would normally be five or ten per cent. Gino's handed over fifty per cent! If a contract of sale isn't honoured, a seller is within his rights to keep the deposit. That's the whole point of deposits, Mamma.'

'There's no risk. If Papá can't help, I'll go to the bank,' blustered Gino.

'You're dreaming if you think the bank will stump up all that money for you,' snorted Marina.

'I don't need your opinion, you fat bitch, ' Gino sneered.

Before she could answer, Gino's mother interrupted.

'There's no need for that either, Marina. Perhaps going to the bank is a good idea. We are well acquainted with the bank manager. He knows we're a good family – why, he even sends us chocolates every Christmas.'

'He knows Papá's business, Mamma. And he's not going to lend Gino a big lump of money just because he's your son. That's not the way it works. Banks want guarantees and proof that the money they lend can be repaid.'

'Of course the money would be repaid. Your brother is a hard worker. I think it's good that he's ambitious and wants his own business,' my mother-in-law defended him. 'The bank could lend Papá the money and Gino could pay it back every month.' She turned to her husband. 'We could do that, couldn't we? I think it's a good idea, don't you?'

Signor Bianchi did not reply.

'Did you at least ask Bartocchi to let you see his accounts?' Marina demanded of Gino. 'I can have a look through them, if you like.'

'I don't need you sticking your fat nose into his accounts! I know it's a good business. I've been working there for years,

208

haven't I? I see clients come every day and they all pay their bills. There's no way I can ask Bartocchi to show me his accounts. He might think I don't trust him.'

Marina raised her eyebrows. 'Nobody should buy a business without looking at the books, no matter who they're buying it from.'

'Did you hear what I said? I *know* it's a sound business!'

'How do you know? You're just an apprentice. What are the overheads? Are the taxes paid up to date? Does Bartocchi owe any money to his suppliers? If he does, will they be paid?'

'I am not his apprentice, I'm his employee!' shouted Gino. 'And whether you like it or not, soon I'm going to be the boss.'

When Lucia began to cry because of the loud voices and arguments, I went to pick her up and console her.

'Fine,' shrugged Marina. 'Do what you want. Do it your way. I'm sure you're right. You always are.'

'Marina, don't be rude to Gino,' said Gino's mother.

'I'm so sorry, Mamma,' Marina said, her cheeks flushed. 'I forgot that your golden boy is beyond reproach in every way. I don't know why I'm even offering to help. Go on, Gino. Go ahead and buy a business you know nothing about. Get yourself in debt if it's what you want. You always get what you want anyway.'

She stood up to leave the table.

'Marina, where are you going? You haven't finished your cannelloni and we still have roast pork,' said her mother.

'I'm going home, Mamma, because I cannot bear this.'

'Now's not the time for jealousy, my girl!'

Marina stopped in her tracks and looked at her mother, open-mouthed.

'Jealousy? Are you kidding, Mamma? I'm not jealous – I'm furious! I'm furious about what Gino's done with Graziella's money. And I'm furious about the totally disrespectful way he treats her and the way he does it right under your nose in your house – and you just back him up. You're completely blind to his selfishness and to his stupidity. Actually, it's worse than that. You encourage him to be selfish and stupid by telling him he can do no wrong. And you always have. And that's why he's such a spoiled, useless little shit!'

Her mother sat motionless. Then: 'Have you quite finished, Marina?' she said coolly, little beads of perspiration forming on her temples.

'Oh, I've barely started – but I know I'm wasting my energy saying anything to you. I really hope you manage to sort something out, because if Gino's stunt causes Graziella to lose all her money, it would be unforgivable.'

'Of course something will be sorted out. If the bank won't lend to Gino, they'll lend to us.'

'The best thing I ever did was to get out of this house,' Marina said, almost to herself, then added, 'I don't suppose you'd be falling over yourself to borrow money on my behalf if there was something I wanted, would you?'

With that, she left.

*

I had no involvement in the arrangement that Gino made with his parents. As Marina had predicted, the bank would not lend him the money, but they would lend it to Gino's father. I had no idea of the guarantees they required, or the size of the repayments. All I knew was that the purchase was going through and that Marina no longer came to lunch on Sundays.

Within a week of the completion of the purchase, made entirely in Gino's name, a fresh new sign appeared above the workshop door: *Gino Bianchi – All Bodywork and Mechanical Repairs*.

Giovanni came and took photographs of Gino standing

proudly by the new sign. There was a spring in my husband's step and a visible self-assurance. He organised a grand opening celebration and invited everybody he knew, except Marina. There was much congratulating and wishing of good fortune. His mother glowed with pride and basked in her son's new confidence. She didn't speak to me at all.

In his state of euphoria Gino was blind to my anger and my unhappiness, although I made no attempt to hide either. He talked excitedly about his plans for expansion and improvement.

'This first year's going to be challenging with both Bartocchi and my father to pay back each month, but next year when Bartocchi's debt is paid off I'm going to get one of those painting booths installed,' he said. 'I'll be able to do full re-sprays. There's good money in that. I'll employ a specialist bodywork painter. And I'll get one of those lifts for cars so I don't have to work in the pit any more. And then I'll get the building finished so it looks really smart.' He beamed. 'What's more, I always told Bartocchi he should have cars for sale at the front by the road. You know, a proper forecourt with all the cars polished and the prices on the windscreens.'

When I failed to show any interest, Gino turned on me.

'Go if you want,' he said smugly. 'Go on – clear off. Go back to the arsehole place you came from and take your daughter with you. I won't stop you. I don't care. As far as I'm concerned, you're free to go.'

We both knew that I was not free at all. It was not as simple as packing a suitcase and catching a train. The little bit of money in the savings account was not enough to start a new life. I couldn't leave with Lucia and throw us into a precarious situation. But above all, leaving Gino with everything that my family had spent their lives working for was simply not right.

With a heavy, angry heart I faced my only choice, to stay and try to make the best of things.

*

The first time I saw the inside of my new home was the day we moved in. It was a wretched, damp-stained place. The rooms were not ungenerous, but they were dark. The only openings which did not look out directly on to a neighbouring wall were the glazed doors which led on to the front balconies overlooking the yard, but as there were no railings, they had been nailed shut.

Bartocchi had been living in the apartment for twenty years and during that time I don't believe that any part of it had been cleaned. It took a whole week to scrub away the oily hand-prints which covered every wall and surface in every room. The grease in the kitchen was so thick I could peel it off the cabinets. Every windowpane was covered in an opaque smear of grime and cigarette smoke. The bathroom was unspeakable. It took two litres of bleach to make it anywhere near acceptable.

The decision for Gino and me to have separate bedrooms was never discussed. Gino installed himself in the bedroom nearest the living area and I installed myself in the back bedroom with Lucia. My room faced the leather-processing plant. The smell of the tanning was inescapable, even with the windows shut. When the factory chimney was smoking, I couldn't see the sky at all.

I hoped I would feel a little better when the furniture from Paradiso arrived, but like me, it just seemed to be in the wrong place, as though it too had been uprooted against its will and forced into a place where it did not belong.

There was a small comfort in sleeping in my old bed. I made it up with sheets from my dowry. Zia Mina's wardrobe was now my wardrobe. It took up an entire wall of my room. I hoped that the mirrors would give the illusion of more light, but all they did was reflect back the gloom.

Although my mood was dark, Gino's was euphoric. He was the

boss of his own business and he brimmed with pride. Every Friday he left me housekeeping money on the kitchen table.

'There'll be plenty more than this once I've paid Bartocchi back,' he said. 'We'll just have to be a little bit careful this year.'

Despite my feelings of rage towards Gino, I fulfilled all the domestic duties that were expected of me. I cooked meals, washed clothes, kept the house clean and ran the household finances competently. Gino ate the meals I cooked with little complaint, unless I tried to give him soup.

'You make a decent risotto,' he said, wiping his plate clean, 'but you really need to learn to make tortellini.'

Through all of this my thoughts of Gianfrancesco were constant. I kept his letters hidden in a pillowcase which smelled of his hair. I read them until I could recite them by heart. But tormenting myself about Gianfrancesco, about the missed opportunity and the misunderstandings, made me feel as though I was drowning. With great difficulty, I put our reunion and our night spent together in its place in my mind; as a stone memory of a happy moment and nothing more – a closure of sorts.

My responsibilities lay in Pomazzo, in my new home with Gino and Lucia. My ties to Pieve Santa Clara had been irreparably severed. My family was gone. My home was gone. Gianfrancesco had made his life in Milan. All I was doing was making myself feel worse.

I hoped that Gianfrancesco would feel the same way and that he would understand why I had not contacted him. I did try to telephone him once to try to explain. It was a few days before his wedding date, but he was not there when I called. The colleague I spoke to said that he was on leave and would not be back for two weeks. I took this as confirmation that he had decided to go ahead and marry Isabella, despite his misgivings. I didn't call again.

As for me, my life as Signora Bianchi, wife of Gino Bianchi, mechanic and owner of his own business was the life which I had.

I could either live in misery, or I could try to be content. I had a home. I had a wonderful daughter. It was up to me to make the best of it I could.

Some things were better. Finally, we had some space. I was no longer tip-toeing around Gino's mother trying not to displease her with my presence. Lucia had room to play, although it was only room to play inside.

I decided that if I was to find some happiness I would need more than domestic chores to occupy me, so I placed my mother's sewing table and lamp by the window and created a workspace for myself. I used the money I had collected from the sale of Zia Mina's bits and pieces to buy an electric sewing machine.

The first thing that I made was a pretty dress for Lucia. When I went into town to buy buttons for it I found that a new shop had opened in place of the old haberdashery shop. The window display showed off an array of lavish ceremonial wear. I went in out of curiosity.

The old-fashioned shelving had been replaced with modern cabinets displaying gem tiaras, satin gloves and silk corsages. Light from a glittering glass chandelier bounced off an enormous gilt-framed mirror and sparkled against diamanté- and pearl-encrusted wedding, communion and christening gowns. The shop was filled with the scent of new, starched fabrics and the perfume from a vase of lilies which sat on the gleaming glass counter.

It was the most beautiful shop I had ever seen. I stood and looked around for a long time at the twinkling fairy-tale kingdom of dream dresses and sumptuous gowns. It was the kind of emporium I might have imagined in a big city, not a place like Pomazzo.

'Can I help you?' enquired a young woman, emerging from the back room.

'I came to buy some buttons. I didn't realise the haberdashery shop was no longer here.'

'I opened last week,' she said. 'But I do have buttons. Mostly fancy ones though. What are you looking for?'

'Fancy ones would be perfect,' I replied and took out Lucia's dress.

'Did you make this?' she asked.

'Yes.'

'It's gorgeous.' She turned the little dress over in her hands, then said, 'I don't suppose you're looking for a bit of work, are you?'

Within a month I had altered and embroidered three wedding dresses, two communion dresses and a christening gown. I was surprised at what I could earn. People in Pomazzo were prepared to pay handsomely.

My bedroom became my atelier. I purchased a mannequin and pinned photographs of wedding dresses to the walls. I sang along to the songs playing on the radio. Lucia sat at my feet chattering and playing with the rag dollies I had made for her. They had ruby-red embroidered lips, huge green eyes and woollen hair, just like the dollies my mother had made for me, except that Lucia's were far more finely-dressed.

Before long I had 50,000 lire saved, which I hid in the box in which I had found my mother's savings. I kept the box on the bottom shelf of the wardrobe, pushed to the back and concealed behind blankets. I always kept the door locked and hid the key under my mattress. By this time I knew better than to place it where Gino could access it.

Being occupied and having an income improved my mood significantly and Gino and I settled into a tenuous domestic equilibrium, helped by the fact that our paths did not cross too much. He opened the doors of the workshop at seven-thirty every morning and often did not close them again until well past eight o'clock at night. I would see him briefly at lunchtime, and by the evening he was usually so tired that he would head for his bed as soon as he had finished his supper.

Gino had taken over the business with little idea of what a commitment it would involve. He had been accustomed to working for a set number of hours per week, unaware of the enormous number of supplementary hours Bartocchi had to put in, doing emergency repairs and dealing with bills and paperwork. However, the heavy workload did not seem to be curbing his enthusiasm.

'The first year was always going to be the toughest,' he said. 'But once Bartocchi's debt is paid off I'll be able to slow down a bit and employ an extra pair of hands. At the moment, I'm doing the work of two men.'

The new domestic harmony lasted less than six months. Gino was becoming increasingly short-tempered. I had put it down to exhaustion since he was working twelve- and thirteen-hour days six days per week. He even stopped going to meet his friends in the evenings.

One day as he was eating his supper he looked up and demanded, 'Is it going to be like this for ever then?'

'What?'

'You know exactly what I'm talking about. By now I thought we'd be sleeping together, like a proper husband and wife. I didn't say anything when you moved into your own room here because I thought that in just a few weeks, or a few months, we'd be together in our marital bed. I gave you time to adjust. But oh no. Here I am, working hard to give you our own home, the thing you said you wanted, but you have no intention of us ever sharing a bed again, do you?'

I had thought about him asking before and had prayed that he would not. I tried to dismiss his complaints with, 'I didn't think you minded.' But that just made him angry.

'You never consider how I'm feeling, do you? I have needs, even if you don't.'

I was not going to argue, but neither was I going to concede.

'We need time,' I said lamely.

'What kind of answer's that?' he spat and left the kitchen.

The conversation put a new tension between us. Suddenly he seemed to be standing closer to me. I felt his breath on the back on my neck as I washed the dishes. Several times I stirred in the night when I heard him go to the bathroom, and held my breath when his footsteps seemed to come towards my room, then stop … but a minute later they would die away and I would hear his bedroom door close.

One evening Gino pushed his plate aside, rubbed his eyes and rested his elbows on the table. He seemed even more preoccupied than usual.

'That place across town which makes awnings is looking for women with experience of working sewing machines,' he said. 'You should go and see if they'd have you.'

'Why would I do that? The pay's terrible for factory work and I'm doing embroidery and alterations for the new boutique.'

'Yes, but that's not like having a regular job, is it? Nothing's guaranteed. One week you could have a load of work and then the next week you could have nothing.'

'I don't want to work in an awnings factory, or any other factory,' I replied. 'And anyway, I have Lucia to look after.'

'My mother could look after her.'

'Absolutely not.'

He put his head in his hands and stared at the table for a long time before muttering, 'Last month I didn't pay Bartocchi and this month I'm not going to be able to pay Bartocchi or my father.'

'Why?'

'Why do you think? It's because I haven't made enough money.' It was an altered Gino sitting across the table from me. He seemed too weary to pretend, and in a rare moment of honesty he confessed that things were not going well.

Gino did not have the skills or experience to carry out every repair. There had been complaints. The regular clients had become less regular and no new clients came. There were many jobs he had to turn away because he simply had no idea how to do them. Most of the long hours when I thought he was working were spent sitting in the back office smoking his way through pack after pack of cigarettes.

In his eagerness to purchase the place, he had never looked at the earnings, or the overheads, or anything else. Marina had been right. Nobody should buy a business without looking at the books first. Bartocchi had earned enough to keep himself and to pay Gino's modest salary, but very little more. The reason for the building being unfinished became clear, as did Bartocchi's readiness to lower his price.

'Bartocchi's a lying piece of shit,' Gino growled. 'He let me believe it was a good business, but it's crap. And half the equipment doesn't work properly. What's more, the tow-truck's fucked and I don't know what's wrong with it.'

Once all the bills were paid, during the first six months Gino had earned less than he had as Bartocchi's employee, but he had not told me this. Nor had he told me that in order to pay the previous instalment of the money owed to the bank, he had sold his precious Moto Guzzi motorcycle.

'I've been trying to sell the car,' he said moodily. 'But it needs a new fuel pump and nobody wants it unless I pretty much give it away.'

When he finally looked up at me I knew he was expecting recriminations, but I just felt sorry for him and perhaps that was worse.

'I can give you some money,' I said. 'Not much, but probably enough to pay either Bartocchi or your father.'

I thought that he would be relieved, but he was not. He just became angry, slammed down his spoon and slapped his napkin onto the table.

'Everything's just shit, isn't it?' he said. 'Shit business. Shit marriage. It's all shit.' He got up, left his unfinished food on the table and went to his room.

Life descended very quickly into endless arguments. Everything was my fault. He stopped liking the meals I cooked.

'Not another bloody risotto,' he shouted, pushing away his dish with such force that it flew off the table. I was glad Lucia was fast asleep in our bed. 'You've got all day to make something decent and all I get are bloody risottos!'

I gave Gino all the money I had earned that month and the following week he asked for more. It became impossible to save anything. Sometimes my box would contain a few rolls of 10,000 lire, but it would not remain there very long before it was needed.

Although the money I earned was enough to cover the housekeeping I could not subsidise the garage entirely. I certainly couldn't cover both loans. Gino managed to arrange an overdraft with the bank, but it was only helpful until the limit was reached, something which happened very quickly.

I learned a new term – 'repossession' – and prayed for a miracle.

'We should sell up,' I suggested.

'No!' he shouted. 'Once Bartocchi's debt is paid off there will be plenty of money! I'm going to make a success of this in one way or another. You don't know anything about business, do you, Graziella, so shut up! I don't need you to tell me what I should be doing.'

Gino would not tell his father about the state of the business and I had also been sworn to silence – or rather, been threatened into silence.

'Don't you dare tell anyone,' he warned. 'I don't want my stupid sister coming over here and gloating.'

I feared Gino physically, and that fear had grown since we had moved out of his parents' flat. At least when we had been living with the Bianchis his mother had been there to soothe him by telling him that he was right, even if he wasn't, and Gino had always bowed to his father's authority. But in our own home I had nobody to shield me from his temper and he knew it. There were many things that Gino didn't understand, but he understood very well how vulnerable my isolation made me. The threat to smash my face was always enough to make me hold my tongue.

As the weeks passed, bills were paid late, or not at all. Bartocchi sent a menacing payment demand via a lawyer. Gino had told me that he was behind by just one payment, but in reality he was behind by four.

There was an argument outside the workshop when a supplier of tyres came to collect what was owed to him, but Gino didn't have the money. I went downstairs and paid him and it made Gino so angry that he kicked over a trolley of tools and didn't speak to me for days.

Gino would not under any circumstances entertain the idea of selling. He was afraid of what people would say. Afraid they would call him a failure. Afraid they would laugh at him. His fear manifested itself in anger towards me and blinded him to any suggestion of common sense.

Somehow we made it through our eighth month and Gino seemed calmer.

'I've been thinking,' he said one day. 'I'm going to specialise in tyres. People always need tyres. It's pretty straightforward work and I can do it by myself. I've got all the equipment I need. It would be a lot more manageable to do that on my own than trying to do lots of different mechanical repairs that need different parts.'

It seemed like a sensible idea. So what was the catch?

'But the supplier's an arsehole,' Gino went on. 'He won't let me have any tyres on credit now, like he used to with Bartocchi. He wants payment upfront.'

'How much?' I asked.

'How much have you got?'

He took everything I had without thanking me. We would have to live on pasta and passata for a while, but two days later a small delivery of tyres arrived. Unfortunately, the damage to his reputation had been done. Nobody came to have new tyres fitted.

Although Gino had made me promise not to tell anyone that he was having problems, I did wonder whether I should take my troubles to Marina. I hadn't seen her for almost a year, since the argument at Sunday lunch. She had never visited and I felt bad for not having been to see her. I had wanted to, but resisted as I knew Gino would have objected. I didn't need to give him any more reasons for acrimony.

At Christmas we had gone for a meal at Gino's parents' and Marina was absent. Gino spent the day spouting boastful lies about how well things were going and how he was planning to expand the business. His mother sat beaming at the table and telling him how proud she was of him, and how clever he was. His father was uncharacteristically quiet. I said nothing at all.

*

It was a piercingly cold day in February 1963, just after Lucia's sixth birthday. I was sitting in a café with her to keep warm. We had not been able to afford to fill the oil tank for the heating and the apartment was so cold that one entire wall of my bedroom had turned black from the damp.

I sat quietly, lost in my thoughts until I was roused by a knocking on the window. It was Marina.

We sat together drinking hot chocolate, exchanging pleasantries and avoiding the subjects of Gino and the garage until she said, 'I'm sorry I haven't been to see you. I've missed you and I've missed Lucia, but I didn't think I'd be very welcome.'

'Of course you'd be welcome.'

'I didn't mean you. You know what I mean. I haven't spoken to my mother since that argument at lunch.'

She sipped her chocolate slowly.

'Graziella, I need to ask you something and I need you to be very truthful. My father's getting nervous. He wants to know whether the garage really is paying its way. Gino tells him things are great and that he's really busy, but his payments are always late, or they don't come at all. He didn't pay last month's instalment because he said he had to stock up on tyres. And there's still no sign of this month's instalment. My father's been paying the bank on time out of his own pocket and it's making things difficult. And this is a small town and people talk. Everyone's saying that Gino's a disaster. I've been past the garage several times and so has my father, and it's plain to see there aren't any customers. The thing is, the debt with the bank is my father's responsibility and he doesn't want to be left with it if the business folds. He was prepared for a few teething troubles, but he needs to know exactly where things stand now.'

There was no point in lying, or trying to sugar-coat the situation, so I explained it to Marina truthfully and in detail. She sat stirring her chocolate continuously and looking very concerned.

'It was obvious to anyone with the slightest shred of sense that this would happen. Gino buying the garage was like giving a child a business to run. And I always had my doubts that it was much of a business anyway,' she said.

'I'm sorry that your father was put in this position.'

'He did it for you, Graziella. He didn't do it for Gino. He did it so you wouldn't lose all your money. I know my father comes across as a bit of a bear, but he's all right, you know. And he might not express it very well, but he likes and respects you.'

I begged Marina not to tell Gino that the information had come from me and she told me not to worry, but worry was all I could do.

The following day I saw Gino's father's car parked outside the workshop. He did not come up to the flat and I did not dare to go downstairs. That night, Gino was in a foul mood, but said nothing about the visit. The next day I made myself scarce.

When I returned home the workshop was closed and Gino was nowhere to be seen. I cooked supper, but he did not appear. There was still no sign of him by the time I went to bed.

I was woken by noises in the night. The clock said 1 a.m. I found Gino in the kitchen, sitting at the table with a bottle of wine and loaf of bread.

'What are you doing?' I asked.

'Taking my holy communion,' he replied, dipping a piece of bread into the wine and stuffing it into his mouth. 'And I'm thinking.'

'Thinking about what?'

'About the fact that you've been lying to me all this time,' he growled.

'What are you talking about?'

'I thought you were hiding money and I was right,' he said, waving the savings account book at me. 'But it turns out that wasn't all you were hiding, was it?'

I felt myself go pale. If he had found the savings book, he would have found Gianfrancesco's letters. The look he gave me was one of utter hatred as he spread the letters across the table.

'You're a lying whore! All that time we were courting, this man was writing to you!'

'It wasn't like that.'

He crashed his fist on the table, knocking over his glass and spilling his wine across the cloth.

'These letters are dated! Right from the start you lied to me. It all makes sense now. You used to blow so hot and cold with me. One day you'd want me, the next day you wouldn't. And you weren't the innocent virgin you tried to make out you were, were you? Sounds like this arsehole Gianfrancesco had plenty of fun with you – more than you ever had with me. You disgust me! I would never have married you if I'd known someone else had touched you!'

He shook a handful of letters at me, then slapped them down onto the table. I stood in silence and watched as Gianfrancesco's words dissolved into the wine. Gino fixed his angry stare on me, wiping his fingers on the hem of the cloth.

'What happened when he got you pregnant? Did he panic? Did he run?'

'What? Gino, no.'

'That's why you didn't tell me you were pregnant as soon as you knew, wasn't it? You were weighing up your options. But you thought I'd be enough of an idiot to fall for your story. You thought I would do the decent thing. And I did! I was your ticket out of the life of a peasant, wasn't I?'

I tried to reason with him, but Gino was not listening. He banged his fists hard on the table again, screwed up the wine-soaked letters in his hand and shook them, showering droplets of wine up the wall.

'I always knew the kid wasn't mine. We couldn't have conceived a child that night. It was impossible. You were so uptight and frigid – I couldn't get anywhere near you! And she should have been born in January, not February. Do you think I'm stupid or something? I can count, you know! I should have listened to my mother. Mamma doubted it from the start. She saw right through you. She said you were a cheap little tart looking for a meal ticket. How could you do this to me? How could you trap me like this? You've played me like a fool!'

He stood up slowly, his face twisted into a snarl.

'So tell me the truth. This Gianfrancesco, is he Lucia's father?'

'No,' I replied firmly.

He seized me by the chin, shoving me back so hard that my

feet almost fell away from under me, and pushed my cheek against the wall.

'You're a liar and a cheating slut!'

He swung his arm to punch me, but I flinched out of his reach and his hand whacked the wall. He cried out in pain, yelling, 'You think I'm going to let you get away with this? You're a whore and an unfit mother! You're lucky I don't give your daughter to the Church! Now get out of my sight!'

I ran to my room, locked the door and moved my sewing table in front of it. I could hear the terrifying sounds of banging and breaking crockery from the kitchen. Lucia was sleeping and I covered her ears with her blanket.

When I opened my wardrobe door I found that its contents had been searched and stuffed back in. My money box was empty.

Almost an hour passed before the noise abated and I heard Gino stumble into his room. I got into bed next to Lucia and stayed awake all night. I needed to be alert in case he tried to break down the door.

*

Gino went out early the following morning and when at last I dared to emerge from my room I found the apartment turned upside down. Chairs were lying on their backs. He had smashed my mother's fruit bowl. The curtains were torn from the windows. The kitchen had been ransacked. Cupboards hung open. One door had been pulled right off. Split packets and their spilled contents littered the floor. There were boot-marks on the stove.

I cleared the wine and the pulp of letters from the table. The mark of Gino's fist was on the wall: he had dented the plaster. As I stood and looked at the damage I snapped out of my stupor and a terrible fear overwhelmed me. The dent in the wall was meant for me.

We had to leave. But I had no idea where Gino was, nor how

long it would be before he returned. We would have to leave on foot, but if he spotted us on his way back, which invariably he would, our escape would be thwarted.

I decided I would phone Marina and ask her to come and get us, but when I went to do so, I found that the telephone was gone. I searched everywhere, but clearly it had been removed on purpose. All that was left was a wire hanging from the wall.

I hurriedly packed a change of clothes for myself and Lucia, but I couldn't open the door to leave. Gino had locked it and had left the key in the barrel on the outside. We were trapped.

I stood at the balcony window for a long time, hoping that somebody would drive into the yard and I could attract their attention, but as there were no clients for the garage, there was nobody's attention to attract and too much noise from the surrounding factories for my cries to be heard.

When Gino returned he unlocked the door, but said nothing about the previous night. He just said that he had been to the hospital, then showed me his bandaged and said that he had broken it.

'Just what I need,' he growled. 'I can't work at all now with a busted hand.'

Clearly he was expecting sympathy. I was frightened, but I didn't want to let him see my fear. I kept calm and cold and asked, 'Where's the telephone?'

'What would you need a telephone for?' he sneered. 'To call your boyfriend, is that it?'

'Why did you lock us in?'

'Because I'm deciding what to do with you. And I'm not sure yet.'

He spoke to me only to hurl insults. He called me a whore over and over again, and when I did not react, he started on Lucia. He called her a bastard child and told me again that he would give her to the Church.

I blockaded us in my room, where we remained imprisoned for three days. I only dared to leave the room when I was sure that Gino was down in the workshop, or asleep in his bed. I took what food I could from the kitchen to feed Lucia, but I myself hardly dared to eat. The kitchen was always littered with empty wine bottles.

On the morning of the fourth day I did not hear Gino leave. There were noises from the kitchen and then I heard his heavy footsteps heading for my room. He rapped hard on the door.

'Come out here!' he commanded.

Then: 'Graziella, come out here now!'

And when I didn't reply: 'Are you going to stay locked in there for ever? Because I've decided what I'm going to do, and what you're going to do. Now open the door or I'll kick it in.'

I opened my bedroom door just a crack. He was standing holding the telephone in his hand. Giving me a leering smile, he waved it at me.

'Right. This is the plan. First of all, you're going to call the bank and get them to send all the money you've been hiding to me. I'm going to stock up with tyres properly so I can earn a living. And then we're going to start again. You can begin by cooking me some decent meals. I'm sick of your vegetable and rice shit.'

I did not reply. Instead, I closed the door and pushed the table in front of it again, but he hammered his fist against it. Lucia began to scream as he yelled abuse through the door.

'I'm giving you one chance!' he shouted. 'You do what you're supposed to do or I'll kick you out! And don't think you can take your bastard child with you because I've got proof of your cheating and it's enough for you never to be allowed anywhere near her again! One chance, Graziella!'

I opened my door again, looked at his glowering face and nodded.

'I'll call the bank,' I said, and he handed me my savings book.

He reconnected the telephone and sat watching as I made the call, but it was not the bank's number I dialled, it was Marina's. I prayed with all my heart that she would answer.

227

'Pomazzo Plumbing. Marina Bianchi speaking.'

'Good morning. My name's Graziella Bianchi. I have a savings account with you.'

There was a pause.

'Graziella?'

'Yes. I'm calling because I have a savings account which I would like to close and I would like all the money to be transferred to my husband.'

Gino was staring at me with a look of victorious self-satisfaction.

'It's very urgent,' I added.

'Graziella, are you in trouble?'

'Yes.'

'Are you at home?'

'Yes. I have the account number here.'

'Do you want me to come over?'

'Yes. As quickly as possible please,' I said, and read out the account number.

Marina remained on the line long enough for us to complete the charade. The last thing she said was, 'Stay where you are. I'm on my way. And I'm bringing my father.'

'Thank you,' I replied.

'Good,' Gino said. He sat back in the chair, nodding smugly. 'Now we can make a fresh start from where we should have started in the first place. You're very lucky that I'm giving you another chance. Tonight you can fulfil your responsibility as a wife by coming into my bed. We've got some lost time to make up for. You're going to be a proper wife. And you can sort yourself out so you look nice for me. Make an effort, will you? You've been looking like shit recently. Our marriage re-starts now, on *my* terms.'

He got up and disconnected the telephone.

'Right,' he said. 'Get this place sorted out. I'm going down to the workshop now to put my order together for the things I need.'

He took the telephone with him. I heard him lock the flat door from the outside and leave the key in the barrel. I waited fifteen interminable minutes for the doorbell to ring. Marina called my name.

'I can't open the door,' I said. 'You'll have to unlock it from your side.'

My relief at seeing Marina standing on the threshold was so immense that I threw myself into her arms.

'What's going on? What's happening, Graziella?' Then Marina took in the vandalised flat. 'My stupid brother,' she murmured, then turned to me and added, 'Has he hurt you?'

'No,' I replied, pointing to the dent on the wall. 'But only because he missed.'

'You and Lucia must come and stay with me. Immediately.'

'I just want to go back home,' I said. 'I'm done here.'

Marina nodded and took Lucia in her arms again. 'I know,' she said. 'But first let's get you out of here.'

Gino and his father were standing in the yard talking in raised voices. Gino was saying something about everything being fine, but as soon as he saw us, he stopped.

'What the hell are you doing?' he said to Marina, then turned to me. 'And where do you think you're going?'

Gino's father raised his hand to silence Gino.

'Graziella and Lucia are coming home with me,' said Marina calmly. 'Where they'll be safe. And if you dare to come round I'll call the police before you so much as have time to ring my doorbell.'

Gino spat on the ground. 'Go on then, leave,' he snarled. 'Good riddance, stinking whore! Take your bastard daughter and go back to the fields where you belong. I never want to see you again!'

His wish was granted. After all, Gino always got what he wanted.

CHAPTER 18

The taxi took us from the station in Mazzolo down the North Road. Lucia was beside me on the back seat, staring wide-eyed at the fields as they rolled past. Flashes of peach and apricot blossom lit the orchards. The verges were green with fresh, new grass.

Our journey from Bologna had been her first experience of a ride on a train and I had spent it telling her stories. She was at an age where she loved stories. I told her about my father and my mother, about Zia Mina, Ernesto and Salvatore. Many of the stories were ones I had told before, but Lucia never seemed to tire of hearing them and I never tired of telling them.

I also spoke to her about my friend, Rita Pozzetti, about how we had played with our dollies together and how I had been envious of her vegetable crate dolls' house. I wondered how Rita was. I hadn't seen her for so many years, but I hoped that as grown women we would forget the childish jealousies which had driven us apart, and rediscover our friendship.

We passed the sentinel gateposts at the end of the Marchesini driveway, except it wasn't the Marchesini driveway any more, although to me it always would be. I couldn't imagine ever calling it anything else.

'I haven't seen you before, but your accent's local,' said the taxi driver. He was a pleasant young man with a broad smile.

'I was born and raised here, but I moved away some years ago,' I replied.

'Ah. I've only been here a couple of years – that's why I haven't come across you. I'm from near Brescia originally, but I married a local girl, Rita Pozzetti. Do you know her?'

In that moment I felt the same tremble of excitement I had felt as a child, sitting in the back of the truck returning from my wartime evacuation to the convent; the same thrill at the thought of being reunited with Rita.

'Of course I know Rita,' I smiled. 'We were good friends. Tell her Graziella's come back home.'

New properties were being built along the North Road. Three were under construction on what had once been Zia Mina's land. Four more plots were pegged out, waiting for groundwork to begin. A large sign advertised that further plots were available.

'There'll be houses all the way from Mazzolo to Pieve Santa Clara before too long,' said the taxi driver. 'It will be like one big village.'

'That was my aunt's land once,' I said.

'She'd have been wise to hold onto it. You couldn't give that land away a few years ago, but since the planning regulations were changed there's been a stampede to buy land. The man who bought it is having ten houses built. I'd buy one if I could afford it. He's going to make a killing when he sells them, that's for sure.'

My heart was in my mouth as we approached Paradiso and I asked the taxi driver to stop outside. Apart from the fact that the gate was secured with an enormous padlock, it looked exactly the same. Nobody had torn it down or changed it in any way. Although the garden was neat and pruned and the weeds had been pulled, it didn't look as though anybody was living in the house. I was filled with such joy and relief that I squeezed Lucia so hard she squeaked.

We walked down to the village together hand-in-hand. During my absence the North Road had been re-named Via dei Patrioti, Patriots' Road. There was a sign bearing the new name in the exact spot where the German soldiers, poisoned by my aunt, had been found dead.

As we stood in the piazza I thought back as far as I could. The first memory I had of the village was from when I was a little younger than Lucia. I remembered being in the village with my mother. There was a war then and I was glad that Lucia did not know the suffering of war-time. I hoped that she never would.

I thought back to the day when Ernesto died and how the last time I had seen him alive he had been keeping a place in the queue for my mother. She had almost left me there with him. If she had, I might not be standing here and nor might Lucia.

The village had changed since then, although not unrecognisably so. The grocer's was still the same, apart from a new sign. The bakery was under new ownership. The butcher's now had a smart modern façade and refrigerated displays in its window.

The bar seemed unaltered. A group of old men were sitting at the tables outside playing cards and smoking. A board advertised the dates of upcoming football matches which would be shown on television. The little trattoria beside it had become a pizzeria, bedecked with strings of Italian flags.

Over the years a bank, a hairdresser's and a newspaper shop had opened. There had been a bicycle shop for a while, which was now a hardware store. A telephone box had been installed on the corner of the road which led to the cemetery.

There were cars too. The days when Signora Marchesini's was the only car seen in the village were over.

Lucia and I sat eating ice cream in the little garden beside the church, then we went in to light candles.

'One for your Nonna Teresa. One for your Nonno Luigi. One for Zia Mina. One for Ernesto,' I said as she handed me each one to light. We also lit one for Odetta Colombino and one for Amilcare Marchesini, just in case.

I found the taxi driver again and requested him to take us to Furboni's practice in Cremona.

Avvocato Furboni was still wearing the same suit. His hair still stuck out from his head, chin and ears like arrows indicating the cardinal points around his face. We snaked our way through the piles of files to his office.

'Signora Bianchi, I'm delighted to see you at last,' he said.

I thanked him, but I was too impatient to waste time on exchanging pleasantries. My dream of returning home felt so close to becoming reality that the words tumbled out of my mouth with great urgency.

'I'm soon to be in receipt of money from the sale of a property in Pomazzo, and with it I would like to buy back Paradiso. I'm here to ask you to contact the property developer who bought it and see whether he would sell it back to me. I realise that much of its land is being built on now, but all I would want is the front yard and a bit of garden to the side. Just the part around the chestnut tree. I will be able to stretch to twenty million but not a lira more.'

Avvocato Furboni raised his hand politely to interrupt me.

'If I may, Signora Bianchi,' he said, settling his spectacles on his nose, 'there is something you should know. The property developer is no longer the owner of Paradiso.'

My heart sank. Suddenly my head was light, but it felt as though I was made of lead from the neck down.

'What?'

'The property developer to whom your aunt sold Paradiso is no longer the owner,' repeated Furboni. 'Less than a week after I last saw you I was contacted by a new buyer who was very keen to purchase the entire property and all its land. He didn't even request a formal viewing or try to negotiate on the price.'

'Would this buyer consider selling the house to me?'

Furboni stroked his gondola moustache and shook his head decisively. 'No.'

'But couldn't you ask them?'

'There is no need to ask, Signora Bianchi,' smiled the notary, slipping a file out from the drawer of his desk. 'Paradiso was purchased by Gianfrancesco Marchesini, who left me with very precise instructions in the expectation that you would come back to see me.'

I could not speak, other than to say, 'Gianfrancesco Marchesini? Gianfrancesco bought Paradiso?'

Furboni continued, 'Yes, and the instruction he left was that the farmhouse and its outbuildings, its garden and the adjoining fields to the north and the east would not be for sale under any circumstances.'

I felt crushed, and could not hide the disappointment in my voice. 'So he won't sell it to me?'

'No. He will not *sell* it, because he wishes to gift it to you. He does not require any payment whatsoever. I have the documents right here, already signed by Signor Marchesini.'

Avvocato Furboni pushed the paperwork across the desk. I stared at the documents in front of me, so astonished that I could barely read the words.

'Why didn't you contact me, Avvocato Furboni? Why didn't you tell me about this?'

'Again, it was at Signor Marchesini's request. He was certain that you would come back, but only when you were ready. Now, if you *are* ready, Signora Bianchi, all I require is your signature to legalize the transfer of the title, and Paradiso will be yours.'

I was ready, and how different the feeling was to the last time I had signed my name. I was overwhelmed with joy, with gratitude and with love for Gianfrancesco. With a few strokes of Avvocato Furboni's gold fountain pen, Paradiso was mine.

CPSIA information can be obtained
at www.ICGtesting.com
Printed in the USA
LVHW032154230223
740320LV00019B/331